Chaos Crown

The Bedlam Boys

Ruby Vincent

Published by Ruby Vincent, 2022.

Prologue

"Wake up. Helllloooo."

Pain lit my cheek.

"I said, get up."

I slowly came to, descending into agony.

My head ached. Temples throbbed. Cheek stung. Wrists burned.

The final realization pushed back on the grogginess. Why did my wrists burn?

Blinking, my vision blurred on a face.

"Finally," a voice said. "I was a minute away from starting the party without you."

Blonde hair came into focus, and little by little, the brown eyes became clear. A round nose. Thin lips.

And a name.

"Zoey?"

My former orientation tour guide beamed. "Look at that. There is intelligent life on this planet. I was worried those knocks to the head rang your bell for the final time, you crazy bitch."

I bristled. Why the hell was this woman talking to me like that? And where was I?

Drifting up, I peered through crisscrossing metal to the clear night sky.

We were outside and on Chaney Bridge by the looks of it.

"Hmm."

What am I doing here? What was I doing before?

"Hmm! Hmm!"

What's that—?

Zoey stepped out of the way, and I fell on Arsenio, Cairo, Jacques, and Legend—wrists bound and suspended from ropes tied overhead. They balanced on a ledge on the balls of their feet. Gags stretched their mouths open.

"Guys!" I raced to them and made it three steps.

My bound hands yanked me off my feet and smashed me against the rail.

Zoey laughed herself sick.

She was dressed in a bright yellow sundress with a matching bow keeping her bangs out of her face. You'd have thought she was going out to a picnic, if not for the crossbow held in her gloved hands.

I squinted. My crossbow.

"Where are you running off to? The fun just started."

"What the fuck are you doing?!" I screamed. "Let us go."

"Now why would I do that... Angel?"

Cold dread climbed my spine. "What did you say?"

"Need me to spell it out," she sang. "I promised I was arranging a meeting for us and here we are. I'd have thought you'd be happy, seeing as you put so much effort into finding me."

"You?" I scurried back as she closed the distance. "But— But how? Why?"

"How and why you already know. But you forgot." Zoey rolled her eyes. "How convenient."

"You're the Letter Man," I sliced in.

"Woman. Thank you very much."

"But you... Blake Jensen..."

My conversation with Craig came roaring back.

"Blake. Is he in this photo? Point him out."

"Blake's not—"

"A guy," I whispered. "He was going to say that Blake isn't a guy. The face he pointed out!"

I snapped up to her. In my mind, I moved past the person I thought Craig pointed at, to the girl I dismissed outright.

Her hair was brunette. The round nose was pointed, but the resemblance couldn't be denied.

"You're Blake Jensen."

"Correction: I was Blake Jensen."

"And Dante? How did you...?" I trailed off, my mind struggling under the new information.

"Oh, I'm not Dante. But the new guy is a friend," she said. "He kindly made a few changes to the show, and added lines to his script when I asked. I have friends, Angel. Everywhere."

"You're not Dante, but you are Blake."

She gestured with my crossbow. "I changed my name to Zoey Mariner the second I hit eighteen. Ugh. You don't know the hell I went through. My parents thought it'd be cool and revolutionary to give me a guy's name. Instead, I was bullied relentlessly. They called me a man. Stole my tampons, saying that guys didn't need them. It was awful."

"Boo-hoo. I don't give a fuck about your sob story." I strained in my binds. "You shot Colton. You killed Bella! And the guys. Get them down from there right now."

Zoey aimed the bow at Legend and fired.

"No!"

He jerked out of the way and the arrow sailed past, missing him so narrowly I heard his jacket tear.

"You're not in a position to make demands, so don't do it again. You are, however, lucky that I'm in a sharing mood. Go on," she sang. "Ask me all about my dastardly plan. Why did you do it? How did you get away with it? I love this part."

I spat at her feet.

She heaved a sigh. "You always were stubborn."

"You don't know me."

"Au contraire. If you want to get technical, I'd say I'm the only one who knows the real you. Come on. Haven't you put it together yet?"

"We met during that blurred-out year of my life while I was on the meds. I get it," I mocked. "But if you think that drugged-up robot is the real me, you don't understand how blackouts work. Anything I did"—I thought of the body at Black Widow Hill—"or didn't do. It wasn't a choice."

Giving me her back, Zoey shot at the ropes keeping Arsenio out of the water below.

"Hmm!"

"Stop!"

"Here's how this goes," she said. "I couldn't have you driving the Crows out of town too early, because they hadn't accepted my price yet. You see, you're not the only one I've sent letters to. But I bet you thought you were special. Aww."

My teeth clenched. I had this person pegged before I knew her.

She's enjoying this.

"Now that Cavendish is dead and the leash is off, I'm offering my services to the highest bidder," she explained. "I sent a few letters to Jeremy Ellis telling him that when he eventually failed against the Bedlam Boys, and he was meant to fail, I'd kill them for fifty grand."

Zoey dropped that like a McDonald's order.

"He kept up that he could handle this himself. That's until the light show in the square. He hired me the second he woke up in the hospital. Only ten grand each. A bargain. Though I am missing one," she muttered. "Should've waited, but we've waited so long to do this."

My heart shot in my throat. One sentence penetrated.

"Kill them?" Tears stung as I took in the ropes, and the death she chose for them. "Don't do this. You said you wouldn't."

"Well, when I said that, I didn't have twenty-five grand in the bank. Keep up."

Tears ran down my cheeks. Behind my back, I wriggled my wrists, working to get free.

"That said, I didn't bring you out here to watch them die. If you do, that will be your choice."

"What does that mean?"

"It means that in honor of our past friendship, I'm willing to let you go in their place." She motioned to the ledge above my head. "Jump and I let the Bedlam Boys go free."

The guys shouted through their gags.

"Refuse, and I keep shooting these arrows till they're either full of holes. Or I get lucky with my aim, catch the rope, and it snaps—gifting them a cold, watery death. Because you broke the rules again, Rainey. You told the police about me even though I've warned you over and over again. I treat you as a friend, but you haven't done the same for me. It's time I stopped giving you chances. You won't talk me out of the decision coming your way. But you can delay it by indulging me and dragging the conversation out as long as you can. So."

Zoey leaned over me and sliced my binds just like that. She backed up and leveled my bow on the guys.

"What's it going to be?"

Straightening, I gripped the railing—cold metal biting my skin.

There were two trucks on either end of the bridge, blocking the opening. One was Cairo's, and the other I saw in the police station parking lot most mornings.

Davidson.

I pushed the name away, focusing solely on Zoey and the healthy stash of arrows in her quiver.

If I keep her talking long enough, I can delay until someone tries to drive across the bridge and sees what's happening here.

"How do I know you won't hurt them anyway? I kill myself and then you loose those ropes, collecting another twenty-five grand."

"If there's anything I honor, Angel, it's a sacrifice." She said that with a seriousness she hadn't used before. "If you give your life for them, they will be spared."

"Okay," I said clearly. "You win. How did you go from that sweet kid smiling with her friends, to a killer?"

"Ah, now that's an interesting story," she mused, pointing my bow at Cairo, Arsenio, Cairo, then Arsenio. She laughed as they shouted at her.

"I met Scott while he was working the youth center, and he saw something in me. By then, the bullies were harassing me just because they could. It stopped being about my name a long way back.

"Scott took me under his wing. He told me about my legacy and that the people I came from didn't take shit from anybody. Then, he taught me how to make anyone who hurt me scream." She winked. "He was a good friend to me. To us. But the guy was paranoid and locked under too many rules. He would not have approved of the little deal I made with the Crows.

"Last year, I made one mistake and he came down on me. Hard. It was no small relief when he got that death wish and ordered you to kill him. Now I'm free to do what I want."

Scott Cavendish was her mentor and supposed friend, and she cheered his fiery death. That answered the question of if sociopaths could make friends they gave a real care about.

No.

"Why do you think we know each other?" I asked. I took a step closer.

"That's far enough." Zoey swung the bow on me. "Hands on the ledge at all times. If you let go"—she flashed and loosed an arrow that struck Arsenio's thigh—"so do I."

"Arsenio!"

His muffled cries shredded my heart in two.

"Stop it," I screamed. "You said you wouldn't if we talked."

She shrugged. "I'm just demonstrating the consequences. I noticed that when I do, I never have to repeat myself."

"You don't." I strangled the metal. "You don't have to demonstrate. I'm listening to you. I'm giving you what you want.

"Hold on, Arsenio." I poured my pleas and comfort into my gaze. "I'll get you down from there."

"Ugh. Enough about him. We're in the middle of a conversation, bitch. Don't be rude."

You're going to see who's the fucking bitch when I'm done.

"How do we know each other?" I forced through gritted teeth.

"Oh, that's easy." She beamed. "We hooked up after your grandma got herself killed."

I reeled back.

"Yeah. You were pretty messed up over it. Wanted revenge like no one I've ever seen," she said. "Scott came to you through work. He did the farm's accounts for free. A favor for your grandmother because she brought his mom free produce when she was laid up with cancer and couldn't get out of bed."

"Oh my gosh," I breathed. "Gran was the connection. Not Walker Lewis. How did I not know this? Why didn't I remember him?"

"You didn't meet till after she was killed. Why would you? I don't know who the fuck my parents' accountant is." She shrugged. "Anyway, Scott got close to you, and you started talking a lot of crazy, violent stuff. He sent you the letters first—checking to make sure you were receptive to the help he was willing to offer. When you didn't go running to the police, he told you who he was, and that he'd gladly help you sacrifice Andrew Clein in the name of your grandmother."

"No," I cried. "No!"

Pain pounded my temples.

I dropped to my knees, eyes squeezing shut as I cried out—from which pain, I couldn't guess.

"You're lying!"

"How would I know this if I was lying?" Zoey laughed. "The three—five—seven of us— I won't tell you exactly how many of us there are. Because all that matters is you, me, and Cavendish had our own thing going on. You and I became friends."

Temper leaked into her voice. "You taught me how to shoot an arrow. Not as good as you, but good enough. I taught you how to break a man's arm in a single twist. That's what you did to Andrew Clein first," she hissed. "Broke his arm."

"Stop it!"

Flashes bombarded my mind. Blurred faces, places, scenes that moved too quickly for me to grab one and make it real.

"We got so close, we started watching that time travel show you like. Every Saturday with a bowl of popcorn and homemade tacos. I called you Angel because the Weeping Angels are your favorite monster in the show. That's who you were to me. My favorite monster."

"No," I sobbed. "It's not true. None of this is true."

"It is true!" she roared. "Snap out of this boring mental breakdown and wake up! We were friends. You know it. You remember."

"No!"

But I did.

Fragmented pieces formed a picture of me and a brunette Blake Jensen, laughing and joking while doing target practice on a hay bale. Who would I let touch my precious bows and arrows from Gran, other than a friend?

"There it is," she hissed. Zoey was suddenly in my face, bending my neck back by the hair. "See? I knew you were still in there, Angel."

"Stop. P-please."

"Oh, now you beg? We begged." She dug the arrow tip in my neck, breaking the skin. "Scott asked you to sacrifice one worthless guy to further our cause, and you refused. Said you didn't get into this to hurt innocent people. We tried to make you see!"

My head shook in her grip.

"No one is innocent, but everyone is honored in sacrifice."

"No."

The pressure in my skull was unbearable. Each horrid word from her snarling lips drove the spike deeper, unleashing a flood of memories that couldn't be true!

"The sheriff had something we needed. All of a sudden, the stubborn oaf grew a backbone. Refused to give Scott what he asked, so he ordered you to sacrifice the sheriff's son."

Eyes huge, Cairo stopped struggling.

"But oh no," Zoey carried on. "Cairo was innocent. Just a teenager. There had to be another way. Blah, blah, blah. Scott said you had two days to gut the guy, or you'd watch while I did it. You walked into the sheriff's station that day and told Davidson everything."

"No," I whispered.

Yes.

I remembered the station bell chiming. Recalled Davidson's smile as he said the sheriff was out, but he'd be happy to help me.

Zoey tsked. "Such a shame. If only Andres was on shift that day. We'd be in prison, and none of what came next would've happened."

"Oh no," I breathed, folding onto the pavement.

My hands came off the ledge and Zoey didn't care. Glee twisted her smile as the spike pried loose the final memory.

"Yes, Angel." Her voice neared a soft coo. "You remember how we punished you. The night we busted into the farmhouse, catching you making a cup of tea like all your troubles were over. What did we do, bitch?"

I tossed my head, shaking roughly. But the vision would not stop unfolding.

The body in the barn. Broken, twisted, and beyond help.

"What did we do to you?"

The woman—for now I knew she was a woman—that I buried at Black Widow Hill, did not answer my calls then, nor did she in the memory.

I heard the name I called her. I saw her face when I flipped her over.

"What did we do?"

"You killed me," I whispered, pain fading as it all came back. "I died that night."

"Yes." Zoey released my hair and stroked my cheek. "That's it. Remember."

"I forgot about dying."

My voice was small. Pleading.

"How could I forget?"

"It's okay." Zoey kissed my forehead. Standing up, she backed away, aiming my bow at my now silent boys. "You were special, Angel. Only you could live on after death. Even so, you must pay for what you've done. Give back the time that wasn't yours."

I rose on shaky knees.

"Scott believed we could bring you back through blood, clues, and letters. But he should have known." Zoey lined the shot at Cairo's heart. The expert marksman I was, I knew this time she wouldn't miss.

"The dead only return through sacrifice."

I looked down below at the black, icy waters.

"Now it's time to make your choice," she barked. "You? Or the Bedlam—"

I climbed onto the ledge and jumped off.

Chapter One

Icy claws bit into my legs, stomach, chest, face—dragging me under. The impact smacked conscious thoughts clean out of my head, filling me with a blank calm. I didn't struggle. Didn't thrash, fight, or claw to the surface.

I shut my eyes... I think. The water was too dark to tell if they were open or closed, and I stopped feeling my face somewhere around the time my guys' shouts faded.

It was better this way. How wrong it was of me to live on after death. My soul walked away from that grave, stealing borrowed time and not even using it for vengeance. There was no point to me anymore, so let my death do some good this time.

Let it save my boys.

The claws loosened their grip—accepting that I wasn't going to escape. Watery arms cradled me, gently sending me on to a place more peaceful than I deserved.

I'm so sorry. My lungs burned... until they didn't. *I'm coming.*

A band wrapped around my forearms, snapping my eyes open. I knew they were open this time, because something was looking back at me.

Black crept in around my vision, blurring the figure. As we burst through the surface, it claimed me for good.

"RAINEY? RAINEY, WAKE up. Dammit, wake up!"

Pain pounded my chest, ripping me from sleep. I shot up, spewing river water from my throat. My eyes focused on Cairo— No, not just Cairo. Jacques and Legend hovered behind him.

"Wha— What happened?"

"You tell us." Cairo scooped me into his arms. The lift jarred my aching head, making me wince. Pictures and scenes were assaulting me. Faces, people, eyes in the dark.

"We ran down and found you on the bank," Legend said. "What the fuck is going on, Rainey?"

I couldn't answer. Burying my face in Cairo's chest, his dry shirt confirmed what he said. He didn't jump in and get me. None of them did.

Someone else pulled me out of the water.

"—out of nowhere." Cairo's voice penetrated. "Killed that crazy bitch and cut Arsenio loose, knowing he couldn't chase after them."

"What?" I croaked. "Cut Arsenio loose? Killed who?"

"That's what we're telling you," Jacques said as the guys made the slow climb up the hill. "That woman— Zoey. She's dead. Headlights appeared on the other side of the bridge, there was a gunshot, and she went down. It was seconds after you jumped."

"Then a guy—girl—who the fuck knows, steps over her body like trash and cuts Arsenio down," Legend continued. "He didn't say a damn word. Just frees him and leaves Arsenio to get the rest of us with one bad leg. It took so long, we knew there was no chance we'd get to you in time."

"And then there you were," Cairo finished.

I heard the question in their voice, but I had no answers for them. If anything, their story confused me more than ever. Someone saved them and me. Who? Why?

Topping the hill, the scene laid out in gory defiance. Zoey lay bleeding on the ground, my crossbow lying inches from her hand.

Propped against the railing, Arsenio's chest heaved as he clutched his leg—bandaged with nothing but a ripped shirt.

"Tell us what the hell is going on," Cairo said. "That girl said you knew her. You two were *friends* until you refused to kill me. What was she talking about, Rainey?"

I climbed out of his arms, making my way to Arsenio. He glared at me with pained distrust. Gazing at the other guys, I saw the same look in their eyes.

"Don't call me Rainey," I rasped, taking Arsenio's hand anyway. "My name is Ivy."

CAIRO

I paced the length of the carpet, glaring at my pet— *Mine.*

Or was she?

The stranger huddled within Legend's covers, the lone lump on the bed. This should've made her look small and vulnerable, and instead I pictured a snake in its burrow—waiting for its chance to strike.

The innocence was gone from her eyes. The softness from her cheeks. She was hard, blank plastic staring back at us, anticipating our first move.

I didn't know this girl. Seems like I never did.

"We're ready for your explanation whenever you are," Jacques said with a calm I both hated and envied.

She flicked to him. "Sit with me." Her hand poked out of the blankets. "Hold me."

"No," I barked.

Those unnerving eyes turned on me. "Why?"

"You fucking know why."

"You're angry with me." She dropped this matter-of-factly. It was just an observation. "Why? I did not deceive you on purpose. I didn't keep quiet about Blake and the others on purpose. In every way that counts, I found out about all of this the same time as you."

"You said—!"

Legend gripped my shoulder, silently staying me. His message was clear even though I shoved him off.

"You said you're not Rainey," Legend spoke up. "In fact, you claimed to be her dead sister. What does that mean?"

She showed her first emotion. Jaw clenching, she turned away—gripping the sheet. "It means what I said. Rainey... died. Blake and the others came that night," she rasped. "They killed her, and when I found her... all I could do was run. I ran so far away, I left Ivy behind."

"You had a mental breakdown," Jacques said like all of this made fucking sense. "You convinced yourself that you were in fact your sister, and to explain where Ivy had gone, your mind invented a story."

"Got it all figured out, don't you, Stone?"

Jacques raised a brow. That deadened reply was nothing like the sarcastic snap we expected from Rainey. "Not quite," he said. "Why don't you fill in the rest? Who is the real Zoey Mariner/Blake Jensen? What were the both of you a part of?"

"Zoey is exactly what she told you. Or she was," the stranger corrected. "She was recruited by Scott Cavendish. We all were. But most of us didn't know his true goal."

I slowed my pacing, eyes narrowing.

"Scott was smart," she whispered. "He went after the broken, the bullied, and the powerless. People who had nowhere else to turn. I knew Gran was murdered for our land, but no one would listen to me. Her killers were going to get away with ruining our lives.

"Then one day, Scott showed up, saying he believed me. He was her accountant. She told him she was getting the farm's financial affairs in order, so R-Rainey and I wouldn't be saddled with debt and struggles. He knew she made a will.

"Once he was in my ear, I was lost. All I could see was someone who wanted to help me. To get me justice. Scott explained that we weren't the first family this was done to. There'd been others who were forced to sell through threats, bribes, and even other murders made to look like accidents. There'd be no justice for me like there wasn't for the others, so I had to get it myself."

"He convinced you killing Andrew Clein was your only choice," Jacques dropped.

She slowly shook her head. "He never used that word. *Kill*. It was always sacrifice. Sacrificed for justice. Sacrificed for an end to corruption. Sacrificed so that no other family would suffer as we were," she said. "It was around then he introduced me to Zoey. Her bullying escalated way past her name like she said. She was getting it constantly from a couple guys on the football team."

My brows snapped up.

"She was walking home one day and they drove up on her, forced her into the trunk, and drove her out into the woods." She gave me a hard stare. "I don't have to tell you what they did to her."

"You don't have to tell us what she did to them either," I replied. "Hudson Olsen, Dylan Meyer, and Thomas Lawson. Years above us, but we all heard about the three footballers who never made it to graduation. They were all found dead in an upstairs room after a party. Everyone said they overdosed."

She nodded. "That's how it was supposed to look. I think there was still a part of me that knew taking the law into your own hands was wrong, but that part died after Zoey. After hearing how she stumbled bleeding and crying into the police station, and they didn't bother to bring them in for questioning. The officer said it would always be her word against theirs, and it wasn't worth the hassle of putting her through a trial that would end in not guilty.

"It wasn't right that those guys got away with what they did to her. It wasn't right that Clein wouldn't be punished for Gran. It just wasn't right, so... how could I be wrong for making him pay?"

"But it wasn't just about Clein and your farm, or giving a bunch of rapists what they deserve," I gritted. "Mariner was a fucking psychopath who took money to kill us. She said you were supposed to kill me."

"That's how it all changed, Cairo. They were about righting wrongs, but I didn't know until it was too late what that meant to Scott and the others. I didn't know that meant all collateral damage was acceptable because they were being *sacrificed* for a greater purpose."

"What purpose?" Legend snapped.

"Stop acting like you don't know! I remember *everything*," she cried. "Including what you and your parents and their parents have been trying to stop since Crystal Canyon became Bedlam. They want it back! Decades ago, this town wrestled away the wealth, power, and lives of the Men of Honor, and they. Want. It. Back."

I whipped to Legend and Jacques, eyes as wide as theirs. "Are you fucking trying to say Scott and all your old friends were—?"

"Are," she sliced. "They are the descendants and recruits to the Men of Honor. They know about the diamonds. They know they once owned the lands filled with them, and by their reckoning, they're reclaiming what was stolen from them. Like *my farm*," she stressed. "Taken over by my great-great-great-grandmother after she joined the riot against her uncle, Jonathan de Souza. He was a bastard that beat his wife and daughters black and blue, until one after the other, they died by his hand—while the sheriff looked the other way.

"My three times great-grandmother didn't lift a finger to stop the crowd when they stormed his home and killed him." Her gaze pinned us through. "But I don't have to tell you this. You all know the story. The townspeople took up arms and wiped out every trace of the Men of Honor and their families. My ancestor was spared because she hated them just like the rest. The next morning, they woke up with wealth and land that didn't belong to them.

"Distant male heirs would inherit the properties and a hell of a grudge to go with it. They were destined to take over and make their lives hell once again. So they said no." Her eyes found me. "You know the history of how they took up arms and violently defended Bedlam from militias and the government. And you three in particular know that after the battle was won, certain people in town banded together to form the Society of Sisters.

"They forged documents and deeds naming themselves heirs and family, so they could keep the town they stole. There had been so much chaos and so many dead, the government couldn't sort out the truth from the lies. In the end, they accepted what they were told—thankful the bloodshed was over.

"Ever since then, they kept the secret of Crystal Canyon. Preventing anyone from digging and building here, and leaving the vast fortune beneath our feet alone." She shook her head. "What's the point of digging it up when it'll just be seized? No one cares about our little speck on the map, but they will if they ever find out we've got millions under our shoes.

"Bedlam would be leveled. The phony papers that gave us our land will be ripped to shreds in court. Either it'll be in the hands of the government, or men like Steven Ellis."

"Ellis?" Jacques repeated. "What's he got to do with this?"

She shot out of the sheets. "He started this. That's what I'm trying to tell you. Steven Ellis isn't moving in on this town for no reason. You know that, but you don't know that he always had his sights on Bedlam. His great-great-grandfather was one of the Men of Honor. Their family name was Eliason then.

"Joshua Eliason, his wife, and their son were spared the blood-shed because they happened to be out of town when it all happened. They came back to a barricade around the town. After the fighting ended, Joshua tried to reclaim what was his, and was killed for it. His wife got the hint and never returned to Bedlam."

My head bobbed on its own power. "She raised her son in another town, feeding him the story of the home that was once theirs, and the barbarians who stole it from them. They passed it down until Steven Ellis decided to do something about that bedtime story."

"Yes," she said softly. "The family had money from when they used to sit on a land of diamonds. That money funded the company Ellis now owns, but it's not enough for him. His legacy was stolen. His town was stolen. In his eyes, all of this should be his." She swept out her hands. "It should be his sons'. You can't steal what was taken from you in the first place. Whatever he has to do to get it back, is just the price of righting a wrong. It's a sacrifice."

Legend stepped forward. "Are you saying Steven Ellis re-formed the Men of Honor? That's how he started this?"

"I can't be sure it was him who re-formed it. It could've been his father who did the legwork, and tracked down the remaining descendants of the Men of Honor, but Steven is the one who tried to use Scott Cavendish to do his dirty work here," she said. "He used the trust he had as people's accountants to push them into selling their properties to Steven's shell companies."

I knew even before she said it.

"One of them was AgriProspects."

"Hold on. Stop." Legend put up a hand. "Ellis was behind AgriProspects? He sent them after your grandmother? Then, why in the fuck did Cavendish approach you after she died? Why whip you up for revenge?"

"Haven't you realized by now? Scott Cavendish is no one's lackey. Steven was setting everything up so that everything—the land, the town, the diamonds—would be owned by him, and the other Men of Honor would have to trust he'd keep his word about splitting the profits.

"What kind of sociopathic monster trusts another sociopathic monster? He saw through Ellis from the beginning, but he used the society he was re-forming to build his own loyal group of psychopaths. Scott broke from him," she explained. "That's why Ellis sent his sons here in the end. Scott took over the Men of Honor, and what was an out-of-towner who was fighting to keep a low profile to do about it?"

"Approaching you was a fuck-you to Ellis," Legend confirmed. "But then why did it go so wrong?"

"They were on opposite sides, but they want the same thing. Bedlam." She folded back onto the sheets. "Thanks to Ellis, Scott's people know the true history, what your mothers do, and what Cairo's father does for them. They believed the drunk, depressed sheriff was the weakest link—"

I stiffened.

"—but he wouldn't give in. Whatever Scott said or did, the sheriff told him to fuck off. So... he and Zoey ordered me to kill the last person he cares about." She met my eyes. "A man who has nothing has no reason to fight."

Her eyes glazed. For a moment, I thought the impostor vanished and Rainey came back. "They taught me that lesson too."

"But why?" I gritted. "What could they possibly have wanted from my father? They already knew about the Society. Otherwise, his job is to make sure outsiders don't have a reason to look twice at Bedlam. How the fuck does that help them take over?"

"I don't know."

"You don't know." My voice was nothing more than a growl. "You've had a whole bunch to fucking say about Cavendish and Ellis—too fucking late after the fact. But now you don't know? How convenient."

Rain— Ivy's gaze darkened. "Oh yes. My sister getting murdered and me losing my fucking mind was *convenient*. Convenient that the beasts who took her, ran around unchecked and laughing at me all this time. So convenient for me, Cairo. The real tragedy is what it did to you. The guy I lost her to save!"

"Don't turn this around. How is it you know everything else except that? More than we fucking know."

"Simple," she rasped. "Scott told me when he thought he had me under his thumb. Naturally, the manipulative shit spun everything to make himself the victim. *Ellis* tricked him into believing they were restoring the town to its former glory, when he really just wanted to level the place and dig it up.

"*Ellis* said they were giving back what was stolen, but actually he was stealing from innocents like Gran. *Ellis* recruited him to save Bedlam, when the truth is he purposely chose descendants from the Men of Honor so that he'd have a handy scapegoat if the truth ever came out. And the person who'd make sure all of his cheating, lying, stealing, and killing would lead back to Cavendish is—"

"My father," I dropped tonelessly.

"Cavendish convinced me your dad helped AgriProspects and Clein get away with killing Gran. The investigation was botched. I had no reason not to believe him about that or anything else. But the problem was it wasn't Sheriff Jack he wanted me to go after. It was you.

"I refused, of course. I wasn't going to kill some random guy. Gran didn't raise someone who hurt innocent people. I was gone but I hadn't lost myself that completely. I wouldn't give in to him. When Zoey and the others came and..." She cleared her throat. "She had a lot of fun telling me how stupid and gullible I was. She was almost impressed with me for finally waking the hell up and pushing back against Cavendish, but I had to suffer for getting in their way all the same. She told me everything. Like she already knew I wouldn't get the chance to tell anyone else."

"But during her gloating she never said what they wanted from my father?"

She shook her head.

"Doesn't make sense," Jacques said mostly to himself. "They went to extreme measures to punish you for not killing Cairo, and after all that, they back off and leave him to walk around free all this time? Why haven't they made a move against Cairo, against his father, or against us since?"

"Why did Zoey Mariner get killed when she finally did?" Legend added.

Silence followed his question.

They were both right. Rain— Ivy's memories coming back hadn't changed a thing. We were no closer to stopping this threat since before we wound up on that bridge. *Steven Ellis wanted to get his filthy hands on Bedlam.* We knew that. *Someone made the girl we believed was Rainey their personal vendetta.* We knew that too. *The Men of Honor were back again.* That we did not know.

But did it really matter what they called themselves? We've been protecting Bedlam from threats since the Men of Honor were founded. These guys were just another in a long line of pricks who found out too much, and tried exploiting our town from the shadows. They could call themselves whatever they wanted. They'd be put down with the rest.

"Who are they?"

"I don't know."

"What the fuck do you know?"

"Everything I just told you," she replied. "Scott and Zoey weren't idiots. They spoke about others, but they never mentioned names or introduced me. They didn't fully trust me, and when I refused to hurt Cairo and went to the police instead..." Ivy trailed off.

"What about the night they came after you and your sister?" Jacques pushed. "Zoey said she didn't show up alone."

"They were like demons," she breathed. "Appearing out of the shadows from everywhere and nowhere. There was nothing to see but black masks, then I saw nothing at all."

The three of us shared a look. As irritated as I was, even I knew it didn't make sense for the Men of Honor to reveal themselves to her. Wanting revenge against someone who murdered your family was a step removed from being willing to kill someone you didn't know.

They couldn't trust that Ivy would carry out their plans against me, and then when she said fuck you and tried turning them in, they'd be stupid to show their faces the night they killed her sister and left her alive. If Ivy did prove anything, it was that she'd hunt down anyone who hurt her family. No, the Men of Honor had no incentive at any point to tell Ivy anything real.

So why did they go after her in the first place? Did they want from her what they wanted from nearly every landowner in Bedlam?

How would they get that when there wasn't a will? another voice asked. *When someone dies without a will, their things don't automatically go to the homicidal accountant.*

"This is illogical," Jacques said, echoing my thoughts. "I can think of no valid explanation for how any of us got here. Why kill Rainey de Souza as punishment for not killing Cairo, and then leave him untouched? Why draw Ivy's attention all this time later with letters and demands of sacrifice? Why Scott Cavendish's sudden death wish? Why did Zoey Mariner offer her services to get rid of us, and then who got rid of her? Who else knew we'd be dangling on that bridge?"

"All we've done is stand around here asking questions." I snatched up my jacket. "There's one man who can give us some answers."

"Your father." Ivy shed the blankets. "I'm coming with you."

"You're not."

"I am." She weaved her fingers through mine. I didn't mistake it for an intimate gesture. "He'll open up to me."

"Why the fuck would he do that?"

She gave me a hard look. "What kind of monster wouldn't... when he finds out what I lost to protect his son?"

I cracked my jaw to argue with her, and found I couldn't. Find my father in a sloppy enough drunken mood, he'd bend to Ivy's pain.

But this was between me and Jack.

"You're not coming."

"Why—"

"Because Rainey I knew!" I burst out, ripping free. "You, I don't. Everything out of your mouth has been bullshit from day one. If my father's involved in this, I'm hearing it from him."

Ivy didn't so much as blink at my outburst. It set my teeth further on edge. I didn't know or understand this hard, blank-faced beauty standing in the space of my pet. Ivy changed more than her name when she deluded herself into believing she was Rainey. She changed her personality too.

The only thing I knew about this stranger was that she was willing to go as far as it took. That should make her a girl after my own heart. But if there was anyone I trusted least on this planet, it was someone like me.

"He is involved," she said. "It's time I knew how. I won't have you two coming up with some story to tell me. If the truth is coming out, I'll be there to hear it."

"Neither one of you is going anywhere," Jacques sliced in. "The sheriff is on shift right now, which means he's holed up in the station with Davidson. Jeremy Ellis put out a hit on us. Arsenio and Roan are in the hospital, and we just walked away from a dead body on the bridge. We need to stop, think, reason. Then, we act."

"Someone must've called that dead body in by now," Legend said. "Davidson's wrapping Chaney Bridge in police tape. The sheriff's on his own."

I found myself shaking my head. "Nah. With all the shit that's been going on, the murder of a pretty little college girl would have everybody out there. Davidson's there, and the old man's right next to him."

"We wait," Jacques said. "Until he's off shift and alone. Wait for him at home."

"Okay," Ivy replied, answering in my place. "What will you two do?"

"We're not sitting around playing dead," Legend said, making for the keys and wallet on his nightstand. "Roan has to know what's going on. Once Jeremy and his boys find out Mariner is dead and we're not, he'll try something."

"I need peace and quiet, but before that, more information. That private detective you hired," Jacques said to Ivy. "I need to know how close he is to tracking down Dante."

"Can't say, but I think the last thing he tried to tell me was that there wasn't an Ivy to find in Chicago."

"Then he figured that out quicker than any of us. He's good at what he does, and now he works for me. Call and tell him so."

I stood apart as they launched into their tasks. Legend arranging for the kind of security only money could buy to stand outside Roan's and Arsenio's hospital rooms. Ivy calling her investigator to tell him confidentiality was waived, and then Jacques taking advantage of that as he barraged him with questions on the way out the door. After far too long, only Ivy and I remained.

We stared at each other across the divide.

"You're angry with me," she stated.

"I've got reason to be."

"I didn't lie to you on purpose, Cairo. I don't have to tell you that I didn't want any of this." She moved in on me, peeling my lips back with each step. "May I remind you that your father covered up my grandmother's death long before Scott Cavendish came into my life and I lost myself?"

Growls leaked through my teeth as her fingers brushed my temples.

"He's been hiding something from the very beginning, and if he'd gotten her justice as he was supposed to do, I never would have been so vulnerable to Cavendish and Zoey." The anger bleeding into her tone didn't match the gentle pressure on my forehead. "Despite my very valid reasons for hating that man, I still refused to hurt him through you. And I paid for it.

"I didn't bring us here, Cairo. Clein did. AgriProspects did. Steven Ellis did. Cavendish did. And yes, your father did. But not either of us," she said slowly. "So why be mad at each other when we have the same enemy? Steven Ellis is close to getting everything he wants, and his son almost served your heads on a platter to go with it. You don't have time to be pissed at me, Cairo. We've got too much shit to do."

"Trust me, de Souza." I pulled her hands off. "I can make time."

She scanned my face. "Why?"

"I'll tell you now. I'll never forgive you... for not being her."

Something flashed behind her eyes. For a second I saw it—saw it all—and I flung myself away from her. Chest heaving, I glared from behind the armchair, fingers gripping the leather.

"I'll tell you something too," she whispered, drawing the mask back over her expression. "I'll never forgive myself for that either."

Turning her back, Ivy made for the door.

"Where are you going?" I barked.

"To get answers." She replied without slowing her stride. "Come or don't. But I won't spend another day in the dark."

IVY

Cairo and I didn't speak on the ride to his father's house. What more was there left to say? He was in love with Rainey whether he'd say it or not, and he was forced to watch Rainey jump off a bridge and Ivy emerge in her place.

All of this started so long before either of us were even born, and I still don't know why.

There was a long list of things I didn't know, even as my missing time and true history came back to me. Cavendish left out so much when he came into my life. All I saw was someone who believed me. Who wanted justice for Gran. After the fucking sheriff looked me right in the eyes and pretended he never saw the autopsy proving my grandmother was murdered, another person stepping in to promise justice, was too hard a siren's call to resist.

But why? Why, why, why, why, why! Why did nothing make sense?!

"If your father's working with the Society, why would he cover up a murder caused by the Men of Honor? Cavendish told me it was so the sheriff could frame him for all of Ellis's crimes, but the man was manipulating me. Everything out of his mouth was a lie. But if that wasn't the reason, what was his motive for helping AgriProspects? Even if he didn't know the Men of Honor were behind the company, he knew they wanted the diamonds. He had to."

Cairo slid into the next lane, attention fixed on the road. "Why are you asking me? You'll get your chance to ask him soon enough."

"Like I haven't gone down that road with him before? I badgered and pelted him for an explanation. He gave as much a shit about my tears as he did my anger. I'm coming because he'll open up to you if anyone," I admitted, "and I'll be there when he does. But before all of that, I want to know what you think, Cairo. I can't be the only one who made you feel betrayed in the last twelve hours."

"Not that betrayal, de Souza."

I bit back a sigh, knowing exactly why he was resorting to my last name.

"He's not working for the Men of Honor," Cairo said. "I've told you before. They've got nothing he wants."

"They could've threatened you."

"Making threats to a sheriff? That's a ticket to prison, not untold riches."

"We're dealing with shadows who leave black let—" I shot up straight. "Black letters come to those wise enough to untangle the prose. Black letters come to men who remember who served them when. Black letters come with a price. Remember what you owe. Bow to the sacrifice."

I gripped his wrist. "Your father used to mumble that when he was drunk."

"Yeah. So?"

Warmth leached from my skin. "So, you weren't the first person to recite that rhyme to me, Cairo. It was Cavendish. I overheard him saying it to himself once and I asked what it meant. He said..."

"What?" Cairo prompted when I stopped. "What did he say?"

"He said it was a reminder to repay your favors. That a man who doesn't uphold his side of a deal is lower than dirt. A letter is a chance to make things right," I said, echoing his words. "As long as they're smart enough to heed the opportunity.

"Why would your father be repeating the same rhyme as a psychopath?"

Nothing showed on his face. "Once again, you're asking the wrong person. I told you everything my father told me about that rhyme."

"Cairo, the most obvious conclusion is that they were sending him letters threatening you. He didn't know who it was. If he did,

Davidson would be in a dark hole where he belongs. The Men of Honor turned him. Against his will, but all the same, they did."

If I expected a loud and harsh denial, I didn't get it.

"Your instinct here is to jump to the simplest conclusion," Cairo said. "I don't blame you, but there's something obvious you're missing."

"Like what?"

A red light finally made him stop and look at me. "Who is in the Society of Sisters, de Souza?"

I frowned. "Your mothers. Nora, the mayor, the judge, the dean, and Legend's mother."

"Who told you this?"

"Zoey did. The night th-they—" I choked on the rest.

"There it is," he said, inclining his head. "If they know who they are, they know all of our mothers have a weakness. Nora couldn't give two shits about me, but she'd do anything for Paris. And Judge Stone, the mayor, and the dean aren't about to shrug it off and sit on their asses if letters fell on their doorstep, threatening their sons' lives.

"So if they're going to haul out the threats and violence toward anyone, why would they start so low on the totem pole? Why not get the mayor and judge to repeal all the laws standing in their way? Why not blackmail Mrs. St. James for all the money in her bank account, so they can buy the town outright?"

My lips parted but nothing came out. Cairo had a scarily good point. There was a benefit to having a sheriff in your pocket, but why would you start there if you could also control a mayor, judge, a dean, and two of the wealthiest women in town?

"Because they don't know who is in the Society."

"You just said—"

I flapped a hand. "No, no. I'm not talking about those who attacked us that night. The people working with Zoey and Cavendish.

I mean Steven Ellis and the Crows. *They* don't know who they're up against. You're right, why waste time in this war with the five of you, when they could've gone straight for your mothers?

"They must have…" The pieces struggled to come together. "Ellis must've made him cover up for Clein and AgriProspects. Cavendish and Ellis broke off their *partnership*. Cavendish wanted you dead as punishment for your dad working for the wrong side, because he didn't remember who served him when."

Cairo shifted back to the wheel, taking off. "It's a theory."

"That makes sense," I pressed. "Steven Ellis would be doing things a lot differently if he knew all the positions of power in town were held by women who were born to stand against him."

"But why didn't Cavendish tell him that when they were on good terms? How the fuck did he find out the truth about the Society in the first place? And why did he have you kill him before he achieved the Men of Honor's goal? Why are his people targeting you now instead of coming for us or the Society? I'm telling you, de Souza, you're looking for a simple explanation." He shook his head. "There's nothing simple about any of this."

We fell silent. My mind twisted and turned going down the myriad of possibilities for everything that'd happen to me. I couldn't begin to guess what Cairo was thinking.

"Do you think Arsenio will be okay?" The sheriff's house came into view.

"Do you care?"

"What?" My brows snapped together. "Of course I care. Why would you ask me that?"

Parking the car, he shoved his door open. "Rainey loved Arsenio. Not you."

"I—!"

Cairo slammed it shut and strode off inside without a backward glance. I fumed, shaking as I stared at the spot he disappeared. It wasn't because of what he said. It was the true meaning under it. What he wanted to say was *I loved Rainey. Not you.*

I had become a different person in his eyes, and he noticed it immediately. There were a lot of things I'd done and said over the years that weren't me but were so Rainey.

I became her in ways that shocked me now. I ate all her favorite foods, watched her favorite shows, redid my associate's degree under another name, and fell for guys I wouldn't have crossed paths with because of our age difference.

But fall for them I did. I remembered who I was in those final moments before I jumped off the bridge. I remembered Zoey taking away the last of my family and the sister I loved more than anything. As she stood there, smirking about ripping my guys away, I jumped to protect them without hesitation.

How did I make him see nothing's changed?

Why would he see that? an insidious voice asked. *Why would any of them? When a person you love changes in every way, they're no longer the person you love. Everything Rainey did to earn their trust and love, Ivy washed away in the river.*

I got out of the car, taking what felt like a mile-long journey to the welcome mat. No, I was no longer the version of my sweet sister that I was playing. The real me was calmer, harder, sharper. She was an endless well of pain and misery that she learned to wield into a weapon. There was nothing pleasant or submissive about the real me... which is why I won't sit back and take Cairo's shit.

He doesn't get to stop loving me. I would have him, Legend, Jacques, Arsenio, and Roan in every way they had me. Their hang-ups—they'd get over it. Their trust issues—they'd let them go.

The Bedlam Boys were mine.

Always will be.

I entered Jack Sharpe's beer-reeking, stained hovel, finding Cairo on the couch. I molded to his side, then tipped over, falling against the cushions when he shoved away from me. Swinging out, I grabbed his wrist and pulled, tugging him on top of me.

"Argh!" Cairo flipped and pinned me flat, securing my arms over my head. "Keep your fucking hands to yourself, de Souza."

My legs snaked around his waist. Looking him in the eyes, I said, "No."

Rage stoked into an inferno. "Let me make this very clear. I don't want you." His lips pressed to my ear. "I never will."

I pushed down the sting. Cairo was never going to make this easy for me. "You don't have to do this, Cairo. I'm not her." The barest peck brushed his lips. "I'm not Nora."

"Careful."

I didn't heed the warning in his hiss. "I'll always choose you."

He snarled, face twisting unrecognizable. "Then you're pathetic. I'm keeping you around until I figure out exactly what's going on in my town. After Jeremy, his boys, and all your old friends are in the ground, I'm done with you."

"We'll see."

"Pathetic," he whispered against my lips. "Waste your time on someone who can stand the sight of you. All I see is an impostor."

I didn't stop him getting up and storming upstairs. Dragging out the conversation was just inviting him to think of more horrible things to say to me. He lost Rainey the night before. When I lost her, I handled it much worse.

Sitting up, I settled in to wait. And wait. And wait.

Minutes stretched into hours. The sun stretched across the sky, giving rise to hunger pains that reminded me of how long it'd been since I'd eaten. Where the hell was Sheriff Sharpe?

"Cai—" I called out as his footsteps hit the stairs. I twisted around, meeting his gaze—still pissed. "Should he be taking this long?"

"This isn't a regular day on the job. Finding a body on the bridge calls for clocking out late."

I nodded. "I'll get started on making us something to eat, then."

"He won't have anything in the house," he said, going into the kitchen. Cairo returned with a phone and takeout menu. He tossed both in my direction.

"What do you want?" I called.

He didn't reply, heading back up the stairs.

Sighing, I studied the Chinese restaurant menu. I recognized the logo as the same one on the bags Paris carried into her room, beaming as we got down to a fun night of movies, board games, food, and geeking out.

Paris.

How was I supposed to tell her all of this? I could hardly say a psychotic death club got their hooks into me while my mental health was teetering on the edge, and then the murder of my sister was the final push that tipped me over.

I'm not the girl you knew. The one you had so much in common with. The one who could still make goofy jokes. Laugh. Smile. That girl died long before she lost her sister.

No, there just wasn't a good way to start that conversation.

"Hello, this is China Garden. How can I help you?"

"Hi. Can I have the honey garlic chicken, cashew chicken, and a small order of wonton soup, please? Thank you."

I gave him the address and wrapped up the call. My stomach was already growling for that cashew chicken.

"So you faked everything."

Jerking, I whirled around. Cairo watched me from his seat on the steps—elbows slung across his knees and gaze boring into me.

"Rainey hated nuts."

Slowly, I lowered the phone. "But I don't. This is strange for me too, Cairo. Imagine how it feels to come out of this fog and realize I was keeping her alive in this way—while her killers ran around free."

"This is just some switch you pulled. Twenty-four hours ago, you were Rainey de Souza. Now you're eating cashew chicken on my couch with that dead-eyed look like nothing touches you."

"If you've got something you want to ask, ask it," I snapped. "You want to know who I am. Who Ivy is. I'll tell you, Cairo. I'll tell you anything, but you need to stop acting like this was all one big plot to trick you guys into falling in love with me." Cairo stood in the middle of my sentence and walked off. "You don't get to make the worst thing that's ever happened to me about you!"

A door slam was my only reply.

Cursing, I clutched my head—pressure building behind my eyes. Goodness, he was such an ass. How had everything about me changed, but I was still in love with that prick?

The question passed through my mind and the answer rose to meet it. I still loved him because one thing hadn't changed. The darkness in him called to me. It had always been there no matter what name I called myself. These were the only guys for me. Anyone else would look in these dead eyes... and run.

Eventually, the food came. I called for Cairo but he didn't come down. There was no use pushing him. I left his food outside the door and continued my silent vigil downstairs. I had plenty of thoughts to occupy my mind.

Who killed Zoey? If the Bedlam's Men of Honor and Steven Ellis's Men of Honor didn't want the same thing, what were they after? Why come for Gran and my family? Were there diamonds on my farm? Had they been there all along?

Back and forth my mind went long into the night. The more answers we got, the less I understood.

"De Souza?" A firm hand shook me. "De Souza, get up."

I shot up, heavy eyes cracking open. Empty containers and fallen couch cushions greeted me. I fell asleep.

"Cairo? Is your father here?" I spun, noting a sunless sky seeping moonlight through the window. "You didn't talk to him without me, did you?"

"I would've, but no." A look I'd never seen before crept across his handsome face. "Old man didn't come home. I ended up calling the station. The receptionist picked up and said he left hours ago. Something's wrong."

"Wrong? You said a new body meant late nights." I got to my feet, vision clearing on the clock. It was two in the morning. "Could he be out tracking down leads on Zoey's killer?"

"He would be, if there was any report of a body found on Chaney Bridge." Cold understanding dawned. "Connie didn't know what the hell I was talking about. She's never heard of Zoey Mariner or that she's dead."

"He took her." The truth ripped from my throat. "Arsenio was bleeding out. Zoey was dead. We had no choice but to get out of there and get him help. After we left, he took the body. Whoever killed her was watching the whole time."

He nodded—a sharp jerk of the head.

"But if the sheriff isn't out chasing her killer, where is he?"

"We've established that I don't know everything that guy gets up to. He prefers to do his drinking alone here where gossip won't spread, but he could've hit up a bar. I'm going out to look, and taking you to Paris."

"No, I'm going with you," I said before he finished the sentence. "Why should we split up?"

In a blink, he was in my face. "Because I want rid of you, but I also want you right where I can find you. You're going to Paris. Stop wasting my time arguing."

Cairo marched to the door, expecting me to follow. I did. I was going everywhere he went whether he liked it or not. Let him drive to Paris's place, unless he planned to carry me inside, I wasn't getting out of the car. I would be there when he spoke to his father. I was getting the truth—all of it. Tonight.

Cairo yanked on the knob, stepping aside to let me through first. I froze, eyes widening.

"Cairo." My lips went numb. "Cairo... look."

Frowning, he followed my gaze to the welcome mat, and the single black letter lying upon it.

He stilled.

A minute passed.

Two.

Three.

I took a step. Then another.

Cairo didn't move or stop me. Bending down, I picked up the letter and cracked the seal.

Cairo Sharpe,

Apologies for our associate. She went rogue and forgot our true purpose. For that, she had to go.

We are now under new management. Mine.

We do not wish the Bedlam Boys dead. You serve too important a function, fighting Steven Ellis and his plans out in the open while we're confined to the shadows. As long as you continue serving that purpose and give up any attempts to find us, you, your friends, your girlfriend, and your father get to live.

Of course, the Bedlam Boys are used to doing what they want, whenever they want. Taking orders is hard for you, so as an incentive to stay in line, we're hanging on to your father until our joint goal is complete, and Steven Ellis is gone for good.

It's for the best. For us to do what we do and assist in the fight, we need a sheriff whose loyalty is without question.

Bedlam will not be had by the descendant of a coward who abandoned the fight. We've stayed right here, bleeding and sacrificing for the legacy that is our birthright. Bedlam will be ours.

So get to work.

Signed,

Dante

Cairo didn't say a word as I read. He still wasn't moving.

"Dante," I repeated, lips twisting. "He is one of them, and he took your father." I reached for him. "Cairo, say something."

Nothing.

I read the letter again, then again. "*We need a sheriff whose loyalty is without question.* He didn't bother to sugarcoat. Davidson—the evil, corrupt piece of shit—will be put in charge." I paused for Cairo's reaction. He gazed at the mat like the letter was still there. "I... I don't even want to think about what this means. Even if we report your father's disappearance, he'll make sure the investigation goes nowhere. And as for everything else these guys plan to do..."

I stared at him. "Cairo? Cairo, say something."

"Okay."

It took me a moment to realize the word came from him. His lips barely moved.

"Okay? Okay, what?"

"Okay," he repeated, finally turning to me. Finally letting me see his eyes.

I lurched back.

"They want a war." Cairo snatched the letter. "They've got one."

Chapter Two

Cairo did drive me to Paris's place. And he did lift me bodily out of the car and carry me thrashing to the gate where Paris yawned on the other side.

My argument that he needed help with the search for his father fell on uncaring ears. My comment that none of us should be out alone right then earned a laugh. In the end, I fought him a fraction less hard than I wanted to. He lost Rainey and his father in the span of two days. Some space wasn't an unreasonable request. As long as he accepted at some point while we were apart... that he was mine.

"Are you okay?"

I shook myself, returning to reality and the breakfast tray Paris carried inside.

"You've been quiet all morning."

"I'm fine." I gazed down at the scrambled eggs, turkey sausage, and sliced avocado. Tears pricked behind my lids.

These were all Rainey's favorites. Gran's breakfast plates for me had fried eggs, fried bacon, and no green in sight.

We've always been so different, baby sister. That didn't stop you from being my best friend. Of course my mind went so far to hold on to you. I couldn't stand for everything you were and everything you loved to disappear with you.

"Rainey?" Paris asked, making me flinch. "What's up? You're not hungry?"

My lips parted, and common sense grabbed hold of my tongue.

I couldn't tell her I was really Ivy de Souza without explaining *all* of it. "Rainey" had been telling people for two years that her sister was living happily in Chicago. To say that I was actually Ivy and the real Rainey was gone, would lead to questions I couldn't answer.

"Starved," I finally said. "It's hard to do something as normal as eating and chatting with you after everything that's happened."

Blowing out a breath, she flopped back on her pillows. "Tell me about it. My attack. The video of Roan's beating. The Crows strung up and branded in the square. To think I wanted to leave Bedlam because it was the most boring place on earth. Now I would give anything to rewind back to the sleepy, peaceful town where nothing ever happened."

I thought of her mother downstairs. "That's what so many people fought for Bedlam to be over the years. A home. Our home," I said. "Where we're safe to live and raise our families without being harassed and exploited by people like the Crows and Steven Ellis."

"Ugh. They are reason enough for why we don't need Bedlam to be like Hunter's Crest. We could use some updates around here, but none that those fucks have had their grubby hands on." Shaking her head, she threw out her hands. "Enough. I don't want to talk about those guys anymore. Let's do something fun today. Get our minds off everything."

"I really want to do that, but would it be okay if we went to visit Roan? A lot's happened and I want to tell him in person."

"Of course, I should've thought of that. Is he doing better? Last I heard they had him on so many drugs, he sleeps all day."

"I don't know if he's better," I confessed. "That's why I want to see him."

She squeezed my arm. "Let's do it. Afterward, we can grab lunch at a theme café. Maybe do some shopping for a get-well gift."

I said yes to it all, thankful she was willing to drive me. The whole being-without-a-car thing was quickly becoming inconvenient. It made it way too easy for the Bedlam Boys to leave me places and take off. It also meant that in all these dark, wooded, secluded places that called my town home, I'd be trapped.

After breakfast, we showered, dressed, and took off for Hunter's Crest Hospital. Nora stopped us at the door, demanding to know where we were going. I couldn't know exactly what she knew, but I had to assume it was more than me at all times.

The Society had been operating to keep people out of Bedlam for a long time. Decades upon decades, passed down from daughter to daughter. I didn't need to tell her Steven Ellis and Foundry were a threat. And maybe I didn't need to tell her Dante and his followers were threats too, but if we could ever have a real conversation, I'd bet there were quite a few things that she could tell me.

Like, why Gran? Why our farm? Why her ex-husband?

I slipped past her, leaving my questions on my tongue. She had no reason to reveal her secrets to me, not unless I revealed a few of my own.

Paris blasted music the whole way. I appreciated it since it gave me a reason not to talk. The guys noticed the change in me right away. For as long as possible, I had to delay that revelation for Paris. The truth would come, but any decent person would insist we go to the police and start the hunt for Rainey's killers. Neither one of us could walk into that station with Davidson in charge.

Paris turned into the visitors' parking lot, pulling me out of my musings. Seeing the three-story, state-of-the-art facility in front of me and comparing it to the small office in the middle of town with a single doctor, I understood why Cairo was working so hard to get Bedlam its first real hospital.

We wasted precious time rushing Roan to Hunter's Crest. We would've wasted even more if we hadn't been able to get ahold of Doctor Nash. My boys were making Bedlam better in their own way.

But what were Foundry's plans? A thriving city center to rival Hunter's Crest?

My ass.

He'd raze the town to the ground to extract every drop of wealth hidden beneath it. When he was done, what was his incentive to rebuild the pile of dirt and rubble? He'd just take his precious stones, return to his mansion, home, and headquarters, and count his money.

"I'm glad those bastards are in jail," Paris said. We paused before the front desk to get visitor passes. "I just hate that it took *this* for them to finally be put behind bars."

"Their first mistake was attacking you, Paris. They were never going to get away with what they did. The Crows underestimated Bedlam. Big-time."

"There's a plaza across the street," she said. "I'll go up and say hi, then I'll leave you two alone. Give you some privacy. I should be able to find a nice gift for him in one of the shops."

"Thanks, Paris. Thanks for driving me and thanks for... everything. You've been such a good friend to me."

She let out a gusty sigh. "There goes that girl crush. Keep it in your pants, de Souza, we're about to see your boyfriend."

A few days ago, I would've laughed. I wasn't that person anymore.

As it was, I tried for a smile. It was gone as quickly as it spread across my face.

"Yeah, I know," she said, side-hugging me. Understanding passed between us, nearly tugging a real smile to my lips. She truly was a good friend.

"He's on the third floor. Room 312. I hope he is awake and recovering," I said. "It's not the same without his Roan-ness around."

She laughed. We made it to the elevator, stepping inside. "I know exactly what you mean. He can be such a dick, but you still can't help but like him."

"Something about someone who is so unapologetically themselves. No masks. No games. No faking. He's just Roan."

"Huh. I never thought of it like that, but you're right." The elevator dinged on our floor. "I guess you can't say that about many people. Roan lets the world see all of him—good and bad. Maybe we're the dicks for always walking around pretending."

I inclined my head. People like Zoey and Cavendish would've saved the world a lot of trouble if they revealed their evil and got locked up in a facility where they belonged.

Roan's room loomed ahead of us. We went in, interrupting a conversation between Legend and Josephine Banks.

"Rainey. Paris." Dean Banks stood and hugged both of us. Over her shoulder, I locked eyes with an alert and watchful Roan. "Thank you for coming."

"Is now a good time to visit?" Paris asked.

"Of course it is. The doctor says he'll be here for a few more days, but look at him." Josephine went over and smooched her son's cheek. "He's getting stronger every day."

"Hey, Roan," I said.

"De Souza." His voice was little more than a thin rasp. The third in our Legend-Roan-Me sandwich looked like a limp and battered piece of lettuce. Faded bruises covered every part of him I could see. His chest and head were bandaged, and the pillows held him up more than he held himself. But he was awake, and watching me with piercing eyes.

Legend told him everything.

"I thought there'd be security on the door," I spoke up, just for something to say.

"I sent them to grab a bite to eat," Josephine explained. "We're here. No one's getting to my boy."

"I'm so spoiled," Roan said, that ever-present smirk hanging on his lips. "They've got the nurses giving me sponge baths with gold-flecked soap. Carrying me to tests on a cushioned litter."

"They call that a gurney."

The smirk widened. "Yeah, it's still her."

I broke his gaze, knowing what he meant.

Paris claimed Legend's seat. I hung back while they talked. Suddenly, everything I came there to say went out of my head.

Legend moved to my side. His shoulder brushed mine leaning against the wall. "What happened with Cairo's dad?" he asked under his breath.

"Did you talk to him?"

"He's not answering his phone."

I flicked to Josephine. I didn't let my voice carry. "Sheriff Sharpe was taken. We found a black letter on his doorstep last night. They said they're keeping him until the Bedlam Boys get rid of Ellis and Foundry for good. The letter was signed by Dante."

The lines around his mouth hardened. "How? When?"

"We don't know. It was two a.m. before we gave up waiting. We didn't see anyone deliver the letter, but Davidson works with him. It would've been all too easy to invite the sheriff for some after-work beers and then..."

Legend nodded, following my thoughts to the natural conclusion. "Where did Cairo go after?"

I just shook my head.

"This isn't good. They've got us running around, chasing after shadows. And those shadows are giving us orders like we fucking work for them."

"The letter mentioned that. They took the sheriff so you'd get over your hang-ups about taking orders. They won't give him up unless we do what they say."

"Do you care?"

"No," I said flatly. I didn't pause to think about it. "They can do whatever the hell they want with Sheriff Jack Sharpe. But I would care if they didn't stop there. I believed I didn't have anyone left to care about, but... Rainey... made friends.

"Frankie, Paris, you guys. You were there for me while I was lost. I'll do what it takes to drive Foundry out, because Ellis has it coming anyway. He's behind AgriProspects and what Clein did to Gran. While we're bringing him down, we'll take the others from my old group down with him."

Legend stepped in front of me, presence bearing down. "Are you sure you don't know who any of the others are? Mariner or Cavendish must've let a name slip. Or you saw them hanging around someone? Think, de Souza."

"What do you think I've been doing since I was pulled out of that water," I hissed. "I've done nothing but rack my brain. Those bastards murdered my sister and left me for dead. No one wants to find them more than me!"

He held up his hands. "Okay, you're right, but... Is it possible there are still gaps in your memory? Did everything about the night they attacked come back? Do you remember how many there were at least?"

"I... yeah." Familiar pressure built between my temples. "It was Zoey and five others. Cavendish wasn't there."

"Are you sure?"

I bobbed my head. "I knew his build. His voice. He wasn't there. With him and Zoey gone, that leaves five."

"Unless they recruited more people in the last two years," he reminded. "But five is a good place to start. What else do you remember about them? Height, build, anything."

I eyed him. "Why are you so okay with this, Legend? Cairo is pissed. I can't guess what Jacques is thinking. But you're not looking at me any differently."

He made a frustrated noise, carding his fingers through his hair. "I'm not going to pretend I understand what's going on with you. Masquerading as your dead sister for two years. That's way the hell beyond me. But..."

Tensing, my breath trapped in my throat.

"I can't think of a single thing you'd gain by doing that. Can't even say you did it to get close to us, since we came after you. Something terrible happened to you and you didn't deal well. You're fucked up, de Souza. Just like the rest of us. I'll cut you some slack until you prove you don't deserve it."

"Slack?" I whispered. "I want more than slack from you. Tell me things haven't changed between us. That me, you, and Roan are still... me, you, and Roan."

Dark locks shadowed those light-brown eyes. "I wouldn't expect more than the slack."

He loped off, joining Paris and Roan's conversation. I hung back, not nearly as stung as I should be. Legend may feel that way now, but he'd change his mind. He'd change it a lot easier than Cairo and possibly Arsenio, because he said the entirely wrong thing if he wanted to break up with me.

"You're fucked up, de Souza. Just like the rest of us."

That's what always bonded us. That's why their revolving door of girlfriends would end with me. The Bedlam Boys had to hide their true selves with everyone else, but they never did with me. You don't walk away from that kind of bond.

"Would you guys give us a minute?" Roan asked. "I sense the lovely wallflower in the corner wants a private conversation."

Legend didn't move. "Roan." Warning laced his tone.

"I'm good, Legend." He probed his eyes—a silent communication passing between them.

"It's all right." Paris stood up. "I'm off to get that list of contraband items for you. Hope you've got a good stash spot."

Roan clutched his heart. "Paris." Already a pretty name, but there was something seductive about it when said in Roan's smoky rasp. "If you weren't my friend's sister... Eh, I'd still give it a shot."

Paris laughed. I did not.

"Careful," I said.

Roan's brows shot up. He looked way too amused for someone plucking my nerves. I would accept a breakup as easily as I'd accept them flirting with other people in front of me. As in not at all.

"Come, Legend." Josephine linked through his arm. "Let's grab a bite ourselves while they talk. Paris, you'll come with us and *forgo* buying any such contraband."

Felt like an eternity before they were gone, and it was just us.

I claimed an empty seat beside his bed. "How are you?"

He shrugged and paid for it with a wince. "Look worse than I am."

"Did they tell you the Crows were arrested? They're in hospital beds too. But unlike you, they're cuffed to them."

"I heard." Dropping his head back, wavy reddish strands brushed his pale forehead. "Doesn't mean much though. Why do you think they rolled into our town acting like they already owned it? The Crows have been doing whatever the fuck they want, and buying themselves out of trouble since Daddy stopped wiping their shitty bottoms. I wouldn't expect any judge in Hunter's Crest to do more than slap them on the wrist."

"The Crows aren't doing whatever they want now." Slowly, I slipped my hand across the sheets, resting my fingers on his. Roan didn't pull away. "You guys put a scare in them that has the Crows wishing their daddy still wiped their shitty bottoms, because they're shaking too hard to do it themselves."

He chuckled softly. "You still sound like you."

I dropped my gaze. "I was always me, Roan. You can copy someone else, but you can't really become them. In the end, that's all I w-was." My throat constricted. "A cheap copy while the real Rainey needed me."

"Hmm."

I waited him out. "Roan, please, tell me what you're thinking. Cairo dumped me yesterday. Legend pretty much dumped me ten minutes ago. Have your feelings changed about me too?"

He pulled a face, tugging on his cut brow, split lips, and swollen eye. "Is your pussy any less delicious than it was three days ago?"

"Roan, I'm being serious."

"Do I not sound serious?"

"No, you don't." I moved up onto the bed, drawing us closer. "Say flat out and plainly that nothing changed between us. You still love and want to be with me."

That pixie grin would never leave his lips. "Okay, I'll say this flat out and plain: I am your sex toy for now until the end of everything. I wouldn't give you up even if you were hiding a sixty-year-old man with a golden shower fetish in that split personality of yours."

A sharp, barking laugh slipped through my teeth. I did ask him to give it to me straight, and this was straight Roan.

Leaning down, I carefully rested my head on his chest. His heart beat beneath my ear. Steady. Strong.

"How can you be so cool about this?"

"Because what's really changed, Ivy?"

My name on his lips stunned me.

"You still lost your family. You're still being targeted by these crazy, black-letter shitheads. You still know the truth about us and don't care. And I assume you still know all of Rainey's sex tricks."

I rolled my eyes. "Shut up. I can't believe the things we got up to. If things were different, I wouldn't have looked twice at a bunch of guys who were younger than me and still in college, but then I would've missed out on the best sex of my life."

"That's right," he hummed. "Technically, you are an older woman. Not my first, but I'm glad you'll be my last. This opens up a whole new world of role-playing for us."

I buried my smile in his chest, amazed it was there. How was he so good at making me do that?

Because he has me under his spell. Another guy who will not use his powers for good.

"The point is nothing's changed for me. So if you rushed up here worried you were going three for three with the dumping, we're good."

I sighed. "I wish Cairo and Legend felt the same way. Plus, I haven't really gotten to talk to Jacques or Arsenio. I know they'll make it difficult for me, but if those fuckers think I'm giving up the hearts I fought so hard to win, they're in for a surprise."

"Mmm. Can't decide if that's crazy or sexy. Either way, we haven't fucked in days. Climb in."

I picked up my head, goggling at him. "Climb in? Roan, you just survived a severe beating. You were pretty much in a coma, and you can't even shrug without pain. Not to mention we're in a hospital," I stressed. "We're not having sex."

He looked at me like he genuinely couldn't see why anything I said was a problem. "What else are we supposed to do?"

"We could talk. A lot more happened on that bridge."

Roan drew my head back on his chest. "Legend told me everything that happened on the bridge and what you talked about yesterday morning." He scoffed. "We thought we knew everything that goes down in Bedlam. We didn't have a fucking clue."

"Cavendish was smart. He played me like a drum. It never even occurred to me to betray him until he overplayed his hand and pushed me too far. The charm he cast still has a strong hold over the others—dead or not. They'll carry out whatever his purpose is, and they killed Zoey to make sure of it."

"Wait, they killed Mariner? How do you know?"

"Oh, Legend and Cairo didn't have a chance to tell you." I explained everything that went down since we found that black letter on the sheriff's welcome mat. "You know the saying that the enemy of my enemy is my friend. Foundry has gotten a lot of families to sell to them.

"All they need is the vote to swing their way, and they had that locked up before the Crows went too far. They're gone now, but we both know Steven Ellis is going to ride back in with more sweet talk, better offers, fancier promises, and then everyone will start dreaming of those chain malls, clubs, music venues, theaters, and all the rest we've been missing out on."

"What are you saying?"

I looked him in the eyes. "I'm saying Foundry's going to win, Roan. They've all but won already. You guys tried, but you couldn't stop people from selling their homes. And you can't stop a bunch of college students from wishing the only real fun around here didn't only happen on Ruckus Royale night. Everyone wants Bedlam to become more modern, but no one knows that we'll lose everything if that happens.

"We've got to do something drastic to get rid of Foundry for good, and Dante and his Men of Honor won't risk losing that fight because they got caught up in one with the Bedlam Boys. They're happy to stay in the shadows while you guys—I'll just say it—break almost every law getting rid of Foundry. Then when it's over—"

"We're the only enemy left standing," he finished. "That is until their pet cop arrests all of us for the exact laws we broke. We don't have Sheriff Jack covering for us anymore."

My lips twisted. "It's neat, isn't it? They play our allies until the war destroys us and Foundry. Then they step in and take over."

"Do we know they want the same thing as Foundry and Ellis? Did Cavendish ever give a hint?"

"He said a lot of strange, cryptic stuff about reclaiming what was stolen from us. The only thing I know that was stolen in Bedlam is Bedlam itself."

"The Men of Honor want to be running things again. Take it all back from the Society. We—"

"Ooh. Hope we're not interrupting." I shot up as three guys entered the room. "Damn, it took forever for Mommy and your security to leave, and still we couldn't get you alone."

The guys fanned out—each one taller, stockier, and smirkier than the last. Two of them wore leather jackets and jeans, while the one standing between them opted for a tight, white shirt and ripped-up, paint-splattered pants that were once jeans.

I put them down as our age. Dark-haired and handsome, they didn't look a thing alike but there was something similar about all of them.

My gaze honed on their necks, and the inky crows flying on their skin. "Who are you?" I flicked to the remote on Roan's nightstand. One push of a button and it'd alert the nurse. "What are you doing in here?"

"There's no need for you to hit that call button you're eyeing. We just came to talk."

"The lady asked you a question," Roan said. "Who are you?"

Middle Guy smiled. "Let's just say we're friends of Jeremy."

"Ah. Did you come here to finish what they started?"

"Like hell they did," I cried, snatching up the remote. "Turn around and get out. Now."

He threw up his hands in mock surrender. "Easy. Like I said, we just came to talk. Jeremy made a mess of things down here in Crystal Canyon. That's what happens when you make business personal."

"It's called Bedlam."

His smile widened. "For now."

The guy on his left stepped forward. "I'm Adriel. That's Nathan. And he's Ethan," he said, going down the row. "Jeremy, Micah, and the other guys are taking a break right now while they sort out some legal matters. On top of the little issue of their being expelled. Since we'll be transferring in at the start of the new semester, we thought we should clear the air before you Bedlam Boy guys saw our tattoos and assumed we have beef with you too. We don't."

My thumb hovered over the button. "So, you lay in wait outside Roan's hospital room like a couple of stalkers just to tell him that? It didn't occur to you to send a text?"

The middle guy, Nathan, grinned. "Rainey de Souza. Heard a lot about you. No, we didn't send a text. An apology should be given in person, don't you think? We're sorry for everything those guys did while bearing our tattoo. Jeremy Ellis doesn't run the Crows. He only thinks he does because of Daddy's money." He thumped his chest. "I'm in charge. We're looking for things to be a lot more civil from here on out."

"Civil," Roan drew out. "You said he thought he was in charge because of Daddy's money. Is that money going to you now?"

His grin widened. "Why would it be? Never even met the guy." Nathan jerked his chin at his boys. "We said what we came here to say. I'm sure you'll pass it on to your friends, because we're not interested in continuing the war. So don't come for us... or we'll have to respond." Turning their backs, they filed out as silently as they came in. Neither of us tried to stop them.

"You heard the subtext in that loud and clear, right?"

Roan nodded, eyes fluttering shut. "They're going to roll into our town, playing innocent. Anything we do to them is going to look like we're taking out our shit with Jeremy and his buddies on anyone with that damn black pigeon on their neck. In the meantime, they'll keep on trying to turn students to voting Foundry's way."

"That tactic isn't going to work as well as they think," I said. "I mean, I'm sure they can turn students, but playing innocent won't protect them. If you do strike, Davidson won't do a thing about it." The truth burned my tongue. "Just like Dante wants."

"We're not his puppets." Roan's speech was slowing. His eyes closed and looked fit to stay that way. "He doesn't tell us how to handle our business. And damn sure he doesn't get to install his pet cop in Sheriff Sharpe's place and think we'll let him stay there long enough for his ass to warm the seat. After what he did to you and your sister... he's gone, Ivy," Roan said, drifting. "They're all gone."

"If we move against Davidson, they'll kill Sheriff Sharpe." I inclined my head. "More reason to do it."

Roan chuckled under his breath. "Oh yeah. You're still... you."

Just like that, he was out. I let him be—content to stroke his cheek while he slept. Cairo may have given up on me. Legend may close off his feelings for me like he closed his true self to the world. But my Roan was so unapologetically himself, he was drawn to the same. This is me in my screwed-up, damaged glory, and he loved it.

Seemed like minutes later, Paris, Legend, and Josephine strolled in with gifts for Roan and a turkey panini for me. I took it and Legend's hand, tugging him out into the hall.

"We need to talk," I said before he pulled away. "We just had visitors..."

JACQUES

I stood in Henry Gold's office, cataloging everything from the worn carpets to the man. He scrubbed his haggard face, sitting down hard in his desk chair.

"This is a lot to take in."

"You knew, did you not? That's what you called to tell her."

"I called to tell Rainey that there's no trace of her sister. No credit card usage, leases, accounts in her name. Anything. I had to tell a young woman who lost her grandmother and was under siege by a psychopath, that her sister was missing and she should assume the worst. I never thought..."

He trailed off, and I picked up the thread. "That the real Rainey de Souza was murdered by said psychopath. Ivy had a mental breakdown and began believing she was, in fact, her younger sister."

"Yes," he rasped. "I don't think anyone could've made that leap. But how?" Gold reached into his desk drawer and came away with a bottle of whiskey and a glass. "How could she just become her sister and no one know?"

"The sisters were homeschooled on a farm until college. Ivy enrolled in Bedlam University and did two years. When she lost her grandmother, she dropped out to take care of the farm and her sister. She also focused all her time on finding out the truth of what happened to Abigail de Souza. When she became Rainey and reenrolled at Bedlam—"

"Everyone who knew Ivy de Souza had already graduated," he finished. "Fuck's sake. All that time she needed help, and no one knew. She's been suffering alone for years. That poor girl."

My jaw clenched. Yes, by every logical way you looked at the situation, Ivy wasn't at fault. She was young, alone, manipulated, betrayed, and the loss of her only family sent her over the edge. It wasn't rational for us to blame her. To look at her and feel like she stole something from us.

"Sure, but everything doesn't have to be logical, does it?"

Said to me by the woman I thought she was, and only at that moment did I accept it as the truest thing she ever said. Nothing about my anger, betrayal, or grief was logical. The Rainey I knew never existed, and the woman I did was the victim of tragedy—not its architect.

These feelings should not exist, and moreover, they shouldn't be taken out on her but...

"I find myself growing attached to you.

"I would not appreciate it if you left," I said. "Don't."

"I won't, Jacques." She rested in the crook of my neck. "I'm not going anywhere."

I asked her not to leave, and she did anyway.

"Mr. Stone?"

Raising my head, I withdrew from the memory of her on my lap. Under my claim. "It's quite unfortunate," I said simply, "but my focus is on what we can do now. Ivy told me you hired someone to track the IP address of Dante's website. What did they turn up?"

"Right, of course. She sent me a report." Setting down his drink, Gold booted his computer. I waited with patience I didn't feel. "Here it is. All right, she was able to track the computer to—"

I bolted upright.

"—132 Chestnut Grove. I'll look up the location—"

"There's no need," I said, sinking back. "132 Chestnut Grove is Bedlam University. Was she able to pinpoint where on campus, at least? A dorm building? A frat house?"

Gold typed something in and then turned the screen to me. Squinting at the map, I made out a building I knew well.

"The computer lab."

He sighed. "I apologize. This doesn't help you."

"No need for apology. Confirmation of a theory is useful in and of itself. We rationalized that the person was nearby and likely a student. You cannot get into the computer lab without a student pass, so now we know. We can exclude the townspeople and focus our search on the university."

"You'll need surveillance equipment in the computer lab. Mine is available to you free of charge."

"The computer lab is five floors with private study rooms on each one. We'd be going through hours of footage waiting for him to come in and update his site. We don't have that kind of time," I said. "He puts on his show much more often. Can your hacker track the broadcasts?"

The look he gave me said it all. "I will ask, but I assume she'll have as much luck as everyone else who has tried to track down the Dantes of your town. It's different with a podcast. He can record from a safe location, and then upload it anywhere else."

"Have her do it all the same. I will pay her fee."

Gold inclined his head. "She is one of the best. I'll get her on it immediately. I hope whatever she turns up brings you closer to finding the Letter Man, but you should know, at this point, I'm passing everything I turn up on to Ribecco. We're dealing with a murderer who shot an innocent kid through the chest in front of dozens of people. This isn't a situation Ra— Ivy is equipped to handle alone. Honestly, she needs to focus solely on her recovery, not all of this ugliness."

I nodded to appease him. There wasn't an argument I could make to convince the man six college students should be in charge of tracking down the new leader of a death cult, instead of an entire police force. Especially because I could not explain that the person who put an arrow through Binari's chest and sent those second round of letters was dead.

It was a good thing our girl thought Zoey/Dante was the same person when she put Gold on Dante's trail. Now he could continue the search for him even though Zoey Mariner was dead. Dante had to be found. The leverage he had over Cairo with the sheriff under his grip was unacceptable.

"There's another matter," I began. "How much do you know about Bedlam's history?"

"I assume you mean how it was founded."

"I mean how it got its name changed. The Men of Honor," I said, leaning forward. "Have you heard of them?"

"I have." He mimicked my movement. "They were a group of men who let privilege turn into savagery. It's said they held hunts and captured innocent young women to do what savage, awful men do."

"Yes, that would be the men I'm speaking of. During the revolt, the townspeople rounded up the Men and their families. Anyone who wasn't quick enough was killed, but a few were spared," I said, thinking of the niece and ancestor to Ivy and Rainey. "Either they weren't in town when the fighting broke out, or some members of their family survived. Can you track down their descendants?"

"Ah. Tracking down heirs and missing family members is work I take on, but when we're talking about lines of descent that go back a hundred years, it's a different matter. Especially taking into account that I'm beginning my search with a massacre. That kind of forensic genealogy would take me months—maybe longer." He reached into his desk drawer again. "I can refer you to a colleague who specializes in this. She's local and might've begun the work of tracing the old families of Crystal Canyon on her own."

I accepted the card. True enough that someone has already begun the work. They found those descendants for Steven Ellis. I had little chance of finding whoever did that for him. As much of a chance of finding someone who could do the same for me quickly, but I had to try. The more people searching for Dante and the acolytes he commanded, the better. Ivy/Rainey had been feeling their unseen eyes on her for years. Now it was their turn to feel the walls closing in.

IVY

My bare feet padded across the hardwood, retreading familiar steps. From Paris's place to Legend's place to the Crows' old place, I'd been everywhere except the only home I found outside of the farm.

I paused in front of the newly replaced window, recalling the doghouse that once sat beneath it. Micah threw a rock through the window that night, waking us all up to what he and his brother did to Arsenio's last connection to his father. They made their vendetta personal, and that's what took them down. These new Crows didn't give a shit about me or the Bedlam Boys. This would be all business to them, and no matter what they claimed, they were here on business.

How much more dangerous did that make them?

"What's wrong, Jacques?" I asked without turning around. I didn't need to. His gaze was drilling a hole in the back of my head. "Arsenio is in the hospital. Legend is camped out by Roan's bedside. And Cairo just up and disappeared. I wanted to go out looking for him, but you listed every reason why it was foolish to drive around aimlessly. Cairo will show his face when he's ready and not before.

"We came back here instead, but I get the feeling you'd rather be anywhere else than with me." I turned to him. "Do you want to search for Cairo without me? It's okay. I'll stay here and get started writing down everything I remember about—"

"I'm not letting you out of my sight."

An entire barrier of wood and stone separated us. Jacques stood in the kitchen, enigmatic eyes watching me from the other side of the island.

"Okay," I said softly. Slowly, I moved toward him. "I'm glad actually. Of course I'm worried about Cairo, but this gives us a chance to talk. Just the two of us."

"We have nothing to talk about."

"That's not true. You forget, Jacques, how well I know you."

His eyes flashed. "But I don't know you. I never did."

I paused for a second, choosing my words carefully. "I don't know that you did even when I thought I was Rainey. Things happened so quickly between the six of us. Our connection was so strong that we fell hard and fast into obsession. The thing with that is obsession always gets a smack in the face when life gets real."

"Real," he repeated like the sound tasted strange on his tongue. "How are any of us to know what's real, de Souza? A few days ago, you didn't know yourself."

My nails pierced my palm. "I had hoped you of all people wouldn't hold that against me."

"I don't— I'm trying not to!" Jacques's fist smashed the countertop. "But she's gone! I told her not to leave, and she did!"

I blew back, eyes huge. I only heard Jacques yell once in all the time we'd been together, and that night his mother was poisoned.

"Don't tell me I didn't know her. Rainey spent her time researching and cooking healthy meals for me. She traded expensive clothes for used sneakers and sweatshirts. Her favorite shampoos smelled of fruit. She loved a ridiculous, implausible show about a time-traveling alien. Nothing scares her other than losing the people she cares about. She'd walk into any dangerous situation."

He barked a laugh. "She lived with us after framing the Bedlam Boys for murder. We were never beasts, monsters, mysteries, or tools to her. But what are we to you, Ivy de Souza? How far out of obsession did reality pull you?"

"Nothing's changed for me," I cried, rushing the island. "I don't feel any differently for you guys than I did before we stepped on that bridge. I love you!"

"You can't," he snapped. "You're not the same person."

"Why are you so sure of that?" Suddenly, I was shouting too. "Okay, maybe I won't watch the same shows or eat the same foods, but I'd still make you healthy breakfasts because those shakes are disgusting, and I love cooking. I'll still massage Cairo's temples because it was me who had those tantrums after losing my parents, but Gran always knew what to do to make me feel better. Cairo didn't have love like that growing up, but he does now—from me."

I thumped my chest. "I'll still tell Roan things I thought I couldn't tell anyone, because he trusted me even before I gave him reason. I'll be the only one Legend shows his true side because even though he doubts it, there's nothing he can do or say to drive me away. My love isn't conditional like his parents'. And Arsenio..." I tossed my head. "That night with Alex Verlice would've sent my sweet, sheltered sister running far and fast, but not me. Arsenio doesn't scare me. He never could. He's my soul mate. You all are!

"Nothing that matters has changed. Why can't you see that?!"

Slowly, rigidly, Jacques moved out from behind the island. "So what has?"

"Excuse me?"

"What has changed, de Souza? We may have to start over, but I'm not doing it at the beginning. Tell me who this woman is who expects to sleep in my bed, serve my meals, and fight a fight with me that she's somehow the center of. Who are you, Ivy?"

I was quiet for a spell, observing him with the same look he gave me. Breaking free, I went to the window.

"What are you doing?"

"I'm answering your question, baby." I drew the blinds and curtains shut. "For some reason, you and I are never closer than when I'm naked and vulnerable before you. Something that was easier for... who I used to be. So, help me get there." Facing him, my fingers skimmed my shirt hem. "Ask me what you want to know, Jacques. Get me there."

He eyed me warily. "Why play games? Just speak."

"Because you never have to figure people out, Jacques. You answered the question of who they were a long time ago, then you filed it away in that storage room and never revisited it. You don't get to take the shortcut with me, and I don't get to keep my walls up with you. That's why we make sense, Jacques Stone. So let's not mess with what works."

He took a step, then another. "I do not understand what you base this theory on."

"I know, but there's no harm in trying it, is there? It's me opening myself up to you. What's the harm?"

Studying him, I read in his expression that he couldn't think of one—which was always my genius love's undoing. His drive to take the logical course of action worked in my favor. And he once said I didn't know him.

Fixed on me, he moved to the couch, slowly setting himself down. I pushed the coffee table aside as he did the many mornings he alternated between spanking my bottom raw, and fingering me to countless orgasms.

"Okay," I said, nudging his legs apart as I positioned between them. "What do you want to know?"

Jacques pointedly grasped my hips and moved me back, edging me out of his space. "What did you study when you went to school here as yourself?"

Of all the things I thought he'd start with, I wasn't expecting that. It took me a beat to answer. "I... studied marketing."

He nodded, expression unreadable. "So, you never wanted the farm."

"It's not that simple." Keeping to my promise, I slowly parted the buttons on my blouse. "I loved growing up on my farm, and I loved my life. But my parents moved out of Bedlam after Rainey was born. I remembered our life in Chicago. Weekend trips to the zoo.

Movie theater nights. Strolling with a hot dog in one hand and little Rainey's in the other.

"We were visiting Gran on vacation when that stupid, idiot drunk crashed into Mom and Dad. The entire course of my life changed in one moment, and it was always in my head that one day I'd get it back," I whispered. "I'd go back home to Chicago and leave the place that took my parents."

My top fluttered to his feet.

"I wasn't worried about the farm because Gran was strong as an ox, and Rainey planned to take over for her. Raise her family there like generations of de Souzas. When I was lost, I just kind of..." I shrugged helplessly. "Tried to give us that dream. It didn't work, of course, because Gran was still gone."

Jacques silently took in my explanation. "The mind can go to incredible lengths to protect itself."

I grabbed a sliver of hope trying to get through, and shoved it back down. That sounded like understanding, but Jacques was a closed-off man. He gave nothing easily.

"What else do you want to know?" I inched closer to him, and was put right back where I was.

Nothing was easy with him.

"We were your first."

I stilled with my fingers on my pants button. The Bedlam Boys were massively, pathologically, and at times adorably, possessive. They've made threats against imagined lovers more than once.

"Cairo can confirm that you were. He said he was too sentimental to wipe my virgin blood from his cock the first day."

"But..." he growled.

I wiggled my pants over my hips, noting his gaze followed its path for all that he wanted to appear unaffected.

"But that was the only first of mine left to take."

Jacques's lips peeled back from his teeth.

"You can't blame me for things I did before I met you guys."

"Can't I?"

A tiny grin teased the corner of my mouth. "No, that would be illogical."

"Give me their names."

"They'd have graduated by now," I said, kicking my pants on his lap. "Lucky for them."

"Then, there's no harm in giving me their names."

I chuckled. "How about I move this along so we don't get stuck on this one? What's my favorite color? Blue." I loosed the clip from my hair, letting it rain around my shoulders. "What's my favorite show? *Stranger Things*." I took off a sock. Just one.

"What's my favorite book? *The Book Thief*." That got Jacques the other sock. I was down to nothing but my bra and panties. "Do I like to be spanked?

"No."

Jacques cocked a brow. "Tough."

"At least not for the same reason," I said, chuckling.

I nudged his legs apart again. Jacques didn't stop me. I straddled his lap, and still, he didn't stop me.

"Before, I happily put my ass up and accepted punishment because I was riddled with guilt. You guys both eased my pain and replaced it with pleasure. But I didn't remember what Scott did to me at the time. I also forgot that grief changed me into the hardest version of myself, and I no longer had any mercy for bullies who pushed me around because they thought I was just another faceless farm girl.

"The true me would've hunted down Scott Cavendish a long time ago, Jacques, so why would I feel an ounce of guilt over the man begging me to kill him? As for framing Cairo, the guy made both a terrible and arousing first impression on me. He screamed bully, and he's the son of the man I hate most in this world."

I splayed my fingers across his chest, heart picking up speed. Jacques would toss me off him any minute now. I'd better get in my delight before he did.

"I admit, things would've gone very differently the night that bound us together. I wouldn't have attempted suicide, and I would not have gone back after giving you guys the slip in the woods." Jacques went rigid beneath me. "I know you don't want to hear that, but I've always been honest with you, Jacques. Even when I didn't know who I was, all I've ever told you was what I believed was true."

My hands left his shoulders and found mine, peeling my bra straps down. "If I was Ivy back then, we'd never have gotten together. Maybe in some strange way, all this pain and tragedy brought me to you."

"And that's a good thing?" he asked. "Sounds like you expect the rules to change."

"Things will change in some ways." My boobs sprang free. "I couldn't give less of a shit about Scott Cavendish. Why should any of us pretend you're still punishing me for killing him and framing you? No, from now on..." My lips pressed to his ear, breasts flattening on his chest. "You'll spank, paddle, and fuck me like a wild animal because that's how we like it. Hot, dirty, and nasty." His cock twitched beneath me. "That doesn't sound so bad, does it?"

"We can't keep going like nothing's changed."

"Okay." I shoved up, walking off. "I don't have much stuff. It won't take me long to pack it."

"What do you think you're doing?"

I tossed my response over my shoulder. "Going back to Paris's until I can arrange a place to stay. If it's really over between us, it wouldn't be fair to any of us to force ourselves to live together."

"Stop."

"Who knows?" I hit the bottom step. "Maybe some distance will be good for us. When you've all accepted that this is who I am now, we can start over and try—"

"Stop," he barked, breaking his even tone for the third time since we met. "That's one. No one gave you permission to leave. Turn around and get back here."

I wiped the victory off my face before climbing off the steps. Giving me a number was the most hopeful thing he'd said to me all day. Spankings were foreplay for Jacques Stone.

Returning to him, Jacques grasped my hips and placed me on his lap before I could squeak. I bit back a hiss as his fingers dug into my ass.

"You're not going anywhere."

"Absolutely," I said, "as long as you answer a question for me. Do you want me to stay because you don't trust me, or because you still love me?"

"This little game made no difference. I do not know you, Ivy de Souza, so the answer must be the former. Because it can't be the latter."

"Yes, it can, Jacques." I glided over his prickly, sexy stubble. "Because everything doesn't have to be logical."

I couldn't stop myself tracing his lips, framing his nose, and sinking in cold, dark eyes. The man I loved both held me in possession and looked at me like a stranger. "I'm still me, Jacques, and you know I am. You can feel it."

"I feel noth—"

Swooping down, I crashed our lips together. Jacques grabbed the back of my head—fisting my hair like he was going to pull me off. Throwing my arms around him, I deepened the kiss.

Our tongues collided in a battle of fury, frustration, and a feeling I couldn't and had never been able to name when I was with Jacques.

He was rude, arrogant, cold, but when I was with him, I felt like we were both with the person who'd never judge us.

Jacques knew I looked at him and saw more than an oddity with a high IQ. He looked at Rainey and just saw her—no prejudices or preformed opinions about the fresh-off-the-farm homeschooler that was clueless about life in Bedlam. I knew he could look at me and just see me. I just had to get through the walls he was fighting to build back up.

I broke from him gasping and head spinning. "Was that real, baby? If I'm someone else, why do I kiss like the woman you love?"

"Argh!" Jacques pounced. Twisting me, he spread me on the couch and crushed me under his weight. His hands were everywhere. Running down my thighs, finding where they parted, sliding them open, and grinding his middle between my legs. I snagged his hands and brought them between us, placing them over my breasts. He didn't need encouragement to tweak them mercilessly, drawing heated moans into our kiss.

Of all of my guys, I didn't think Jacques would be next to fall after Roan. They were all mine. They would have to accept that this was me, and the real Ivy was still the woman they needed... because she was just as ruthless and possessive as the Bedlam Boys could ever be.

I scrabbled at Jacques's belt, half expecting to hear a number. His mouth was too busy plundering mine to deliver.

The belt came free, making the most delicious sound clattering to the floor. "I won't leave, Jacques," I gasped. "I'll never leave you again."

A deep, feral noise rumbled in his chest. "That wasn't an option." Slipping under my thong strap, he tore it clean off me. Heat prickled my skin anticipating what was coming next.

Roan, Legend, Cairo, and Arsenio had their way with me often and every chance they got, but Jacques and I were together one time, and that time I drove him over the edge—basically making it clear he wasn't leaving the living room without ending the tease.

It was right that our second time would be as myself. Jacques was there when I needed to heal. Now he'd be mine as I rose from the ashes, and burned everything else down around me.

"Is my kiss different, Jacques?" I slid between his waistband. "Are my hands?"

Fisting his cock, I stroked him quick and rough—ripping the yummiest groans from those deceptively soft lips.

"Is this different, baby?" Freeing him, I positioned him at my entrance.

Jacques looked almost dazed. Glassy pools reflected my swollen lips and red cheeks. I sensed his internal war of mind and body. Logic said I wasn't the woman he fell for, but this woman had the same wet pussy and firm breasts, and his body wanted that bad.

"Don't hold back, Jacques—"

Thud!

"Isn't this nice?"

My neck snapped in half, looking upside down to see our new arrival.

"My father's been taken by a death cult who is conspiring to take over our town, but at least the impostor is keeping my best friend's dick wet."

We didn't spring apart like two sixteen-year-olds caught under their parents' coats. That was for people who felt shame, and I felt none for being with my boyfriend in front of my other boyfriend.

"That's not what this is, Cairo."

"Oh?" There was more ferality in his snarl than normal. "You telling me you two were consoling each other out of worry? Or more likely celebrating"—he narrowed on me—"because the man you hate most is likely dead."

"Neither," I said, swallowing my disappointment as Jacques climbed off me and picked up his belt. "Why would I want your father dead before I get the answers I've been waiting years for? I want to help you find him, Cairo. Were you able to find anything out? Where were you?"

I wished the state of him gave me a sign. Besides the red rimming his eyes, giving away that he hadn't slept, he looked no different than he did the night before when he deposited me at Paris's house. No scratches, blood, or swollen knuckles, so my love hadn't gone out and picked a fight. Or he picked a fight that he won.

"You first. You're giving a great impression of someone who cares. What did you find out about our missing sheriff?" He flicked to my fallen clothes. "Before you turned your attention to making sure we keep you around."

I bristled. "Is my leaving an option? Because I told Jacques the same thing I'll tell you. If you want me gone, say the word. I'll pack my stuff and be out tonight. Consider us broken up."

His face changed, making me shoot to my feet. I was wrong... this was the most feral I'd ever seen Cairo Sharpe.

He stalked toward me, handsome face in mine. "This isn't the time to test me, de Souza. You're not going anywhere."

"Glad to hear it." I reached for his temples and he was out of reach in the space of a blink. I dropped my hands. That reaction wasn't a surprise, even if it still stung.

Cairo abandoned me and tugged Jacques into the kitchen. I listened in on their conversation while I dressed.

"—asked Andres where Dad went after his shift. He said he told him he was going home, so they must've grabbed him on the walk. Spent all fucking day asking everyone in the stores and houses along that route if they saw something last night. Nothing."

"Nothing?" Jacques said. "The man is six feet tall, over two hundred pounds, and trained law enforcement carrying a weapon. He didn't go anywhere quietly."

I inched closer.

"Doesn't make any sense," Cairo agreed. "Someone should've seen or heard something. I'm thinking he didn't go home like he told Andres. He was lured somewhere."

"On foot?"

"Andres said Davidson left the same time as Dad."

They shared a look that said everything I was thinking. The sheriff's traitorous deputy had his grimy hands all over this disappearance.

"We have to pick Davidson up. An hour with me, he'll spill everything."

"Why tell me? Why aren't you out there chasing after him?"

Cairo swore, punching the cabinet. "Bastard called out sick today. Why do you think I was able to have that chat with Andres uninterrupted? I swung by his place but no one's there. Sat in front for hours until I busted in around the back."

Of course he did. My Cairo didn't know a law he wasn't happy to break.

"He's not living there," Cairo said. "Sure there's furniture, electricity, cable, and shit, but there's no food in the fridge and dust is covering everything. These guys aren't stupid. During the day, Davidson is sitting pretty in a sheriff station with cameras, guns, and witnesses. He knows we can't grab him there. And at night, he's sitting at who the hell knows."

"We'll find out where he goes. Tail him."

"A cop will know how to lose a tail." Two heads swung to me. "Especially when he's expecting one."

"We don't have a choice," Cairo said, "and you don't get a vote."

"Wait." I darted in his path as he made to leave the kitchen. "I know you don't believe this, but I really do want to help you find your father. I may not know who Dante is, but I know what he and his followers do to people. They don't give a shit about innocent people. They're just *sacrifices* for a greater good.

"If you take a swing at Davidson and miss, Dante will find out and punish you for it. That punishment will be taken out on the sheriff. All I'm saying is your plan has to be foolproof. It has to work fast, the first time, and Dante has to stay in the dark."

"She's not wrong," Jacques said. "Davidson is the one member of their group that's known to us. They know we want him, and they know the consequences if we get our hands on him. A decoy house? They will not make it easy to get him."

"Do you think I came here to listen to you bleat that we should give up!"

"No," Jacques replied in that even, lazy way of his. "I'm saying I will assess the issue from every angle, and create that foolproof plan. Fast, the first time, and with Dante none the wiser."

"Wonderful." Cairo mockingly bowed. "You have twelve hours."

Jacques said nothing to that improbable deadline. He just cast me one final unreadable look and left us alone. I watched Cairo as his footfalls faded up the steps.

"There're some other things you should know," I began.

"Then I'll find out from someone else." He brushed past me.

Teeth gritting, I followed hot on his heels. "Roan and I got a visit in the hospital today. Three guys with crows on their necks came in to tell us they're enrolling at Bedlam U for the new semester. They claim they come in peace and have nothing to do with Steven Ellis or Foundry."

Cairo didn't slow his stride.

"They also said they don't have beef with us, but they will if we come at them."

I could've been talking to the wall for all the response I was getting from him.

"I had a thought while you guys were talking about Davidson." Cairo burst into his room. I threw myself inside despite his attempt to slam the door in my face. "Jacques wants to track down the descendants of the Men of Honor. Cavendish told me that's how Ellis made contact with him."

Cairo riffled through his closet, ripping out clothes. He was about to slam another door in my face. I got comfortable on his bed all the same.

"I don't think that was a lie. It makes perfect sense that descendants of the Men would join in with Ellis. Technically, they are the rightful heirs of the land and the riches that go with them," I said. "But at some point, Cavendish split from him to do his own thing with his little cult. When he started preying on the bullied and vengeful Blake Jensen, was that because she was descended from the Men or because she was easy to control?"

"What's your point?" he snapped.

I loved him too much to smirk at my victory. I forced him to acknowledge me, and Cairo didn't make that easy for anyone.

"What I'm saying is Davidson is a grown, middle-aged man. He took a job that's high stress, but not for the cowardly. I don't see him bawling his eyes out on Cavendish's shoulder while he whispers in his ear that he can give him the strength to stand up to his bullies."

Cairo shifted to me, frowning. "Okay...?"

"I'd bet anything that Davidson is just one of the descendants. He's in this for the money and doing whatever it takes to get it. But Zoey?" I shook my head. "It's way too much of a coincidence that one of the descendants would be someone Cavendish was already grooming. I think she proved that too by going rogue and offering to kill you guys for Jeremy. She's not about Bedlam or the Men. She just likes hurting people.

"What I'm saying is tracking down the descendants will take a lot of time, and if I'm right, it'll only help us find some of them. But if we want to find the kind of people who'd throw in with a man like Cavendish. Who'd k-kill innocents like my sister, and stand by while Zoey murdered Bella and shot Binari with an arrow, then... you need to be looking for people like me."

Cairo beheld me, his expression changing as he got it. "Young, vulnerable, alone. People who were bullied or denied justice. People filled with hate who are primed for someone like Cavendish to come in and do exactly what you said, whisper in their ear."

I nodded.

"Just like the original Men of Honor. They weren't all wealthy landowners. A good many of them were just violent, sadistic beasts who enjoyed terrorizing a town. Cavendish was the same, and he wanted all the members of his little clubhouse to be like him." His gaze locked with mine. "But he underestimated you."

"And I him," I said softly. "Rainey paid for it."

"That's why Ellis and Cavendish split. Ellis wanted a group of heirs salivating over a big check. They'd sabotage, bribe, and cheat to help clear the way for Foundry."

"But Cavendish didn't want the Men's money. He wanted their power. He wanted to bring back the days of fear and control they had over Bedlam. Bedlam wasn't meant to be run by the Society. It was meant to belong to the Men."

"And if Ellis gets his way, Cavendish would've ruled over a pile of dirt," Cairo said, dropping by my side. "If the bastard kept his word, they'd have gotten some money out of it. But they wouldn't have gotten the town, or the glory of ripping it from the Society's grip. All of them Men of Honor, but two groups chasing after different legacies."

"Yes. Yes, exactly." Again I loved him too much to show my relief at him engaging with me.

Cairo made a noise in his throat. "Begs the question, why did Cavendish develop a sudden death wish?"

"That day outside his house, he said he didn't want to die. He had to sacrifice himself because of me. I'm a hypocrite and he'd prove it even if it cost his life. I have my memories back, and all that stuff still doesn't make sense. I have no idea what his death was supposed to accomplish, other than clearing the way for Zoey to take over torturing me."

"Can't believe that was the endgame." Cairo stretched back on the sheets. His shirt rose up, drawing my eyes to his sculpted abs. Before, Cairo didn't go a day without touching me. Every morning I was sliding over his sudsy body in the bath. Right then, I was inches from him and a few feet from the bath, but I never felt further away from that couple who couldn't keep their hands off each other.

"Cavendish didn't have to die for Zoey to play her sick games with you," he continued. "His death was supposed to set off something else. The question is, did it?"

Gingerly, I joined him, curling up close to his side. "At this point, I don't know how we'd find out without questioning Dante and whoever is left of their group. I know Jacques is figuring out a way to get our hands on Davidson, but we can come at this from the other side. Find out who in town was in Cavendish's orbit, and ripe for his grooming."

"You mean that little after-school club he volunteered at?"

"I mean my love Roan's highly unethical and illegal access to Bedlam U's therapist's records. That's how we found out Blake Jensen existed in the first place. It's how we'll find a bunch of young, vulnerable loners who are pissed at the world."

A slow, feral smile stretched his lips for an entirely different reason. "Ivy de Souza," he said. "You may just grow on me."

Chapter Three

A*rsenio*

"It's smart. Honestly, we should've thought of it first." Cairo, Legend, and Jacques leaned on various pieces of furniture in my room. I sat on the bay window—my bad leg propped on a mound of pillows. I flicked between them and the busy street below as I clicked my lighter. "Josephine denied us access to the database as punishment for sloppiness. I assume that ban is lifted."

"It is," Legend replied. "Josephine doesn't give a shit at this point. She shoots off curses I've never heard of whenever I mention Steven Ellis or the Crows. She wants them taken down."

"And yet she just enrolled three more in our fucking school," Cairo said.

"It's not like they put their gang affiliation on the application. She's ready and waiting for them to give her a reason to kick them out."

"They won't," I said, shifting away from the window. "They've learned from Jeremy's mistakes. They're not going to underestimate us this time, and they won't strike first. Doesn't change the fact that we have to get them out of our town. I'm not too fond of doing it under this Dante's orders. I don't wear the leashes."

Jacques spoke up. "Once we have a clear path to Davidson, we'll free the sheriff. Ivy is correct that a swing and miss will result in torture or death. Dante and his crew are fond of both." The vein popped in Cairo's jaw. "She was also right that the best and fastest way to identify that crew is to find all the Ivys and Zoeys in town. Those that were perfect candidates to his grooming."

"I'm bringing up Roan's laptop right after I leave this room," Legend said. "He'll get started tonight."

"Good. So while the conversation is on her, we can talk about what we're actually here to talk about." Jacques swept over us. "Ivy de Souza."

"What's there to talk about?" I asked. "She doesn't get to walk away after everything she's seen. All that she knows." I sat up, anger hooking into me. "Why? Is she trying to leave?"

"No," Legend said. "The opposite. She thinks nothing's changed and we can all keep going as we were. Doesn't fucking help that Roan is singing the same tune. He doesn't care that we've been living with a woman who has needed psychiatric help for the last two years. She thought she was her dead sister, and acted like it. We don't know who the real Ivy is. We only know who she thought she was."

"Doesn't matter. She's ours now."

"How are you of all fucking people saying that?" Cairo barked. "Ivy got spun up in Cavendish's web. He turned her into a killer, and she's still got people on her hit list—including my dad and the person who got him to cover up her grandmother's death. We're not after the same thing. What happens when we get in the way of her revenge?"

I laughed. "What? You think she'd plunge a knife in our sleeping backs? Didn't Mariner say she already had that opportunity with you?"

"Yeah, and she didn't take it. The real Rainey died as a result. She won't make the same mistake twice."

"No," I said with absolute certainty. "She's got no one else to lose now, except us. We have her loyalty."

"She's got no one else to lose." Legend's face cloaked in shadows as he propped against the wall. "But she's got plenty to avenge. If those shits murdered my family, can't say I'd let any of you bastards get in my way."

I chuckled. "You think she's playing us? Biding her time until she's got a clear path to Sheriff Sharpe and Dante? If that's true, it's more reason to keep her exactly where she belongs—with us. Can't watch her if she slips back into the shadows like her old friends taught her to do."

"Agreed," said Jacques. "We don't yet know why, but Ivy's a lightning rod drawing the Men of Honor to her. Cavendish resurfaced after years of peace to send her those letters. Mariner came for her turn after his death. Dante demanded the Crows' punishment after they attacked her and Paris. And Steven Ellis bribed her into a contract for the sale of her farm. Jeremy told her the guys in his crew got way less than she did, and they were beating on women and blowing up cars. A lot more risk than reporting on us.

"The more we learn, the more certain I am that understanding why her grandmother was killed and what makes that farm so special, is the key to connecting all these seemingly random and unnecessary events. So no, we're not in Ivy's way. We want the same thing."

"Don't we know what makes her farm special?" Legend asked. "It's what makes every patch of dirt in Crystal Canyon special."

Inexplicably, he shook his head. "Remember what she said? I'm not sure she realized the significance of it herself, but Ivy told us AgriProspects was one of Steven Ellis's investment companies. Just another front like Foundry, but that one went bankrupt after Clein murdered Abigail, so they never bought the farm." He flicked between us, clearly expecting to see understanding dawn on our faces.

"Want to finish your thought?" Cairo returned.

"AgriProspects was a front, guys. What the fuck did it matter if they couldn't buy the farm? It wasn't as though Ellis went bankrupt too. If he wanted that farm, he had two fucking years to buy it like he's done every other scrap of land he could get his hands on. Why—?"

"—did he wait until he could use it as leverage over Ivy?" Legend finished. Understanding was clear in his expression now. "Did any of us ever read that contract?"

One after the other, we shook our heads.

"Now you see," Jacques said. "There is more going on here than either of us comprehend. We don't find out what that is without her close. In the meantime, her insights have already proved useful. She's twice as smart and three times as ruthless as any of us. On that bridge when Mariner gave her a choice of our lives or hers, she jumped without a second's hesitation."

Jacques turned on Legend. "Mariner admitted to killing her sister. The real choice was to live and make her suffer for it, or die and save us. Seems to me she already chose us over revenge."

Neither Legend nor even Cairo had a slick-ass response to that. Good. There was never any question of them sending Ivy away. I didn't have an off-the-charts IQ like Jacques, or a half a psych degree like Cairo, but I know what I saw that night I took my prize to visit Axel Verlice.

There was a moment there when I asked her to decide his fate, and the sweet, innocent freshman faded and a coldness bit her soul. *Rainey's* eyes changed. Her voice deepened, and surety squared her shoulders. She became someone harder, fiercer, and a mirror to me in every delicious way.

Now I knew who that someone was. Why in the fuck would I reject her? Ivy's the girl who put her pool cue through my heart.

IVY

"Rainey, you okay?"

I started as I always did when I heard that name. I looked around before I could stop myself, half expecting to see my sister walking up behind me, beaming away as she came to join us for breakfast.

The vision vanished, taking hope with it.

"What? Sorry, Elise, I'm out of it."

"I'll say. You lost half your breakfast again."

I looked down. Half of my breakfast bagel was gone, and from the unrepentant smile on Amy's face, I knew where it went. She liked to say losing my food was my fault. I should stop ordering better than her.

"What's up?" Paris asked.

I shifted back to the sight that caught my eye. "That's what's up. Doesn't it feel like we've been here before? I don't know about you guys, but I'm not interested in round two."

Amy, Paris, Elise, Zara, and Presley followed my line of sight. Five pairs of eyes hardened at once.

Adriel, Nathan, and Ethan kicked back on the deck. It was the first day of the new semester, and Paris wanted us to spend it doing our morning ritual of Bagel Glory and sunshine. I wasn't expecting to come out onto the deck and find it haunted by Crows.

"—wasn't us," Adriel said. "The whole thing makes me sick, man. I saw that video of them kicking that red-haired guy's ass. Brutal. That's not what the Crows are about."

"Then, what are they about?" asked a shaggy guy in glasses. The three of them were gathering a listening crowd. Against my will, I was one of them. "I heard you guys are a gang. Steven Ellis wants to split the town and bring back Crystal Canyon. Jeremy and Micah decided to back up Daddy's construction plans by rolling through with his gang to fuck with our people."

Adriel, Ethan, and Nathan burst out laughing. "A gang? Us? Nah, man, you've got that all wrong. We're a fraternity," Adriel said. "One of the underground ones at Hunter's Crest College. We all got in it freshman year. The day you become a brother, you get a crow tattoo. It was just fun and games at first, but you know how it is with the rich boys." Adriel tossed him a wry grin like they had an inside joke. "Jeremy started throwing his money around. Why should the older brothers treat him like a scab when he could buy their whole lives and burn it down for fun?

"Him, Micah, Gael, Jonah, and the rest of them got a little too hard core. They got off on acting like the kings of campus. With that fucking tattoo on their necks, they gave the whole fraternity a bad name. Now they got people thinking we're some kind of gang?" He tossed his head, feigning actual disappointment. "I'm glad you ran those jokers out of here. They got everything they had coming to them."

My jaw clenched seeing students exchanging glances, dislike bleeding away. They were buying this.

"If you've got nothing to do with Jeremy or his father's company, why are you here?" I called. "Because I'm counting the minutes until you bring up smoke shops and nightclubs, and how Bedlam would be so much better if we modernized."

Adriel slid to me. "You know I've got nothing to do with that because I couldn't give two shits about this Crystal Canyon crap. What's it got to do with me? After I graduate from here, I'm looking at grad schools on the East Coast. What you all do with your town is your business. Change it or keep it the same. You won't hear my opinion about it, because, once again, I don't care," he said, all smiles.

Couldn't put it past him, it was a nice smile. Bronze kissed his skin. Steel hardened his jaw. Sunlight bleached blond streaks in his brown waves. If he wasn't going full-time as the duplicitous, sweet-talking banger I knew he was, Adriel would kill as a model.

I gave him a smile to match. "East Coast? Very cool. Which schools were you thinking?"

His grin twitched for a moment, as if he wasn't expecting such a pleasant response. "Top choices are Columbia and Yale."

"Ooooh, definitely Columbia. That's where my father went. He swore there was nothing like living, studying, and partying in New York."

He laughed. "Not gonna lie, New York is pretty tempting after living the small-town life. I might go your dad's way too."

"Good luck." I turned back to the remains of my breakfast.

"That's something, at least," Zara said. "They don't care about the vote and they're not here to start that Crow/Bedlam Boy rivalry all over again. No more attacks. No more Riot Royales. We can just chill this semester."

"No, we can't," I replied, tone mild. "Everything that came out of his mouth is pure bullshit. Tuition for Columbia University is eye-wateringly expensive, and he just said he's not one of the rich boys. I bet Daddy Ellis's money would go a long way toward that student loan debt." I chanced a peek over my shoulder. Adriel was still watching. "This guy is much smarter than Jeremy Ellis. What he does next, we won't see coming."

Amy shuddered. "Yikes, that's ominous. You've gotten super intense lately, Rainey. Is everything cool with you? Are you fighting with your boyfriends?"

Bringing up the Bedlam Boys got my mind off Adriel and the Crows quick. Things had been weird between us in the weeks since we counted down the start of the new semester. Roan made a full recovery, but walked out of the hospital with some scars he was immensely proud of.

Jeremy and his Crows were radio silent the entire time. With Zoey officially declared missing, maybe Jeremy thought she was lying low before she struck the Bedlam Boys their final blow. Or maybe he thought she was missing because the Bedlam Boys got rid of her.

Either way, he and his brother holed up in their Hunter's Crest mansion dealing with their legal problems, and the ankle monitors made sure of it.

The six of us moved back into our house on campus, and things had been chilly to say the least. Cairo only spoke to me to pick me clean about any and everything I remembered about Cavendish, Zoey, and the others. Otherwise, I didn't exist and I certainly wasn't allowed in his bed.

Jacques ended his morning sessions with me. No matter how much I provoked him, and I was getting outrageous with my attempts, he brushed me off without uttering a number. It wasn't surprising that a genius knew when he was being baited, but he was in for a surprise if he thought I didn't know why he held back.

I felt in my heart that Jacques didn't blame me for losing Rainey, but he lost her all the same. He opened himself up to her on accident, then she was gone. After that, how could he open himself up to me on purpose?

No, my time with Jacques was limited to short conversations in the morning while we made breakfast side by side. The rest of the time, he closed himself in his room doing homework or helping Roan narrow down the list of Cavendish's recruits.

That left only Roan's and Arsenio's beds open to me. Both of my guys were recovering and very interested in the healing power of my pussy—as Roan put it. It was like nothing changed between the three of us— No, it was like things were even better between me and Arsenio, and me and Roan.

Arsenio said a lot of things to me that still didn't make sense. That he'd been trying to find me for weeks, and he rewarded my loyalty with more orgasms than I could stand. Whereas Roan said it all in the hospital. I was still the same person to him, but now even more delectable because I'd finally bared my pain to him. Knowing all the ways I was fucked up was an aphrodisiac going by the way that man was always on my ass.

Not that I was complaining. If I was in Roan's bed, Legend wasn't. There'd been no threesomes. No lessons from Roan on how to please him. No waking up sandwiched between my favorite couple.

My love and sex life had taken a serious hit, and having Arsenio and Roan by my side was the thing keeping me sane.

"No, we're not fighting," I said, plastering on a smile. I did that so much easier when I thought I was Rainey. No wonder my friends thought I was too intense lately. None of my smiles reached my eyes. "Everything's good between us, which is why I can't stand the idea that those guys are going to restart the war. His *frat brothers* attacked Paris, blew up Arsenio's car, poisoned Jacques's mother, and beat Roan half to death.

"I just want the people I love to be safe. After everything I've lost..." I dropped my gaze. "I just want you guys safe."

"Oh, Rainey." Amy threw her arms around me. "Of course you do. Ugh, I've been such an insensitive idiot. Who wouldn't be stressed after all you've been through? I'd hate anyone with a damn crow tattoo too."

Paris hugged me from the other side. "I am safe, Rainey. I swear. Whatever those guys are planning, they will not catch me off guard again. We know how they operate and what they're after. They won't get Bedlam, and if they try, my brother and your boyfriends know how to get the garbage to blow back out of town."

"Thanks, guys."

We traded more hugs, then I let them change the subject. We could talk about other, happier things for now because I'd be spending the rest of my day figuring out Adriel's play. He said he wasn't expending his energy on the fate of a town he didn't give a crap about, but I had a feeling a big enough check from Ellis made them care.

Whatever they were up to, I had Mass Media Law, American Legal History I, and Logic and the Law that day to spend thinking about it. Becoming a lawyer wasn't Rainey's dream. It was the mission she adopted after we lost the farm and envisioned one day having the power to get it back.

Now that the contract with Steven Ellis was signed, I had the farm. I didn't need to pretend like this degree was what either of us wanted. At this point, I was going through the motions until I figured out how to tell the world I was Ivy, and switch back to her major.

After breakfast, I walked into Mass Media Law and fell on a tall, handsome figure sipping water in the third row. How like my bespectacled love to not bother telling me we were in the same class. Marching up the steps, I dropped my butt in the seat right next to his. Jacques didn't look up from his textbook.

"Mass Media Law." I bumped his shoulder and didn't pull away. "I wouldn't have thought you were interested in a class like this. I'm only taking it because it's as close to marketing as I can get."

"What about this subject isn't interesting? Media lawyers mostly deal with copyright infringement, defamation, and privacy. As a child, my name and face were plastered in newspapers and on television as the boy genius who won another academic contest against people twice his age.

"Despite my objections, journalists were allowed to violate my privacy again and again because my parents gave them permission. That's one of the many issues I would address during my career. Privacy is an individual right. No one else should be able to decide whether or not you have it."

"Hmm," I said, thinking deeper as every conversation with Jacques made me do. "You're right. Having half the world knowing your name should've been something you and you alone said yes or no too." I rested my hand over his. "Especially because I know people treated you like an oddity. Bad enough from classmates, teachers, and neighbors. You didn't need it from thousands of strangers too."

Jacques eyed our hands. "Are you attempting to reestablish our relationship through feigning empathy and interest in my field?"

The corner of my mouth curled up. "Did you read a few books on relationships so you could anticipate my next moves and block them? No, baby. I'm not feigning anything. You and I just happen to think alike. It's what makes us perfect for each other."

"Hmm. I don't believe in the concept of a soul mate. Neither do you," he dropped. "Or you wouldn't have five."

"I do believe in soul mates, actually. I just don't believe in the idea that you have to find one single person to be all things for you all the time. The six of us connect in different ways, but just because you've broken my soul into five pieces, doesn't mean I can live without a single one of them."

His response was another noncommittal noise and pulling his hand free. In Jacques speak, that was far from a rejection. We had an actual conversation about us. This was the first real progress we'd made since Cairo caught us on the couch.

One after the other, I was getting my guys back.

"You have two hours free after this class," Jacques said. I didn't know his schedule, but of course he knew mine. "You'll help me with something."

"I will?"

"You will."

"Can I get a hint?"

Jacques pointedly looked around the filling classroom. "After class."

I accepted this, leaning back. Eventually a man in dress pants and a blue blazer walked in, introduced himself as Professor Clarence, and the lesson got underway. As promised, I spent it scribbling in my notebook, jotting down every legal and illegal method Steven Ellis and Adriel could bring about the return of Crystal Canyon.

There were still five months before the vote could be called. Five months to undo the damage Jeremy and his boys caused, so what was their plan?

Bedlamites know Ellis is behind Foundry now. They know if they vote to split the town, Foundry will be free and clear to develop all the land they purchased. If only we could tell them why that'd be such a disaster. If only they knew why a snake like Ellis shouldn't win.

What he was doing was as slimy as an appraiser who tells you the painting Nana left you is only worth five bucks, and turns around and sells that Rembrandt for millions. He's paying pittances for gold mines—make that diamond mines, and the landowners don't know they don't need to fund their retirement with a cheat's check. Their fortune is right under their shoes.

My mind drifted to Gran. Every day, sunup to sundown, she worked herself to the bone to provide for my father, and then for me and Rainey. She never complained. She never quit. But when she dared to tell that cheating snake no, and deny him what was never his to take, he had her killed.

My pen strangled in my grip. *Foundry will not win. I don't care what I have to do. I don't care if it costs me my life. Neither Steven Ellis nor the Men of Honor will have Bedlam.*

"—essay on those chapters." Professor Clarence clapped, snapping me to attention. "All right, everyone, good work today. Great discussion. We'll pick this up again on Wednesday."

The class filed out. I fell in step with Jacques, planning on getting the assignment from him later.

My silent companion led me across campus, back to the Bedlam Boy house. I held my breath as we climbed the stairs and stepped over the threshold into his room. Was my *helping* him with something code for helping him with his blue balls? Because I was way past ready to do that.

Jacques bent over his desk. Slipping my arms around him, I melted against his back, reaching for his belt.

"Unless you're taking that off for me to use on you, let me go and sit down."

I hummed. "We both know that's not a threat."

Jacques made a noise. Was that... a laugh?

Before I could be sure, he peeled off my fingers and towed me to his bed. I didn't hide my disappointment when he reached into his desk, pulled out a sheaf of papers, and dropped them on my lap.

"What's this?"

"These are the possible members of the Black Letter Crew—for lack of a better name." Jacques pulled his desk chair over to me. Our knees bumped as he sat. It cheered me that he didn't pull away. "Took a while to sort through the therapist's notes, and then cross-reference to check if they ever crossed paths with Cavendish.

"You're the last step."

"Me?"

His chin dipped. "You know how he worked. What he said. How he spins his webs of manipulation. You can tell me which of these people were more likely to fall prey to him."

"But you blocked out the faces," I said. "And the names."

"Naturally. I just told you I believe in privacy. Dante and his acolytes might be in there, but the rest are students who didn't consent to us knowing what they told their therapist."

Sighing, I leaned back against his pillows, making myself comfortable. "Fair enough. There has to be a line somewhere. This is a good one. I'll need your help to fill in some things for me, though. Since you know the people behind these reports."

"Neither one of us has anywhere else to be for the next two hours."

With that, I got to reading. Dean Banks made seeing the therapist mandatory for everyone who experienced a trauma. That was how Scott Cavendish himself ended up in the chair, talking about sitting by his dying best friend's bedside. Too bad the woman didn't pick up that Scott killed said best friend. It would've saved a lot of people trouble if she had.

"This one." I tugged a page out of the stack. "Do you know her?"

Jacques scanned the page and nodded.

"When she lost her boyfriend, did she have friends or family around? It says she broke down after his death and attempted suicide, but what happened? Did she go through treatment alone?"

He shook his head. "As I recall, her parents flew in and stayed with her. And it was a friend who found her and called an ambulance."

"Then, she's not one of them." I put her page facedown on his desk, the start of my discard pile. "Think about me and Zoey. Naming her Blake was just one of the many reasons she resented them. Her dad ditched when she was eight. Her mother checked out soon after. She had to deal with the bullying alone, and after she was raped and the cops did nothing, she dealt with that alone too.

"It was the same for me," I said, wanting to look away but trapped in his gaze. "We were so isolated out there on the farm. I dropped out of school after Gran died, and my friends could only stand my grief and rage for so long. Pretty soon, they wanted to go back to drinking, frat parties, and hooking up. I was buried under the pressure of keeping things together for my younger sister, and then I discovered the murder and cover-up.

"I was totally vulnerable to a snake like Cavendish coming in and swearing he could help me when I was on the edge of losing hope. Someone with a strong support system wouldn't fall so easily to him."

"Sound reasoning. Actually, I have to agree with you." Jacques took the papers and flipped through, taking some out and dropping them on the pile. "Someone with a loving family and supportive friends doesn't just up and join a death cult. How about the rest?"

I took them back, going through the ones he had left for me. One caught my attention. "This guy.

Raised by a single aunt. He was sent to the therapist because she was killed in a domestic violence situation. Sadly, the string of abusive partners could've started way before then. Maybe he was put through it too when he was sent to live with her."

"There's no maybe," Jacques replied. "He came to school with bruises more than once."

"Fuck's sake," I breathed, massaging my temple. "I could be holding Dante's notes in my hands, but it's still awful if years of bastards beating on him turned him into this. Monsters aren't born, Jacques. They're made."

His eyes glazed out of focus. I could only imagine where that comment took him. But I didn't ask, and he didn't say.

"So, you think it's possible he fell prey to Cavendish?"

"How is he connected to Cavendish?" I asked.

"Same way Blake Jensen was. The after-school program."

"Shit, yes, then. Definitely. The kid likely signed up to delay the time he had to go home for as long as possible, and there's Cavendish noticing the bruises, and seeing another victim to make his victim. After all that time feeling helpless, Scott swoops in and tells him the legacy of men who were beholden to no one. They took what they wanted, and nothing could hurt them. He convinced this kid he'd get his power back by becoming the one people feared. Does he have friends or other family?"

"No family. I have seen him around campus with a group of guys, but some of us get good at leading a double life."

I placed his sheet beside me—the start of my possibles pile. "Here's another that got my attention. Why did you include her?" I asked, showing the page. "This says she wasn't sent to the therapist because she went through something traumatic. She was there because she caused trauma."

I read the page, putting "she" where Jacques blocked out the name. "*Accounts say she was the ringleader of the hazing. It was her idea to force pledges to give blowjobs to members of the brother fraternity. It was also her idea to secretly film it and threaten to upload the videos to the internet if they didn't go on to do more degrading acts to get into the sorority.*"

"Ugh," I spat. "This person isn't a socially isolated victim of bad self-esteem. It says right there that she was *laughing* during the sessions, and didn't feel a lick of remorse. The only reason she wasn't expelled is because they couldn't prove she made those videos, and they didn't end up on the internet either way. This girl is a grade-A bitch."

He chuckled. "I don't dispute that, but don't you think that's exactly what would draw her to Cavendish? And her to him? She gets off on pain, control, blackmail, and manipulation. Zoey laughed about the night they murdered your sister. Were the others enjoying themselves too?"

My throat tightened. "Yes," I forced out. "They were definitely... enjoying themselves."

"I figured I should include the ones who became monsters long before they met Cavendish."

Saying nothing, I put her on the possibles pile. For the next hour and a half, we worked through the stack, discarding the unlikelys and discussing the possibles. By the end, we had nine students who could be running with Dante, or Dante himself.

"What will you do now?" Stretching, I slid off the bed and began gathering my things. "How will you confirm they're in the Black Letter Crew?"

"I admit, it'd be easier if they sent their threats through texts or emails. Give us something to trace. But I have ways of finding out what I need to know."

"You're trying to find the descendants of the Men of Honor too. Did you get in contact with Gold's colleague?"

"I got an automatic email response saying Dr. Lopez was currently on sabbatical and would return my email at her earliest opportunity. That was weeks ago. Gold gave me her professional contacts. I need her personal email to get through to her."

I paused in checking my books. "Are you sure we need her? She can't be the only genealogist."

"She's the only one in Hunter's Crest," he said, swinging his desk chair. My attention drifted to his pants, and the thigh muscles bulging as he swayed side to side. I thought Jacques couldn't deliver a punishment harsher than his belt. Then he discovered celibacy.

"I've been doing my own research, but Gold was right," Jacques continued. "It's slow, painstaking work. Work that a local genealogist might've done already."

"Especially if she's the one the Ellis family hired in the first place."

"Exactly. Gold gave me the right recommendation. He just gave it at the wrong time."

I found myself back on his bed. "Do we know where she's doing her sabbatical?"

"Some remote town in Scotland. She works in HCC's history department. Her fool of a teaching assistant didn't remember the town she's in, let alone where he put her contact information."

"Fuck," I cried. "It's been dead end after dead end for weeks. These shits aren't that good or that lucky. How are they always a step ahead of us?"

Tension rippled through his jaw. "Because we just found out the game we're playing. They've known from the beginning."

I sighed, getting back up. It wouldn't do to be late to class on the first day. "There's one thing that should help us. Remember one of the Black Letter Crew smokes. That wasn't Zoey unless she developed the habit recently."

"Never saw her with a cigarette in hand. I also didn't smell any smoke when she was hanging us on that bridge. This fact does help us narrow down the others."

"At least we're finally making some progress," I said. "Cairo has not been patient. I know he spends his nights either searching for his dad, or trying to get into that safe and figure out what started all this. He must've tried a million combinations by now."

"I've heard you liken him to a wolf, but Cairo is a shark, de Souza. If they stop moving, they die."

That image followed me throughout the day, stealing the focus my classes didn't really have. Cairo had to get up every day and do *something* to find his dad, even if it was futile. This was the same person who, as a child, tried to take on his burden of being a vigilante cop. He looked after his drunk, depressed dad long after everyone else abandoned them. Cairo didn't give up on the people who earned his loyalty.

That's why he's so angry. He'd never have given up on Rainey, but he was forced to. Because he lost her before they ever met.

In between thoughts of my wolf who incorrectly believed I was no longer his mate, I kept flashing to those nine people I picked out of a pile. Was Dante among them? The person who killed Zoey, abducted Jack Sharpe, got that shit stain Davidson promoted to acting sheriff, and held an anvil over my guys' heads.

I left my last class of the day and cut through Homer Green. Students basked in the evening sun—stretching out on blankets, passing around textbooks, slurping lattes, and laughing it up like it wasn't just last semester that the Crows kicked off a brawl in this very spot.

Everyone went on like it was just another blip in their perfect college lives, but somewhere...

My eyes narrowed, scanning all the laughing, carefree faces. *Somewhere you're hiding among all these normal, happy students. Waiting. Watching me. Pulling our strings.*

I understood why Jacques wouldn't let me know the names and faces that went with the deep secrets and painful truths. I even agreed with him. But right then more than ever I wished I knew which faces to pick out of the crowd. The night they came for us, I saw only their eyes.

I was me again. My memory was back. The next time I looked, I'd know, and they will pay.

Shaking myself, I forced myself to continue on. My phone buzzed within sight of our place.

Roan: I'm in bed right now and for some reason you're not handcuffed to it. Explain this cosmic wrong to me.

The beginnings of a smile teased my lips. Roan just gave me a great idea.

I walked the path leading to our place, pausing before the mailbox. Dropping the lid, I was almost unsurprised to see what was waiting for me.

Damn them for getting smart and using the mail. Damn them for figuring out the police were watching the drop boxes.

I withdrew the black letter.

Damn them for the evil, lurking monsters they are. And damn me for not seeing who they were until it was too late.

I glanced at the house but made no move to go in. The letter was addressed to The Bedlam Boy House.

Seems I overestimated how attached you are to Jack Sharpe. You left him in my company over the holidays, and I can assure you he didn't enjoy himself. I figured you'd have made your move against Ellis by now, but I guess I have to spell it out for you.

We'll find out how much you care about him, because if you don't do exactly what I say, the sheriff's body will be next to hang in the square within a ring of fire.

The latest of Steven Ellis's tools has arrived on campus, but he's gotten smarter. He's sending disposables to continue his work, and if they're sacrificed, he'll just send someone else. Six months gives him plenty of time to help people remember that whatever his sons did, the Bedlam Boys have done worse. The return of Crystal Canyon will free them from their rule.

That makes Ellis just as much your enemy as he is ours. Word is Foundry is planning another community event to raise support for the vote. I don't care how you do it, but you're to sacrifice him before he gets up before the crowd.

Of course, what the father loses, the sons inherit. After he's gone, Micah and Jeremy must go too. It's unlikely the Ellises told Foundry's board exactly what makes Bedlam so special.

With the family gone, their financial backing of the project dries up, and Foundry will be left with land they can't develop, and a town that's finally learned what becomes of those that try to change Bedlam.

That event is your deadline. If it passes and Steven Ellis is still alive, I'll take that as your goodbye to Sheriff Jack.

Then we'll see if the next person I take does a better job of inspiring you to action.

Signed,

Dante

"De Souza." A presence fell over me.

I didn't say anything. Just held out the note for Cairo to take.

"Fuck!" Cairo lashed out, striking the mailbox square. It ripped out of the ground and showered my shoes in dirt. He slammed inside, rattling the windows. The letter stayed behind in a crumpled scrap on the welcome mat.

Honestly, he handled that much better than I expected.

JACQUES

"Community event? What the hell is he talking about?" Arsenio asked. "If there was an event planned, my mother would know about it. She'd have told us."

I smoothed out the wrinkled page, reading it through for the fifth time. It was me, Legend, Roan, Cairo, and Arsenio in the kitchen. I didn't know or ask where Ivy was. My need to know where she was at all times was temporarily put aside by the kill order we just received for a man and his sons.

"Pretty sure Dante didn't waste our time and his by writing down a bunch of bullshit," Legend said. "There is an event. They must still be planning it. Haven't booked a venue yet."

"Then how would Dante know about it?" Arsenio threw in. "Does he have the man bugged? Reading his emails? Tracking his fucking event planner? If he can do all that, what does he need us for?"

Roan got up and left the room.

"Hey," Cairo barked. "Are we fucking boring you!"

"Not at this moment," floated back.

"Sex-addicted fuck." Cairo snatched the letter. "Kill Ellis, then Jeremy and Micah. Worst thing is, he's probably right. Get rid of the family and funding dries up. They'll give up on Bedlam unless they know."

"The fact that we can't answer that is why we didn't take that route the first time Legend suggested it," I reminded. "We don't know who's on the board, or how Ellis convinced them to buy large swathes of land in a town that doesn't allow development. With the way things are going, it's probably made up of all the Men of Honor descendants that didn't break from Ellis.

"Slaughtering the Ellises and an entire board of directors would make Foundry national news, and even the slowest, most dim-witted investigator would make the connection between them and Bed—" I halted, holding stiff as the storeroom that was my mind shifted, spun, and re-cataloged itself, putting what I needed to the forefront. "Not between them and Bedlam. Between the Ellises and the Bedlam Boys."

I met Cairo's eyes. "They can get rid of Steven, Jeremy, and Micah themselves. Of course they fucking can. They could walk right up to them, and they wouldn't know they were a threat—unlike us. Dante is setting this up so that after they're gone, the cops have the motive, means, opportunity, and suspects all wrapped up in a neat bow. None of this gets back to him."

"No, we'll have the letters," Arsenio argued. "We'll have the sheriff singing of his abduction. Either way, we can prove duress."

"We won't get the chance," Cairo said, fists balling on the counter. "Dante's going to kill us. Get rid of the Ellises. Get rid of the Bedlam Boys. Fuck, get rid of our moms too. None of us are meant to survive this. After we've gone—"

"—Bedlam will be theirs," Legend dropped. "Davidson the new sheriff, and the Black Letter Crew stepping into all the roles our mothers have. The Men of Honor retake Bedlam."

"Your father isn't meant to live through this," I said. Cairo wasn't one for platitudes blown up his ass, and I wasn't one to deliver them. "Even if we do everything Dante says, they're going to kill him. We have to find him before the event, while Dante is still using him as leverage."

Cairo threw up his hands. "I look like I'm going to fucking argue? We should've found him weeks ago—"

"And now we've got days." Roan climbed off the steps, carrying his laptop. "Guys, the reason we didn't know about this *community event* is because it's not being held in our community. Steven Ellis is throwing it at a country club in Hunter's Crest"—he spun the screen around—"this weekend."

Cairo pounced on the thing, eyes ping-ponging in his head. "You are cordially invited to the Hunter's Crest Country Club for— How the hell did we not know about this?" He snapped to Roan. "How did you?"

"I didn't know," he replied. "The fact is nothing goes on in this town without our mothers knowing about it. That was a hint right there that the event isn't in our town. If this is already planned, then it's got RSVPs. There are a few families in Bedlam, besides ours, that have the influence to sway things to Ellis's side. I called up one, said I misplaced my invitation, and she forwarded this."

More than once I defended my friends' intelligence to Mother. The fact remained they were clever in ways I'd never consider.

"Friday," Legend read over Cairo's shoulder. "We have until Friday night to kill Steven Ellis, or Sheriff Jack is the first of us Dante takes out."

"We can't do it." Arsenio shoved away from the counter. "Getting close to this guy was short of impossible when we thought we had weeks. Now we have days."

"No, this doesn't change anything," Cairo said. "We find my old man before the party. Take away his leverage. Jacques, you said you were close to finding them."

I shook my head. "I have a list of people who could be a part of the Black Letter Crew. Five men and four women."

"Perfect. We'll pick them all up." Cairo headed for the door. "Question them."

I knew exactly what *question* meant. "I'm not opposed, but we saw what happened with Zoey Mariner, and then with Scott Cavendish. One dies and there's another to take their place and continue the plan. Our next strike has to take them *all* out."

"He's right," Legend said.

"Then what do you all fucking suggest!"

His bellow didn't so much as blow my brows up. "Let me handle the Black Letter Crew. If my list of nine has secrets, I'll devise a way to make each of them crack by Friday. You have my word on that, which is good because the four of you will be too busy."

"Busy doing what?" Arsenio said.

"I can get to all nine, but doesn't mean I'll get to the entire crew." I met their gaze in turn. "If I don't, you all need a way to get to Steven Ellis before the party.

"You need a plan to kill him."

If I expected an argument, I didn't wait around for it. We had very few options while a masked group of psychopaths held our balls in a vise. Abductions, murders, and attempted murders. There was no bluff to call. They proved they were serious multiple times.

We would prepare for the best, but plan for the worst.

I pushed on my door, mind turning to those names. Ivy said six people attacked them that night. That meant at least four people on my list were innocent, and there was nothing to admit to.

But I have to be sure—

I stopped dead, landing on my bed. I flicked around, checking for a second if I walked into the right room.

No, I was in the right place. And the woman handcuffed to the bed frame wasn't.

"Ivy," I said slowly. "Seems you've gotten lost. Roan's room is three doors down."

She peered at me over a bare shoulder. Ivy wore nothing on top. Stretching belly-flat on my sheets, I followed the curve of her spine down to a pink lace thong that she needn't have bothered with. It covered nothing.

My pants tightened.

The reemergence of Ivy put an end to the "home clothes." She bought herself a new wardrobe, and Cairo was too busy barely speaking with her to do anything about it.

I should've handled it my-fucking-self.

Ivy kicked her curled toes, beckoning me forward. "I'm not lost. I'm right where I'm supposed to be."

"Out."

She laughed. "Even if I wanted to"—Ivy shook her cuffed hands—"looks like I can't."

"Where's the key?"

The devil lived in her smirk. "Somewhere interesting."

"What did you hope to accomplish with this?" I asked with my traitorous dick hardening by the second. It had been a very long time.

Ivy shrugged. "I hoped to break a few rules."

"This will not happen." I took a step, hands traveling to my belt buckle. "You think you can seduce me? I'm not some lovesick fool who loses his mind at a bare back—"

A sharp hiss escaped my throat as Ivy rose on her knees, shaking that bare backside at me. It was shameless how loud it begged to be spanked raw.

"If you're so unaffected, find the key, uncuff me, and carry me out of here. I'll get the hint loud and clear. But if not..."

My grip tightened on the buckle. "You don't make the rules here, de Souza. You don't test me to see if I'll break. Much has changed, but that never will."

She pinned me through. "Then do something about it."

That challenge was the sounding bell to charge. To whip off my belt and give her what I denied myself while she positively begged for it. But I didn't move. It was possible I wasn't breathing.

She got me all those weeks ago as we played her little game of "ask me anything." Ivy slipped in my head, and then into my pants. Cairo walking in was both welcome and unwelcome.

Rainey burrowed into my head without me realizing, then was ripped out. Catching me off guard once was a statistical probability, but the same woman winding me around her finger twice was the action of the lovesick pathetic fool I just swore I wasn't.

I will not do this with her again.

My belt slipped its buckle.

She will never have that power over me.

It slipped its loops, leaving my waistband to slide an inch down. I unbuttoned and it went the rest of the way.

There was nothing more illogical than the concept of love. It was nothing more than a rush of chemicals in the brain—as real as the trick Ivy's mind played to make her believe she was her sister.

The bed dipped beneath my knee. Drawing my shirt over my head, it joined the rest of our clothes on the floor.

What I felt wasn't real. It didn't exist to be lost again. It didn't make sense to say it never truly went away.

I pressed her flat, palm warm on the small of her back. As warm as the legs wrapping around me.

My love was nothing more than a delusion that had taken hold of me, and experience said there was no controlling when those released you.

I tightened around the leather.

So why fight it?

Thwap!

"Uh," Ivy half cried, half moaned. My balls squeezed in time to her pale cheeks. "Again."

My jaw clenched, penning in a hiss. Her alter ego didn't demand more. She'd offer herself up to me in total submission, even if she didn't pretend she wasn't enjoying it.

But I was dealing with Ivy now. She wasn't shy about taking what she wanted, and that did nothing good to the dominant alpha beast that logic, reason, and genius were never able to tame.

Thwap!

Her back arched against the sheets, bending like a finely crafted bow. I ran my fingers up the curve of her spine. "Ah, yes, Jacques. Don't—" I closed over her mouth, muffling the rest of her order beneath my palm.

Much better.

Thwap!

Ivy vibrated beneath me, pain and pleasure rippling through her body. It had been so long. Too long.

My erection honed in on her like a heat-seeking missile. Precum gathered on the tip, unashamedly giving away this woman's power over me. Half-naked and three spankings in, and I was so hard there was a chance all of me would explode when I came. So much for the genius who was always in control. Always—

Pain sprouted from my palm. Ivy scraped her teeth along my bitten palm and closed over my finger.

"Ugh." My cock twitched violently as she sucked me into her mouth. Head bobbing, she found something else to do with her mouth and I pictured all the other uses I could put it to. Where the fuck was that handcuff key?

"Where's the key?"

"Can't recall," she sang.

My lips peeled back from my teeth. "Where is it?"

"You'll just have to find it."

Thwap!

"Ahh," she moaned, tightening around me.

"You don't want to play games with me."

"Oh, but I do. I really, really do." Ivy tossed a smirk over her shoulder. "Everything comes easy for you, Jacques Stone, the self-controlled genius. Even the woman of your dreams walked right into your house and got ensnared in Cairo's web."

My reply was immediate. "Actually, she framed me for murder and accepted she was better off serving her sentence under the Bedlam Boys."

Her smirk widened. At that second I realized I just confirmed she was the woman of my dreams.

I glared at my cock. Fucking hell, so much for the self-controlled genius.

"I'm going to make you work for it when it comes to me." She wiggled her red ass. "Just a little bit. So the next time you get it into your head that it'll be easy to throw me away, you'll remember how hard you fought for me in the first place."

The vein under my left brow twitched. Irritation like I'd never felt before swelled in my chest. I raised my belt... and tossed it over my shoulder. Ivy's eyes widened as I prowled over her.

"Is that so? You think you're going to teach me a lesson." Eyes locked, I bit her shoulder, enjoying the soft exhalation of breath. "Train me? Make me the pet at the end of your leash?"

I felt her toes caress my backside. "That wasn't exactly what I was going for. I was thinking something more like equals."

I laughed, lips trailing along her shoulder. "There's no such thing as an equal relationship. Someone always holds the power." I kissed just under her ear. "Whether it's the partner that makes more money. Or the one that's out of their league and knows it. Or loves just a little bit less. The balance of power can only swing one way."

"Which way does it swing for us?"

Tipping her head back, I captured her lips, kissing her hungrily. I fisted her strands, opening her mouth as wide as it'd go as I plundered her warm, sweet mouth to my heart's content. "Asks the woman currently cuffed to my bed and vulnerable to my mercy."

Glazed eyes held my reflection. Swimming among it, mischief danced in her pools. "I've been exactly where I want to be, Jacques. So who's vulnerable to whose mercy?"

"Hmm." Just like that, I released her and sat up. "It appears we have an important question to answer. The only way to handle it is to collect the data, and come to the conclusion it grants us."

"How do we do— Oh," she cried—soft, tight body shuddering as two fingers dipped inside her pussy.

"The data is how many times I fuck, tease, and punish you to the brink of orgasm and refuse to deliver until you say I own you in every way and make me believe it. That should give us definitive evidence." Her juices coated me, calling me to weep more precum while I slipped in and out, scissoring my fingers to the most delicious moans.

"That's cheating. The only way the results would hold up is if the experiment is replicated. After this, maybe I'll handcuff you."

My laugh was deep and free. "I almost want to see you try. But what I want even more... is to hear you say it." I crooked my finger, stealing a gasp. "Who do you belong to?"

"Like... I'm going to give it up that easily." Shuddering, she melted into the sheets.

Much like the spankings, she enjoyed it too much to call it a punishment, but it changed nothing for me. Ivy was at peak perfection when she was on her knees, captive to my mercy and yet begging for more. That at some point she wound me around her finger wasn't news. I was a logical man.

I didn't feel anything in particular for Quinn, or our previous girlfriends. I agreed to sharing them because once again, the logical thing proved to let them come to me. It was different with Ivy from nearly the beginning. She talked back to me in front of an entire class, daring to tell me that I was wrong. If that wasn't a fatal enough mistake, she dumped water on me and landed me in an interrogation room.

She had a spirit that was hard to break, but secretly thrilled me to try. She challenged me. Questioned me. Made me see things her way. It was only right that she come to see things my way too.

"Who do you belong to?" I smacked her ass—the first time I traded belt for hand. The feel of her warm and quivering beneath my palm nearly made me come on the spot.

"Ah," she moaned, rocking back on my fingers. "Technically, I belong to five men, so—"

Smack!

Ivy squealed, tightening around my fingers. I withdrew so abruptly, she gasped.

"Jacques!"

"I already know my name." I bore over her, my cock skimming her ass and leaving a weeping trail. Cum marks the spot. "There was something else you had to tell me."

Swirling clouds of defiance and desire darkened her eyes. She was not going to make this easy for me, and damn, it wouldn't be so hard to let her go if she would.

"Say it."

Ivy nipped my bottom lip, nuzzling my cheek. "You first."

I plunged inside her pussy, tasting her cry on my tongue. Other men would've given her time to prepare, adjust, catch her breath.

That's why Ivy wasn't with any of them. She was with us.

I rammed her against the headboard, taking savage pleasure in her screams. *Bang, bang, bang.* Ivy's cuffs clanged against the headboard. Maybe I wasn't a genius. Why of the two of us was she the one to think up handcuffs?

Her smooth ass cradled my hips on every thrust. The arch and curve of her spine mesmerized me with each rock. It was akin to physical pain when her pants grew hoarse—giving the signal. I drew out and groaned, grip strangling the headboard.

"Jacques, no," she cried. "Please."

"Say it."

"You can't keep this up any longer than I can!"

I grinned. "We'll find out."

My hands traveled down her back and around her waist, indulging the slippery perfection of her damp body. Gliding over her stomach, I cupped her breasts—tweaking her nipples to moans and pants that changed and increased in pitch with the barest change in pressure. Who knew ten years of piano lessons would pay off in this way?

"Ah, yes, Jacques. That feels so good."

I slid inside her, no less gentle than I ever was. Ivy's cries ratcheted to insane levels. If the other side of the wall was another room in a cheap motel, the occupants would assume I was paying a woman I met off the street to fluff my ego as well as my dick, but there was nothing fake about her sinful juices coating my cock. The sweat slicking her skin. Her curled toes smacking the bed. Her nipples rock hard and wanton beneath my touch.

I pulled out.

"Ahh!" she shrieked. "Jacques, please."

"Say it." The growl was fitting of the animal I'd become.

"I... belong to... you." Ivy strained against her cuffs, rocking back to bump my erect and equally frustrated cock. Even when she begged, she demanded. "I'm yours, Jacques. Always." Ivy twisted, lips curled into her dimpled cheeks. "Glad you finally accepted it."

My control snapped. Lurching forward, I secured her wrists and yanked, snapping the post clean free of the board. Ivy let out a tiny shriek as her world spun. She found herself flat on her back and her wrists locked around my neck. Cuffed to me. Anchored to me. Where she belonged.

I settled between her legs like I was coming home, inwardly cursing myself for all the time I wasted while she was ass up and kneeling before a doghouse, ready and willing to go as far as I'd take it. Ivy was mine. She had to say it... and I had to accept it. It didn't matter what she called herself or who she thought she was. I owned her body and soul, and she was going nowhere.

We moved as one. I assumed she wasn't expecting slow, sweet, or tender because she got neither. Ivy bucked her hips, meeting each strike to hit that spot dead on. Her legs strangled my hips, pulling me deeper still. Arms locked around me, Ivy buried in my hair—tangling my strands under soft strokes.

Such a tender, intimate touch amidst our frantic rutting. Our gazes locked—hers swirling and enigmatic. Mine no less open or readable, and still... everything that needed to be said passed between us.

Ivy rose as I dipped. Lips clashing, I slipped inside. Tongue tangling with hers, swallowing her moans, grunting as she strangled my dick, I said, "Hmm mh mhh."

Her eyes flew open. Breaking away, Ivy's lips parted and I struck, nailing that spot without mercy.

"Ah!" Back bending, Ivy came hard—any words that had been about to leave her lips washed under the wake of her orgasm.

I held out for all of a millisecond. Milked by her tight pussy, I spilled every drop of cum in me. We came in a shower of writhing, moaning, sweating, and surrender to the only force that'd ever claim our weakness.

I collapsed on her, flattening into the sheets and not caring. She wasn't going anywhere. Why give her the chance to try?

She didn't. Sighing, Ivy wrapped her arms and legs around me, settling my head in the crook of her neck. Gentle strokes glided through my hair, both irritating and soothing me. I was curled up on her and being petted like a faithful lapdog. I should re-cuff her to the bed. Deliver an actual punishment for breaking into my room, disobeying me, breaking rules to taunt me back into our morning sessions.

I should do any fucking thing other than lie here and accept the change of relationship that she was assuming.

"Me too, Jacques." Ivy's red-painted toes caressed my thigh. "I love you too."

Teeth gritting, I balled my fists and put them to better use tracing the dips and curves of the body beneath me.

I was a logical man. I knew when to admit defeat.

IVY

"There has to be a way to get in," Cairo argued. "Roan, you scored a copy of the invitation. Now get us a real one."

"We wouldn't make it past the door. Ellis will have security. Even if by some miracle he let us in, he'd have his guys on us all night. Our only choice is crashing."

I listened with one ear while I gathered the ingredients for Jacques's smoothie. Our bedroom activities were hardly over. It was like the man was possessed. Months of celibacy unleashed, and I was only too happy to catch up on lost time. At one point, I snuck the key from its hiding spot, slapped the cuffs on Jacques, and mounted him.

He destroyed another bedpost and made me pay for that so swiftly and deliciously, my juices were still drying on my red cheeks.

I was only allowed out of his presence to get us sustenance. We were in for a long night and neither of us intended to sleep.

But it looks like I came down at the right time. I flicked from our food to Arsenio, Roan, Legend, and Cairo huddled in the living room. *They're talking about Dante's latest letter and the community event.*

"—disguise ourselves as waiters or the cleaning crew," Legend said.

"Not waiters," Arsenio said. "I'm sure the Ellises don't normally pay attention to the help, but the guys who beat and branded Jeremy won't be ignored when they're standing over his table. There can't be any chance of getting caught before."

Before? Before they assassinated Steven, Jeremy, and Micah? They can't seriously be discussing this.

"Why are we wasting our time with this?!"

I jerked, spilling apple juice over the rim of the blender.

Cairo shot up. "We don't take orders from the likes of Dante. Forget Ellis and his fucking party. I'm finding my father. Davidson has to know where he is. I'm doing what I should've done weeks ago and picking him up."

"You didn't do it weeks ago because you couldn't." Roan darted in his path. "We don't know where the hell he goes after his shifts."

"Then I'll drag him out of the station."

"And get yourself shot?"

Four heads swiveled around—to me. They looked like they didn't know I was standing there.

I pushed on. "Cairo, you know you can't do that or you would've already."

"This doesn't concern you, de Souza."

"The hell it doesn't." I abandoned the blender and stormed out of the kitchen, planting myself in front of them half-naked in nothing but Jacques's shirt. "He's ready for you to come for him. That's exactly what he wants: an excuse. Why all of a sudden do you want to give him one?"

"Because as our resident genius just reasoned," Roan sliced in, "it doesn't matter if we kill the Ellises. Dante is never going to let the sheriff go. If I was Dante, I'd let my enemies take out my other enemies, have my pet cop throw them in prison for it, then one by one clean up the rest of the people in my way—without the Bedlam Boys around to stop me."

"Of course," I whispered, sinking onto the couch. "Why would Dante let him go? He has no reason to even if you do everything he asks. Davidson as acting sheriff, then *actual* sheriff, works out just fine for him."

"We have to get to my dad before the party," Cairo said. "Which is this Friday."

My eyes bugged. "Friday? You've been looking for him for weeks. How are you supposed to find him in five days?"

Cairo swung around. "See? Even she sees the problem. Why are we wasting time on this party and giving Dante what he wants when we know it doesn't end well for us either way? The only move is to find my dad and take away the leverage he has over us."

"Jacques is on it," Arsenio reminded.

"Jacques seems a bit busy getting his dick wet." Cairo smiled mockingly at me. "You've got one tasty pussy, de Souza, but my old man isn't dying for it. You helped Jacques come up with the list. Tell me their names."

Was it wrong that I was secretly pleased he complimented me? I hadn't gotten a nice word out of Cairo for weeks. "I don't know their names. Jacques blocked them out before he let me read the reports."

His eyes narrowed to slits. "You're lying. Why the fuck would he do that?"

"To protect the privacy of the innocent people who didn't consent to us sneaking into their therapy sessions. Cairo, if Jacques said he can find the Crew, and therefore your father, I believe him," I said, talking over what would've been a scathing retort. "Of course you can't kill an entire family just because Dante tells you to, but the Black Letter Crew knows us. They're watching us.

"For now, you guys should go through the motions like you're following orders. Don't give him a reason to think you're going to disobey him because Dante is not bluffing." My voice grew thick. "They'll kill him and then move on to someone else you care about.

It'll never end, and we'll still be right where we started—under their thumb."

"I'm not under anyone's thumb," he snapped, but had nothing else to say to me. None of them did.

I got to my feet. "I say you crash that party. Get close to Steven Ellis, lure him somewhere private, and tell him he and his sons are in danger. Show him that note," I said, gesturing to the crumpled letter. "Dante wants it to be everyone against us, so flip the tables on him. One thing we do know is that if Ellis was a crazed, homicidal nutjob, he wouldn't have broken with Cavendish. He doesn't want you guys dead, but I bet he'd join forces against the people who want him dead."

"Ridiculous," Arsenio dismissed. "The guy has no reason to trust us, or us him. He could betray us just as easily as we know Dante will. We're talking about a fortune that'll keep the Ellises rich for generations to come. People tend to find the homicidal nutjob within themselves when that kind of money is on the line."

Shrugging, I padded to the kitchen to return to making my sandwich and smoothie. "Okay, it's your families on the line, so I won't tell you what to do. It just occurs to me that a man who has spent years secretly surveying and snatching up every bit of land for sale in this town, would know all the best and secluded places to keep a hostage."

I jabbed on the blender, drowning out any response to that. But the looks on their faces quirked my lips up all the same.

Chapter Four

L*egend*

We took another lap around the country club, eyeing the grand iron fence, manned entrance, and cameras sweeping the lawn.

"Ellis chose this place like he expected trouble."

"He does and so do the bastards that accepted his invitation." Cairo marked a check on his list. He spotted yet another security camera. "There's a reason we didn't hear of this sooner. Jeremy and his boys messed up the offense. Now they're going back on defense, making their moves in the shadows."

"So is Dante."

"But he's using us to do it," Roan said, speaking up from the back seat. "We're being put in the middle of two shits we have to take down. I hate to say it but—"

"Then don't," Cairo cut off.

"—we should think about telling Ellis what's going on. The man has money, resources, security, spies, and more on Cavendish than likely even Ivy had. He could help us take down the Black Letter Crew. He'll be motivated to do it anyway when he finds out they want him and his sons dead."

Cairo made a harsh noise in his throat as I turned the corner on Rivera Street, coming up behind the club. Hunter's Crest Country Club was the kind of place you expected to house the uber rich. A two-story mansion converted into restaurants, meeting rooms, ballrooms, and a golf course and tennis court in its backyard. It wasn't like there were armed guards ready and waiting to tackle us, but sneaking in unnoticed became more and more unlikely with every check on Cairo's paper. The cameras would pick us up coming and going.

"You have to admit she has a point," Roan pushed.

"I'll admit she's slippery. Her manipulations slide and stick in your mind like she has in your, Arsenio, and now Jacques's bed. Tell me, how long did it take for you to fall for her moon eyes and promises that she loves you?"

Roan smirked in the rearview mirror. "Fell for it instantly. Never actually unwound my dick from around her finger, if I'm honest. But what's that got to do with us, Ellis, and the fact we now have four days to either find your father, or gamble that Dante will stay his execution if we kill the Ellises?"

"It's got everything to do with it. The way she thinks. The stuff she says. Ivy is colder and more manipulative than—I'll fucking say it—either of us could be. Ellis isn't giving us shit for free. He'll strike back to help himself, but he damn sure won't do it for my dad. And if he did, it'd be at another cost we can't pay.

"This is all a game to her. She doesn't care about the pawns getting sacrificed because she's already got what she wanted. The farm and us."

"She wants the Black Letter Crew dead," I heard myself say. "We know whatever moves she's making, that's the endgame."

"She's not in charge or calling the shots," Roan said. "It's one fucking suggestion."

"Yeah, she always has those at the right time, doesn't she? After swearing up and down she didn't know anything about the Black Letter Crew, she floats the idea that they broke off from Ellis because he wants the money and they want the town.

"Then again, she perches over Jacques's shoulder, whispering in his ear that Cavendish filled his crew with bitter, vulnerable little bastards that were ripe for grooming. And then again with Dante's deadline hanging over our heads, she shares the thought that Ellis would know a few places to hide a hostage."

"Cairo, it's not some big conspiracy. Ivy isn't playing us."

"Yes, she is," he said, low enough he could've been talking to himself. "She has from the very beginning."

"What's that mean?" I asked. "Are we warning Ellis or not?"

"How the fuck is that conversation going to go? *Some unseen guy is blackmailing us to kill you and those bitch boys you spawned? Oh, who's that you're calling? The cops? Makes sense.*"

Cairo had become three times as sarcastic and twice the asshole since he stopped screwing Ivy.

"No," he said flatly. "There's no reason approaching Ellis would end the way we want. We're in the same place with him that we are with Dante—no leverage."

"Then, what do you suggest?" Roan asked. "If we can't get to your father in time, we're not actually going to kill them just because Dante says so. We're all smelling a setup."

"I've said it for the last time. We don't take orders from anyone. If we don't find my dad before the party, we buy him more time by making the world think they're dead. Jeremy, Micah, and Papa Ellis are going to meet a violent, grisly *end*. The party will never happen."

"How do we pull that off?" I asked.

"Stop the car."

I hit the brakes, easing out of traffic and pulling up to the curb. Cairo pointed in the distance. "See what I see?"

Following his line of sight, my brows drew together, shot up my forehead, and finally smoothed out—stretching with my grin. "Now, that could work."

"It'll definitely work," Roan said. "Even better, this will be fun."

JACQUES

Bark scraped an uncomfortable greeting against my back. I barely felt it as I watched her—one of the names on the list only I knew.

She tossed her head back, laughing with her friends over salad bowls and smoothies. The normal college student living the normal college life.

I told them I had ways of finding out if the people Ivy picked were the ones following Dante, or even Dante himself. A fact I overstated.

I'd been going to school with them for years. Some since high school. Most since elementary school. If I didn't see what they were in all that time, observation wouldn't reveal something to me now.

I needed proof. Evidence. A confession.

And I needed it in four days.

I peeled myself off the tree, approaching the group. She glanced up at my call.

"I need to speak with you. Do you have a moment?"

Zara glanced around like I couldn't possibly be talking to her. I've never addressed her before. Her surprise was understandable.

"Uh, sure."

That's why I must choose my words carefully. Zara and I strode away down the path from Homer Green. *If she is one of the Black Letter Crew, I've raised her suspicions just by talking to her.*

"Is something wrong?" she asked, pulling up under an oak tree. "Is Rainey okay?"

"This isn't about her. I saw you have two classes with Adriel Burton. What's he like? How does he act when a Bedlam Boy isn't around? Is he pushing for the return of Crystal Canyon?"

Zara's expression smoothed out. "Ah, this is about Adriel. Well, honestly, I haven't seen or heard him do anything. He just sits there, takes notes, and walks out at the end of the period. Maybe he doesn't care about the vote or Crystal Canyon like he keeps saying."

"Or maybe he knows that after everything Jeremy and his Crow buddies did, he has to play this much smarter." I gave her my back. "Goodbye."

"Huh? Wait— That's it?"

I peered over my shoulder. "Do you have something else to say?"

She blinked. "Uhh, guess not. You just... You looked so serious when you walked up, I thought someone died."

"I'm told I always look serious—"

"Hey! Look out!"

Zara snapped around, eyes bugged. The cyclist squealed his brakes, bellowing as he barreled toward us. Swerving, he was too late.

The handlebar clipped some random kid, popping him off his feet and landing him flat-backed at Zara's. He groaned—wind knocked out of him.

Everyone watched, and rushed, the scene, but I watched Zara. My attention fixed on her—nothing and no one else. Before that day, I never saw a trace of the homicidal monster who descended on Ivy's house in the middle of the night, killed her sister, and fractured Ivy's mind. I had no formed opinions on anyone outside of my circle. I didn't bother to get to know them, so it didn't register if they did something out of character.

But in this case, the person who surprised me was Paris. She, of anyone I knew, was a good judge of character. She saw Cairo, me, Arsenio, Roan, and Legend for exactly who we were—even if she didn't know the full extent of what we did for Bedlam. But if someone told her, I figured she wouldn't flap an eyelid in surprise.

Zara Singh had been Paris's friend since middle school. She had two involved parents. She obviously had a circle of friends that backed her up and supported her, but still Ivy picked her out of the pile due to something that happened long ago.

When she was a little girl, her parents left her at her great-aunt's house and flew off on a week-long second honeymoon. That night, her great-aunt dropped dead from an aneurysm.

Zara didn't know to call nine-one-one. She didn't know to go to a neighbor for help. So, for three days she was alone in that house with a corpse. The three days it took for her parents to freak out over their calls going unanswered and end up calling Sheriff Jack to check and see if everything was all right.

Again, she had parents who fussed and cried and comforted her. They put her in therapy immediately, and over the years, she's had no trouble making friends and living a seemingly happy life.

I questioned Ivy on this pick—her unaware she chose one of her own friends as a possible member of the Crew.

"Why did you choose her?" I asked. "She didn't go to see the school's therapist because of that ill-fated visit. She went because she was having a hard time after her boyfriend announced he was transferring out of state and dumped her. Her great-aunt only came up because it was in her history."

"Believe me," Ivy told me. "She found someone she loved dead. She felt the horror, pain, and confusion of calling their name while lifeless eyes stared back at her. She stayed there for days while the cold realization that they weren't coming back bit into her. That changes you, Jacques. It changes you permanently."

Zara flicked down to the groaning man at her feet and—

My gaze sharpened, seeing a look in her eyes that I would've missed if I wasn't watching at that exact millisecond.

"Oh my gosh," Zara cried, dropping down beside him. "Are you okay? Stupid idiot, racing around campus like that. Did he hurt you? Can you get up?"

Her fussing faded into noise in the back of my mind. *Ivy de Souza, it's your judgment I will never question again.*

I stood to the side, my back once again scraped by bark while Zara and two other guys helped him up and carried him to the health center. Show over, the crowd melted away—leaving only the cyclist. He came up to me.

"That was fun," he mused. "I'm putting 'do my own stunts' on my actor résumé. Got something for me?"

I smacked two hundred dollars on his palm as promised.

"Pleasure doing business with you, Stone."

I nodded, my mind returning to Zara the second he left. I had to get creative to get the nine to reveal something without suspecting I was looking for it. If only I could count on the others making it this easy for me.

I set off, heading to the first class of the morning, which happened to be held in the same building where the next person on my list also had a morning class.

One down, eight more to go.

LEGEND

I blinked awake in the dark, my vision coming into focus on my darkened canopy. I couldn't say what exactly woke me. It wasn't the tightness nipping at my wrists—that was nothing new. It also wasn't the weight and warmth pressing into my left side. Put it down to naturally honed instincts that tell you something was off, but the reason my hands were now tied to the bed and someone was sleeping next to me, wasn't due to Roan.

"Ivy."

She wiggled, burrowing deeper into my side. "Hmm?"

"Do I need to ask questions, or are you going to explain this yourself?"

Her husky, sleep-deepened voice found me in the dark. "Seems pretty self-explanatory. I miss waking up next to you, but you've been so irritatingly stubborn, I've had to take matters into my own hands."

"So you tied me to my bed." Saying it out loud wasn't helping either.

"Untie me."

"No."

My brows shot up my forehead. If I needed further proof this wasn't the woman I knew, she gave it to me. The only one she'd ever taken charge with before that night on the bridge was Roan, and that was because he demanded no less. The woman currently dropping kisses on my jaw did not take no for an answer. She had taken back Roan, Arsenio, and Jacques. Looks like I was next.

"I never thought I'd say these words before, but I'm not having sex with you. Walk out of here with some dignity, de Souza. Whatever the hell you're trying to do won't work."

"Roan seems to think it'll work. Who do you think told me where you guys keep the silk ties?"

Irritation ticced my jaw. "Roan put you up to this?"

"Yep, but he only confirmed what I knew. The key to you is persistence, Legend St. James. Your parents didn't work very hard, or at all, to have a relationship with you. They turned you over to nannies and housekeepers and went about their lives—only noticing you when you were useful to them.

"You may be the one pushing me away, but if I give in. If I let you go without a fight, I'm only proving I'm like all the rest. I love you, Legend, and I'm not going anywhere. I won't get you back until I prove it."

A rough snort rocked my chest. "I wish the lights were on so you saw how hard I rolled my eyes. Save the lonely-little-rich-boy, psychobabble nonsense for someone else. I'm not pushing you away as some kind of test. I just don't want to be with you," I dropped. "I'm not attracted to you anymore, and I sure as fuck don't love you."

I shook my wrists. "Matter of fact, this little stunt shrunk my balls and sucked them up in my body. That's how turned off I am right now. Rainey was a tasty, submissive little treat who dropped on her knees and took a paddle on command. Have you met my fucking boyfriend? What made you or him think that this would work on me? Untie me and get the hell out. I wouldn't fuck you again if you paid me."

Ivy propped her chin on my chest. I saw the outline of a smile traced in moonlight. "This is also what you do. Get vicious. Think if you hurt my feelings, I'll go running off, and you'll have protected yourself from losing another person like you lost who I thought I was. It's not going to work, so relax, baby." She caressed my stiff chest. "I once promised that I'd never let you sleep alone."

My lips peeled off my teeth. "Ivy, get out."

"Make me."

"You do not want to play this game with me."

That smile melted into a smirk. "What are you going to do? Spank me? I learned my lesson with Jacques and tied you to the metal frame. You're not getting out of these."

Zeus save me, why the fuck didn't I stick with men? I'm bi. I have no excuse.

"You'll have to let me out sometime."

"And I'm looking forward to it. You'll find out how well I take a paddle then." She kissed me bold as shit. "It's three in the morning. I'm going back to sleep. Want me to fix your pillow, or pull the blankets up?"

My glare burned her alive.

"Okay, then, good night, baby."

I stared in complete disbelief as she pulled up the covers, dropped her head on my chest, and dozed off.

The doorknob rattled. Roan snuck inside, wearing nothing but silk boxers slung low on his hips.

"Good, you're here. Let me out of these things."

He cocked his head, closing the distance. "Why would I do that? You'd only kick our shared pet out of bed."

"Roan." I barely recognized the growl as coming from my throat. "I fucking swear."

"Can't do it, love." The bastard popped another mocking kiss on my lips. "But I promise you can punish me for it in the morning."

"Count on that."

"Oooh," he teased, sliding in on my other side. He slung his arm over the both of us—his erection poking my thigh. Even the thought of his coming punishment turned him on. More threats would only get him harder, and would not secure my release.

I stewed for a full two hours, alternating between yanking on the ties and glowering at the schemer and traitor using me as their pillow. At some point, I drifted off and woke to the shower running. A look from left to right confirmed I was still tied to the bed, but Ivy and Roan weren't with me.

The water shut off and Roan padded out, clad in a towel.

"Where is she?"

He shook out his hair, splattering me in droplets. At this point, he was being an ass to increase the number of lashes his bare ass had coming. The shrink was right. Roan's need to make a situation worse was pathological.

"She's gone. Had an early morning class." Dropping the towel, Roan straddled me. "You look tense, love. Want a blowjob?"

"Did you tell her to do this!" I strained in the ties, bellowing. "What the hell are you thinking, Roan? Were you trying to sabotage her? Because you know the only thing that was going to do is piss me off."

Roan reached between us, palming my cock. I was surprising my-self with the feral snarls I was making. This guy was doing a terrible job reading the mood.

"No," he said, his palms slick and wet sliding on my dick. "I wasn't sabotaging her. It was the best way to get you two in the same room and talking. You're being very stubborn and I'm getting tired of it. She isn't a different person, Legend. Not in any way that matters. Why are you holding this against her? Ivy didn't want any of it."

I gritted my teeth, fighting the wave of pleasure spreading up my chest as he rolled his thumb over the precum gathering on my tip. Distracting me with sex would work as well as guilting me.

"She is a different person. How do you not see it? Everything is different from the way she talks, eats, thinks, and what she says. We're the sum total of our experiences, Roan, and for two years, she had someone else's experiences in her head. What is it that you're not seeing that everyone else is!"

Roan didn't slow his pumping. "I do see all of those things. She orders a latte with her cinnamon sugar bagel instead of iced tea, and watches crime shows instead of sci-fi now. But all of that is surface, Legend. Know why? Because she never had her sister's experiences in her head. She didn't live her life, love, she only shared it with her.

"Ivy copied the things she saw and heard Rainey do, but all she was ever doing was playing pretend. Everything else was Ivy. The pain of losing her grandmother—that was real. The effect of Cavendish's and the Black Letter Crew's torture—that was real. Falling for five unrepentant bastards and choosing not once, but twice to stay with us—that was real. Sacrificing herself to save us—that was real, Leg-end."

He picked up the pace, trapping a grunt in my chest. Pissed or not, I couldn't deny the man gave good hand jobs.

"What other experiences could possibly matter besides those?" Roan demanded. "Everything else is trivia. Ivy is loyal. She's ours.

And she still wields a riding crop like the yummy little minx she is." Roan released me the moment my balls tightened, climbing off the bed.

"Hey!"

"Admit it, Legend. This isn't about Ivy, it's about you. Whatever hang-ups you've got, you're going to get over it because I'm sick of this. We finally found the perfect third, and you're screwing it up." He loosened the straps on one hand. "You've got a week to work it out with her, because if I'm not fucking her pussy while you're doing me up the ass by then, your sex life is taking a hit too."

Roan slammed out the door—naked and uncaring. He really was angry with me. He didn't even wait around for his punishment. That didn't matter of course because I stormed after him and delivered it anyway, but his eyes said clearly what the ball gag didn't. I either handled my problems with Ivy, or for the first time in years, the two of us would have some of our own.

IVY

Wednesday morning, I curled up on the couch, drinking coffee, and pretending I didn't see the skin-peeling glare coming from the kitchen. Legend wasn't pleased with me tying him to the bed. He wasn't pleased I did it again the night before either.

Not my fault the man's a heavy sleeper.

Arsenio came in carrying shopping bags. He dumped them on the kitchen table, the only invitation I needed to snoop.

"Polos? Khakis?" I blinked at him. "Is this some weird sex thing? What are you doing with these?"

"One animal tail butt plug and she thinks I've got some role-play fetish."

My face heated remembering that interesting day. He claimed not to have a fetish, but as I recalled, Arsenio very much enjoyed walking his pet on a leash from room to room, and screwing me in each one.

"No," he replied, dropping next to me. He snaked his hand around and under my shirt, teasing my nipple with his usual casual ownership of my body. "This is for Friday. Hunter's Crest Country Club is hosting a golf tournament. It's open to outsiders as long as they pay the obscene buy-in fee."

"Will you play in the tournament?"

He dipped his chin. "We'll have to, but in exchange, we'll get weekend passes that'll give us access to the entire club. When crashing won't work, get an invitation."

"Wow. It's genius in its simplicity. Everyone else goes home for the tournament while you guys hang back until the party starts."

"No one's going to look twice at us carrying golf bags or clubs either. We'll pack the shit to knock out and tie up the Ellises, use the clubs to smash the security cameras, and then haul their asses onto a golf cart and take off."

"And now we've left simplicity behind," I cried. "How in the hell do you expect to pull all of that off?"

Arsenio pinched my nipple, eliciting a soft squeal. "I believe you meant *we*, de Souza. We're buying three passes for three participants and three caddies. That includes you. You'll find a way to get the Ellises alone. You're the only one who can claim to have business with them because of the contract."

"A contract that's probably void now. I betrayed Micah and Jeremy. Lured them into a trap and got their asses tied to stakes in the town square. That's got to be a breach."

"And finding out is the perfect topic of discussion." Arsenio tipped my chin, capturing my lips. I melted as he swiped my lips for entrance, then plunged in without permission. His tongue wrapped around mine, demanding its surrender as he plundered me down to my very soul.

I broke away dizzy. His kisses were all the more powerful for how rare they were. And the jerk knew it. His smirk stirred my middle.

"This is the only way. They're hardly going to step into an empty room with one of us."

"So, you're really going to do it," I whispered. "You're going to kill them."

Arsenio didn't answer right away. My skin tightened with each passing second.

"No." He slid out from under my shirt. "We can't be sure of who knows what. Killing the Ellises and then having Foundry's board carry on in their place would solve nothing. We won't be forced into what's ultimately a stupid move. We won't benefit from it, but Dante will as long as he has the power to put us on death row."

I blew out a breath. "Okay, then I'm in, but what if I came at it another way? Instead of showing up out of nowhere, I could call Steven Ellis, say I'll be in town on Friday, and ask if he'll give me ten minutes to talk."

"There's no guarantee he'd say yes or invite you to the club."

"But what if—"

"The plan's all worked out, de Souza." Legend shoved away from the kitchen table. "Stop trying to change it."

He came over, plucked my coffee from my hands, and drew me up. "Let's go. It's time for class."

I blinked. "Let's go as in... let's both go? Together?"

"That's right." Legend grabbed our stuff and made for the door. I didn't move.

"Are you luring me away somewhere to kill me?"

His grin did not reassure me. "Why would I do that? You're not worried a little thing like holding me hostage in my own bed and turning my boyfriend against me would set me off?"

I am now, I thought, spine stiffening as that grin widened.

"You coming or not?"

"I'm coming." I approached him slowly, eyes narrowing as he swept open the door and gestured for me to go ahead. "Bye, Arsenio. I love you."

"Last words, de Souza?" Amusement laced Arsenio's reply. "I'll put them on your tombstone. Make sure the world always knows you're mine."

That was his asshole version of saying he loved me too, so I accepted it and let Legend close the door behind us. We set off in silence.

Bare trees led our way—stripped by winter's chill. The dark events that happened in this town—that have followed it since its creation—should've cast a pall that clung to every stone, twig, and branch. But the fact remained that Bedlam... was beautiful.

Our town didn't get cold enough for snow, winter coats, or dreamy nights curled up by the fire while the sky hid the grass until spring, but we did get couples walking the lane sharing warm cups of cocoa and a scarf around them both. We had fairy lights in the trees, leaves crinkling beneath our feet, and an excuse to cuddle up by that fire whether we needed it or not.

I drifted closer to Legend, indulging his warmth. I couldn't help but be close to him. Why else would I tie the guy to the bed just to sleep with him again?

"Aren't you going to say something?" I spoke up. "I assumed that's why you're walking me to class. To tell me exactly what you think about holding you hostage and turning Roan against you—Which I didn't do, by the way. I told him what I did to get Jacques's attention and he told me to do the same to you. It was all his idea."

"Why do you think he can't sit down right now instead of you?" Legend grasped my waist and pulled me in, doing point-blank what I was aching to do. "But no, I've got nothing to say. You're going to do the talking now."

I stopped in the middle of resting my head on his shoulder. "What does that mean?"

"Roan claims that you're not a different person. Everything that really matters about you and us hasn't changed."

"It hasn't."

"He also says," Legend plowed on, "that if I don't make up with you, he'll turn off the tap and deny me sex."

My brows blew up my head. That was news to me.

"I'm not sure if he's capable of such restraint, but I won't find out."

Pressure swelled in my chest. "Does this mean...?" Slowly I cupped his cheek, turning his jaw. I placed the lightest kiss on the corner of his mouth. "We're back together?"

"Course not."

The pressure burst like a balloon.

"You didn't think it'd be that easy, did you?" He snorted, setting my teeth on edge. "No, what it means is I did all the work the first time. Tamed my little pet. Made her obedient and semisweet. Fashioned her into the perfect slice of bread for our sandwich. If you want back with me, it's your turn. Seduce me. Convince me. Make me want you so badly, I'll do the impossible and forgive everything that's happened."

His speech spread through my swirling mind. "Seduce you like you did me? Are we calling chasing me through the woods and paddling SLUT on my ass seduction?"

"Seeing as it got you wetter than a Slip 'N Slide, yes. Don't pretend like we haven't given you exactly what you wanted. There's no lock on the front door, de Souza. You could've left whenever."

My boots click-clacked on the path, the echo to my heartbeat. "No, I couldn't. You guys would've chased me to the ends of the earth. This is who we are. We don't let go of what we own. What we love. I can show you how much I want you, Legend, but would you really give me a fair chance? Are you open to getting back together, or is all this just to make sure Roan doesn't turn off the tap?"

He shrugged. "You know me. What do you think?"

I think it's the latter one hundred and ten percent, but that changes nothing. If Legend truly wanted to be done with me, he shouldn't have opened the door the tiniest crack. Seducing him will be my absolute pleasure, and greatest accomplishment.

He walked beside me—expressionless but still so achingly handsome, it hurt. Wind chill teased his skin, teasing dots of color along his cheekbones. Cold chapped his lips, and I immediately pulled my lip balm out of my bag, drawing it on for him. Our gazes locked over my fingers.

Legend wasn't roughly handsome like Cairo. Coldly beautiful like Jacques. Impishly gorgeous like Roan. Or uniquely dishy like Arsenio.

There was a softness to his perfection. A warmth in his autumn-brown eyes that shone through whether it truly existed or not. His full, plump lips made you lean in for a kiss in an almost trance. The soft waves tickling his brow begged you to run your fingers through them. Everything about Legend was designed to draw you in. Whether he invited you to or not, you wanted to make Legend St. James love you.

"Okay, you have a deal, but if you want me to tell Roan you gave me a real shot, you can't make it difficult for me by kicking me out of your bed, or refusing to talk or be alone with me."

"Starting right off with blackmail. Interesting choice."

I cracked a smile. "This is how we are, Legend. I won't give you what you want, but I'll always give you what you need. Meet me here after class," I said as the poli-sci building came into view. "Since Roan's holding out on you, I'm sure you're in need of a blowjob, or three." Winking, I drew out of his embrace. "I'll make that happen for you."

"De Souza, if I drop my pants, I'm putting my dick in more holes than your mouth."

A shiver climbed my spine. "That's fine with me."

"I bet it is," he replied, chuckling. "But I'm no cheap date. You want to get in my pants, you'll have to work for it. I'll be back here after your class. Better come up with something to keep me around, or we can call this a fail on day one."

I watched him lope off, stuck between loving him and wishing I'd left him tied to the bed, shouting all day for someone to free him.

I was even more useless in class than I usually was. Most days, I jotted down notes to give myself something to do. That morning I didn't bother putting on the show.

Roan's ultimatum wouldn't make a difference. The guy loved riding Roan's ass as much as I loved him riding mine, but Legend didn't bow his head and surrender to anyone. He would make this needlessly difficult because he was still in love with me but admitting it... was too much like surrender.

So what could I possibly do to make him bring down the walls he's building back up? Especially if he won't let me use sex as a side door.

An hour and a half dragged into eternity. I was first out of my seat when the clock struck ten, weaving through shuffling students and coming outside to a brighter day.

The sun escaped the clouds, raising the temperature on campus a few degrees. Legend abandoned his coat and leaned against the stone railing in a tight blue sweater and black pants. It wasn't right that people spent hours choosing their outfits, putting on makeup, and accentuating their features just for him to slap on the simplest, if expensive, clothes and achieve model-like beauty.

"You're here."

"I said I would be." Legend didn't react to me molding myself to his body and resting my head on his chest. "You'll get a fair chance to screw this up, so Roan can't give me any crap."

"We're not just here because of Roan." I kissed his smooth jaw. "You missed me."

"Now I see how you sustained that delusion for two years. You have an active fantasy life."

That was meant to sting, and it did, but I brushed it off. He could call it lonely-little-rich-boy, psychobabble nonsense but I knew him. Legend put on a fake, gentlemanly show for people he didn't care to know, then he brought out his acid tongue and vicious tricks for those that tried to know him. Only those who saw past the first and cared enough to fight through the latter were worthy of earning his loyalty.

He wasn't scaring me away. I've survived much worse than an obstinate ex-boyfriend, and the *ex* part was only true in his delusion. According to me, we never broke up.

"Are you ready to go?"

"Go where?"

"On our date."

His tone sharpened. "I never said it was a date."

"Nope, but I did." I tugged him after me, setting off across Homer Green. "Come on. We're taking your car. My next class isn't until four, so that gives us plenty of time. Although, I'm not bothered about skipping."

"Taking my car where?"

"It's a surprise." I tossed a smile over my shoulder. "I'm driving."

"The hell you are. No one drives my car but me."

"You don't know where we're going."

"That's why you're going to tell me."

We stepped off the sidewalk into the parking lot. Legend's car—one of them—was a Bentley Bentayga. Very sleek. Very sexy. Very expensive. But that's not why he didn't want me to drive. The man just had to be in charge every minute of every day.

"My date, my rules."

"It's not a date."

Spinning around, I grasped his shoulder and shoved him up against his car. Legend raised a brow at this, which rose higher as I slid my hand between us, rubbing him through his pants.

"Come on, Legend. Trust me. I have something special planned for you. I know you'll love it."

"What is it?"

"A surprise," I teased, tracing the outline of his cock. My not-so-small friend raised his head in interest.

"I hate surprises."

"You know, for someone who said they'll give me a fair chance, you're being very difficult right now. Give me the keys and I keep this"—I cupped his package—"up the whole way."

He plucked off my hand. "I told you you're not getting in through my cock." I shrieked when he picked me up. Legend rounded the car, unlocked the door, and plopped me in the passenger seat. "And you're not driving either. Tell me where we're going."

I didn't tell him shit. Instead, I just said to drive and told him when and where to turn. He was not going to find out until he saw the signs. In between directions, I told him stories.

Stories of growing up on the farm. Stories of my early life in Chicago. Stories of my parents—the few that I had. And stories of Gran and Rainey. Legend listened in silence, neither commenting nor offering memories of his own.

But he listened.

"Gran and Dad had a real relationship. They were close," I said. "He'd talk to her on the phone every week. We visited as much as we could. One year, Dad paid for a farm sitter, so she could come on a cruise with us. It's funny now, remembering her in a floppy hat and floral muumuu, kicking back on the beach with a fruity drink. I never saw her that relaxed and free again, but at least I got to that one time. That one memory of my family all together and happy. At least I have that," I whispered.

For a long time, neither of us spoke.

"We weren't always this way."

I stilled—not moving, not looking away from the trees whipping by my window.

"My folks and I," he clarified. "Right now, they seem like the stereotype. A rich couple that's too wrapped up in their money and each other to remember they spat out a kid twenty years ago. But it wasn't always like that.

"My mom suffered six miscarriages before becoming pregnant with me. I was their miracle baby. The child they longed for. When I was born, Dad took leave, and left the running of the business to his second. The two of them were all over me when I was little. They took me everywhere. We did everything together. I had three shadows."

I chanced a peek at him. His expression was as blank, relaxed, and handsome as it always was. Was it hurting him to tell me this? I couldn't tell, but he was telling me.

"What changed?"

"It's what changes for nearly every family. They're no stereotype, de Souza. They're like every other parent who wakes up one day and discovers they've given birth to an individual, not a copy of themselves. I was their only child. The one they poured all their hopes and dreams into, and I was perfect—as they told me every chance they got. Their perfect son. Their angel.

"Until I started showing interest in men and women, and Dad didn't know what to do with that. Then Mom started organizing acting auditions and modeling shoots for her handsome little boy, but all it taught me was how to act like I enjoyed it. Their interests, plans, and hopes for me weren't mine. So... they pulled back."

Cautiously, I touched his thigh, rubbing soothing circles. "I'm sorry, Legend."

"Don't be." He didn't take his eyes off the road. "I never thought they did it because they stopped giving a shit about me. The opposite actually. I had a feeling they were just... scared. Scared if they pushed too hard, I'd hate them. Scared if they said the wrong thing, they'd damage our relationship beyond repair.

"They thought I wanted them to stop smothering me and"—he inclined his head—"some days I did. But what I really wanted was for them to accept me the way I was. But that's nothing new. Like I said, billions of sons and daughters have said the same about their parents. It's almost boring how typical the St. Jameses are."

"It may be typical, but that doesn't make it hurt any less. Not being accepted by the people who are supposed to love you unconditionally? That's how Dantes are made."

He chuckled. "I'd be offended, but considering what I do as a Bedlam Boy, you may have a point."

"That wasn't a dig at you." Sitting up, I pointed out the window. "Right here. Take this right.

"I'm just saying. Humans don't do well when they don't feel loved. That's one thing Jacques and I agreed on. No one from a sweet, loving family with great friends and a support system is running with the Black Letter Crew. Those monsters are broken," I rasped, fist balling. "They're broken beyond repair."

"Hard to argue that," he said simply.

He's talking. We're having an actual conversation. A depressing one, but real.

"Can I ask you something?"

"You will anyway."

I laughed hoarsely. "It's the Society of Sisters, so your mom is one of them. She gave her perfect and only child the green light to become a Bedlam Boy. Why?"

"This town means just as much to her. Before she became a St. James, she was a Lyman. Before the revolt, there were three Lyman sisters who inherited their father's tailor shop when he died. They were the only women in town who owned their land and a business. That—"

"—made them a target of the Men of Honor."

He nodded. "They were relentless in their harassment. Raiding their shop and destroying their fabrics. Bricks through the window. A mysterious fire started in their home in the middle of the night. It all escalated to one terrible night when they chose one of the sisters for the Hunt.

"The things they did to her were so horrific, Mom wouldn't let me read it in the old journals that survived and were passed down. She still won't and I'm a grown man. I just know it was an attack so brutal, it left her unable to have children."

I squeezed my eyes shut, sickened by the people who did that, and those today who raised them up as some kind of heroes.

"When the revolt kicked off, the Lyman sisters not only took up arms, but they shielded women in their shop—defending them when the Men descended with guns and torches. When the fighting was done, only one sister survived. She rebuilt her family's legacy and passed it down to us," he said. "Mom would say that if she wasn't willing to fight half as hard as they did to protect what we have, she didn't deserve it in the first place.

"She's proud of me for being a Bedlam Boy. In this, I've made my parents very proud."

I gazed out the windshield, his reply turning in my mind. Gran's voice came to me so clearly.

"That's the blood that runs through your veins. You came from the strongest of people. The fiercest. People who would give up their lives before surrendering their freedom. Never forget who you are, girls. Fighters."

"I think my grandmother would be proud too. She raised me to fight. Like she fought for our home and family. Like I'm fighting for them now. I haven't done everything perfectly," I admitted, "but me here with you guys—stopping Ellis and Dante. I know that's what she'd want."

If Legend planned to say something, he was interrupted by me spotting the final turn.

"This is it. Turn here. I bought our tickets online, so we can go straight in."

Legend slowed, then hit the brakes short of the sign. "Hunter's Crest Zoo? You're taking me to the zoo?"

"Yes. Go on, pull in."

He didn't move the car. "Why in the hell would I want to go to the zoo?"

"You'll find out in approximately ten minutes."

"I won't find out shit. I was brought here half a dozen times when I was a kid. There's nothing in there I haven't seen."

"Ah, your parents brought you back here to see the python family they adopted you from? It's good to be among your kind. We'll drop in and say hi on the way out."

His brow twitched. "Cute."

I bit back a smile. "Legend, if you haven't been since you were a kid, then you haven't seen what I'm about to show you. It's a new exhibit. You'll understand everything when we're inside. Now, take your foot off the brake, find a parking spot, and stop being the most stubborn date on the planet."

"This isn't a date."

"What did I just say?"

I thought I glimpsed a grin as he finally pulled off and turned into the parking lot. Early morning on a weekday, there were few people about. That didn't stop Legend turning into a deserted part of the lot—far from everyone and backed by trees. He wasn't risking a ding to his ride by parking next to a stressed-out dad, too focused on wrangling his sugar-crazed kids into the car to pay attention when he was backing out.

"You have a need for control," I said, linking my arm through his.

"That a problem?"

"No, I find it very attractive. Especially because it gets you so deliciously riled up when I tie you to the bed."

"You will not like the consequences if you try that again."

Oh, but I would. I knew my guys. Roan was the only one of them who enjoyed being at my mercy. Legend, Arsenio, Cairo, and Jacques would unhinge like wolves in a trap, chewing off their own leg. Thinking of the resulting effect on my pussy made me stumble. I wouldn't walk right for weeks.

Together we walked past the ticket booth, heading inside. I'd also been to Hunter's Crest Zoo many times. When I was searching for the kookaburra in Cavendish's letter, it brought me here even though the park employees kept telling me they didn't have any here. After the first time, I'm not sure what I kept coming back to find. But I did keep coming back to walk under the canopy of leaves, finding an odd sense of peace as a light mist washed over, and critters chirped, screeched, and huffed around me.

Animals didn't know malice. Yes, they killed to survive, but only to survive. They didn't taunt their prey. Drag out the fear and pain for their own enjoyment. *Sacrifice* a creature to advance selfish ambitions. They just lived their lives in the only way they knew how.

On my worst days living Rainey's life, I came here to be surrounded by innocence.

Legend and I passed by the panda habitat, spotting the fluffy, lazy creatures lying on a rock slab and watching us go by. He let me hold on to his arm, my chin propped on his shoulder. I loved being this close to him after weeks of him keeping a football field's distance between us.

"Are you hungry?" I murmured. "Afterward, I was thinking we'd eat lunch in the café. They've got a perfect spot on the balcony that overlooks the giraffe habitat. We can eat chicken wraps and shortbread cookies while we watch them graze."

"Watch them? How closely do you watch me? How do you know I like shortbread cookies?"

I poked his side. "Don't act like I'm some kind of stalker. We do live in the same house. The only thing sweet or sugary I've seen you eat are shortbread cookies. Not too big a leap to guess they tickle your sweet tooth."

He grunted something in response.

"My favorite are white chocolate strawberry cookies," I went on. "You never see them in stores, but Gran made them special and she taught me. I'll bake you some one day."

"Why?" He was genuinely asking. "We just confirmed I only like shortbread cookies."

"You'll like these too. Trust me."

"I won't," he dismissed, turning to the tiger exhibit.

I sighed. "How did you and Roan get together? Is it because your stubborn refusal to give in to him brought out his devil imp side? Every no just made him work that much harder to have you."

I didn't imagine it that time. A definite lopsided grin teased his soft lips. "Would it surprise you that I pursued him? I decided I wanted Roan, so I had Roan. The one who didn't get to say no is him."

"Hmm. Actually, that doesn't surprise me. Roan wouldn't give me anything until I took it from him too. So, was your seduction routine the same for him as it was for me? Did you chase him through the woods and paddle him until he came screaming on your couch?" I was very glad there was no one else nearby on our walk.

"A hunter doesn't use the same tactics on different prey."

I eyed him. "Do you truly see me as a different person now?"

To my surprise, he turned and gazed at me head-on. "Do you see yourself as the same person?"

"I..." Looking into his eyes, I tried to say something, anything else. "I don't. The person I was the last two years wasn't me."

Vindication curved his lips.

I quickly added, "But the way I feel about you and the guys hasn't—"

"You said there's something you want to show me," he sliced in. "Where the hell is it? I'm getting bored."

Swallowing my annoyance, I led him right on a forking path, heading for the exhibit that had seen a lot of me since I received Cavendish's letters. Legend unwound his arm from me and followed behind. The mood shifted between us, but I would get it back. Legend knew what it was to play a part. If anyone should understand that didn't make the person underneath it any less real, it was him.

The path narrowed, bringing the leaf canopy close enough to block the sun—shading us in cool and mist. A small, darkened tunnel entrance loomed at the end of our path. I reached behind, lacing my fingers through Legend's. "This, baby, is what I want you to see."

We stepped out of the gloom into a vibrant, living paradise.

Birds of all colors zipped through the trees, flitting from the greens, purples, pinks, and reds of the flower-filled paradise. The sweet scent of honeysuckle blanketed the space, filling me with calm as I gazed up at him.

Legend looked around, his face unreadable, but something—the tiniest flicker—shone in his eyes. "They're hummingbirds. You brought me to a hummingbird habitat."

"Some of the rarest species in the world live here. They started a program three years ago to ensure their survival. They've got glittering starfrontlets and royal sunangels. Hummingbirds get the most beautiful names," I said. "They're free to roam the whole habitat, so there's no guarantee we'll see one, but we can try."

Legend flicked to a bird flying overhead. "I didn't realize you thought I was this sentimental."

"You did get a hummingbird permanently inked on your body." I bumped his shoulder. "You don't have to say I nailed it. I know I did."

Legend let me link our arms again. He didn't say much while I led him down the winding paths. Actually, he didn't say anything at all. He looked at the birds I pointed out, and nodded a few times at the things I said, but otherwise, I didn't have a clue what was going on behind those brown eyes.

Twice we did the rounds—me just enjoying holding him close. On the last lap, I asked, "Anything else you want to see while we're here?"

"Since I'm not a seven-year-old girl, no. If we're done, let's go back."

My smile dimmed. "Don't you want to get something to eat first? The shortbread cookies here are really good."

Legend wasn't asking anymore. He hooked around my waist and took off, ducking through the exit and taking us out of the zoo and into the parking lot.

I didn't know what to say or do, so I said and did nothing. Was he annoyed? Mad? Done with me? Had I ruined my first and last chance to win him back?

All I wanted to do was show him that I knew him. I listened to him. The late nights we spent in bed, talking about the little things while Roan slept pressed against my back—they mattered to me just as much then as they did now. I could live a thousand lives and that would never change.

"I'm sorry, Legend." He beeped the car open. "I truly thought you would enjoy it. I'll think of something better for next time." Legend's hand rested on the small of my back, guiding me around the trunk to my side. "What if I make us a romantic dinner? Shortbread cookies from scratch. Or we could do something the three of us. You, me, and Roan—"

A hand clamped on my jaw, constricting my gasp. He hauled me to his lips, eating another gasp as he bit my ear.

"Damn, woman, you need a lot of validation. You know you nailed it, so stop fishing for me to say you did."

My eyes went round. "But— You said—"

Legend crashed his lips on mine. I responded instantly, twisting around and linking my arms behind his head. A faint beep sounded in my ear. I didn't register what the sound meant until Legend picked me up and plopped me back-flat in the trunk.

"Uhh. If this was a trick to lock me in here, I'm telling you right now, you're the one who'll face the consequences."

His grin could only be described as wicked. "I'm almost tempted to find out what those would be, but no." Calloused fingers tickled my leg, leaving a teasing trail under the hem of my dress. "I had something else in mind."

"What—"

Legend tore my panties clean off. I choked on a noise when they went sailing over his shoulder, into the trees. *This is why he didn't want cookies. He had another kind of dessert in mind.*

"Leg—" He pushed two fingers past my folds and they were off, pumping and finger-fucking me as my legs flailed for purchase and found none. The man really didn't want me to talk, which was good because all thought of doing that flew out of my head.

My head bumped against the rough fabric. I was only half in. My ass was propped up and hanging over the lip. Legend flipped my dress up and it fluttered over my face, muffling the moans I was already fighting to hold in. Thank goodness there were barely any people here on a Wednesday morning. That didn't mean I needed a homeschooling family of four to stumble on this sight.

I batted my dress out of my face, just in time to see Legend free his cock. I tightened on his fingers, whimpering in anticipation of that smooth, thick rod moving inside me.

It had been a very long time.

Legend crooked his fingers, angling them to undo me while his thumb caressed my clit. My eyes crossed. He added a third finger, stretching me just to the point of my limit. Goose bumps rolled down my flesh, the visual proof of what this man did to me. Intensity rippled through me again and again like a thumping bass—reverberating in my soul.

He caught one of my legs and hooked it around his waist. "Take your dress off."

I scrambled to heed his order. Wasn't easy when I was the wrong side up and maneuvering in a tight space. Finally, I got it off and quickly shoved it under me when he reached for it. He wasn't tossing that into the woods too.

Chuckling, Legend drew a line through the sweat collecting between my breasts, over my stomach, and slipped among the digits working my pussy. He swallowed that finger to the knuckle. "You're wrong, de Souza. Shortbread cookies aren't how I indulge my sweet tooth. You are."

I swallowed hard. As I thought, I nailed the date and it stirred something in Legend I didn't understand, but wasn't about to stop for all the money in the world. If he wanted to forget how angry and distrustful he was of me, who was I to remind him?

"Tease me," he ordered.

Rough pants heaved my chest, and it was getting his divided attention as he palmed his cock. I cupped them without a thought—pushing them together and delighting the hitch that small act caused in his breath. My nipples were hardened pebbles, begging for Legend's mouth on my breasts, or his dick pumping between.

They settled for me rolling and tweaking them between my fingers as his eyes glazed.

My time was up.

Legend tore his fingers away without so much as a goodbye. Positioning my hips, he buried inside me to the hilt—rolling my eyes up into my head.

I clapped a hand over my mouth when he started pumping—No, when he started jackhammering my hole like he was looking for diamonds. Moans leaked through my fingers. My pelvic bone bounced on the rim, collecting bruises that revealed the proof of my first time in a trunk.

Legend's perfectly coiffed hair was a mess. It flopped in his eyes, sticking to his damp brow and drawing my attention to those plump lips—now tinged red and pulled back over his teeth as he tried to hold in his groans. It was unnatural how gorgeous he was, but I didn't mean his looks.

Somewhere along the way, the sweet kid who was doted on by his parents was buried under the feeling that he'd never measure up to their expectations, so why try? I didn't care about what he told himself, or what others led him to believe to make him think something so ridiculous could be true. Legend never needed to be anyone other than his searing-hot, possessive, domineering, hummingbird-loving self. He would fall in love with me again because we both knew... I loved Legend St. James, and wouldn't change a thing about him.

The car bounced with his thrusts. We both did. Over and over, my hand smacked the roof and my head banged against the trunk. I was too far gone too long ago to care.

Legend grasped my hips, lifting me up and angling me into place for one, two, three punishing thrusts dead center on my—

"Ahh!" I screamed, contorting my body in a shape it was never meant to go.

I came hard—flopping, kicking, and scraping my back on the unforgiving fabric. Throwing his head back, Legend went rigid.

"Yes, baby. Come for me."

Sticky warmth spilled inside me, setting off another orgasm that bowled me over, filling me with bursts of heat and electricity. Felt like I grabbed a downed power line and bolts of sinful pleasure were coursing through my veins. I had no doubt it'd kill me if it could, and what a beautiful way to go.

My hips jerked, rocked by a violent spasm.

"Whoa— Shit!" Legend popped off his feet. Scrabbling, he grabbed at the lid to stop his fall, and down they both went.

"Ah!"

One hundred and sixty pounds of man collapsed on top of me, then the lid dropped on us—concealing us in darkness. For a breath, neither of us moved.

A sound leaked through my lips. I covered my mouth, trying to stop it, but it was too late. I laughed so loud and hard, if the entire parking lot didn't hear us having sex, they definitely heard that. Two seconds after me, Legend cracked up too.

"Date Roan for a week and you don't think you have any firsts left," I giggled. "Guess we proved that wrong."

"Definitely the first time I fucked myself into a locked trunk in the parking lot of a zoo."

"Tell me we're not really locked in."

"Nah." Legend was nothing more than a vague outline in the dark. "I've got the keys in my pocket, but..." There was shuffling, the clink of his belt, then hands found my hips. "We don't need to go anywhere just yet."

"I was about to say the same thing."

Chapter Five

That night, I showered and changed in Roan's room, then went out to Legend's. The more-than-a-rich-boy opened the door wearing silk drawstring pants, a bare chest, and a smirk. He propped against the wood. "Something I can do for you?"

"You can step aside so I can climb into your bed."

He cocked his head. "Why would I do that?"

Our interlude in the parking lot came roaring into my mind, and on my face if his widening grin proved anything. "Why wouldn't you? I thought we made up."

"You take me to see some birds, and you think that's all it takes for us to get back together? How easy do you think I am?"

"Very," I said, crossing my arms. "You put out on the first date."

He laughed. "That's because I'm a slut, gorgeous. Not because you're forgiven. I'm still feeling the need to be wooed."

My teeth gritted. Did I say I loved *everything* about him?

"What's this? Fixed things up already?" Roan sidled up next to us. "I knew you were missing that Roan sandwich as much as I was."

"Not fixed quite yet," Legend replied, throwing an arm around his boyfriend. "Ivy wants to take me on a few more dates. Show me how much she really cares. Who am I to say no?"

Roan shrugged. "Yeah? Okay. Well, I'm still in the mood for a dick in my ass, so join us, Ivy. You can watch."

"Yes, please."

"Oooh, afraid not." Legend expertly slid Roan in his room and blocked my entrance in one smooth move. "Wouldn't be nice to tempt you with what you can't have yet. But here's a tip for our second date. I like red wines, expensive gifts, silk, and amateur porn. Night, love."

My retort shot at his closed door. "You finally admit it was a date!"

"I guess knocking us down isn't going as easily as you thought."

I faced the handsome figure hanging out of his doorway.

"I never thought it would be easy, Cairo. But it is worth it."

"Is it? Then why have you given up on me?" Nastiness curled his lips. "You haven't batted your eyes in my direction for weeks."

"Because I'm giving you space," I said, hips rolling as I closed the distance. "Your dad is in trouble. Wouldn't be right to make it all about us right now."

"Oh, how thoughtful," he mocked.

"Was that the wrong thing to do?" I placed my hand on his chest, my heart picking up speed as his thumped slow and steady beneath my palm. "You know how badly I want to make things right between us. Tell me how to do that."

"You can't, de Souza. It's never going to happen between us." He brushed my hand off. "Besides, I've already moved on."

"What do you—?"

Cairo pushed open the door. Peering over his shoulder, I landed on the slim, pretty, young blonde... stretched out on his bed. Red bled into my vision.

"You fucking bastard."

"Now that's not very nice."

"You shit-covered piece of garbage!" I shoved him. "What do you think you're doing?!"

"Whoa, man," the girl said. "I don't want any trouble."

"Get out!" My bellow popped her eyes out of her head. "Get out right now."

She scrambled off the bed.

"No, you stay," Cairo barked at her. "And you."

The world spun. In a blink, I was hanging off his shoulder—pounding his back in the midst of being carried off.

"Put me down, you cheating piece of shit. If you touch her, they'll never find your corpses! Put me down," I shrieked.

Cairo hauled me into Roan's room and over to his bed. I had no idea why until I heard a faint click. A cool metal bite encircled my ankle.

"Cairo!"

The guy flipped me on my back, plopping me on the bed I was now handcuffed to. With that, he strolled right out.

"Come back here! Cairo, I swear, if you sleep with her, you'll regret it for the rest of a very short life."

I shouted and raged at the shared wall all through the night. None of the other guys came in to free me. Legend was likely getting a kick out of the karma, while the others were thinking I'd carry out my many violent, graphic threats.

All night I screamed and threw everything in reach at the wall. It was the only thing I could do. I was afraid if I stopped, the tears beating behind my eyes would drag me deeper than the river under Chaney Bridge ever could.

JACQUES

I sipped my smoothie in silence, eyes fixed on the same sight everyone else at the dining table was looking at.

Ivy slammed around the kitchen, white-knuckling a large knife she needed to open the package of bacon, but certainly did not need now that she was making eggs.

Cairo kicked back next to me, looking entirely too cool for someone unlikely to see tomorrow.

"One of us should probably take that away from her," Legend mused.

Bang!

Ivy flung the pan in the direction of the sink. It bounced out and clattered on the floor. She paid it no mind in favor of banging the drawers open and shut.

"You first," Roan said.

"Why did you free her in the first place?" Cairo breezed.

His guest left two hours before. I watched her go from the living room. I had woken up early and gone downstairs, away from Ivy's shouting, to mentally sort through the information I collected on the seven out of nine on my list. It was Thursday. Our last day to finalize a plan to either rescue Sheriff Jack, or kidnap the members of one of Hunter's Crest's richest families.

Roan shrugged. "I wanted to see what she'd do to you."

It wasn't hard to answer why people were tempted to beat Roan unconscious.

Ivy stepped out of the kitchen, snapping five heads up. She carried a plate of bacon and eggs... and that knife.

Spines stiff, we didn't say a word as she went back and forth to set a plate down in front of Roan, Legend, and then Arsenio, accompanying each one with a kiss on the cheek. "Here you are, baby."

She returned for the last plate, and narrowed on Cairo. She approached fast, raising him half out of his seat. "Here." The plate went flying, crashing on the table and tipping half the contents on his lap. "Choke on it."

He chuckled with a bit of egg decorating his nose. "Thanks ever so, sweetie."

A fierce growl was her reply. Ivy went into the kitchen and finally dumped the knife in the sink. We didn't resume conversation until she stomped up the stairs.

"We've lapsed on our pet's training," Cairo said, brushing off his pants. He wisely pushed his plate aside. "Jacques, we've got one day left. You said you'd have something by now. Who's in the Black Letter Crew?"

"Out of the seven I've gotten to so far, I can eliminate two. I had to go back in and recall the information, but the night Rainey de Souza was killed was the same night as Stacy Becker's party. Those two were there."

"How do you know they didn't duck out early? You weren't watching two random guys all night."

"Because when I saw them, they were passed out drunk on the couch. I doubt they collected themselves and became coherent enough to murder a girl and chase the other through the woods an hour later."

Cairo inclined his head, accepting this. "That's two out of seven. Who are the other five? Let's stop fucking around and bring them in for a real chat."

"We're not at that stage yet. I'll find out what I need to know about the final two in"—I checked my watch—"three hours. After that, I'll have a clear picture of who I'm dealing with. When I know who to move on first, I'll pick them up."

"Three hours. That's all you have."

"That's all I need."

Arsenio pushed away from the table. "Then, we're good. We're not making that trip to Hunter's Crest after all."

I didn't reply. Finishing the last of my drink, I washed out my cup and headed out the door, returning my mind to the train of thoughts Ivy and her knife interrupted.

Yes, Mia Collins and Roderick Murphy were saved suspicions by my memory. That left the five I did get to, like Zara Singh. In that moment as a hurt, moaning man mewled at her feet, there was the briefest flash in her eyes where I saw... nothing at all.

No concern. No shock. No compassion. No empathy.

Zara could've been looking at a gum wrapper on the sidewalk for all the emotion reflected in her dark-brown pools. Then, just like that, it all flicked back on as if she remembered faking human emotions was required to fit in.

Then there was Jackson Hyde, the one who was abused by his aunt's boyfriends. He did not have a tight-knit group of friends or loving parents. The guy wasn't exactly a loner. He regularly attended the school anime club and got on well enough with the other members, according to what I dug up. But he didn't have a girlfriend, boyfriend, or even a close friend he hung out with on a regular basis.

Arranging another accident in front of him wasn't worth the two hundred dollars. I had no doubt he'd keep walking like it wasn't his problem. Instead, I went with the direct approach and broke into his dorm room while he was at the aforementioned anime club.

He had a single room and the cheap lock that was on all the doors. I was in without much effort. The look inside his private world was eye-opening. Nothing so obvious as black envelopes on the nightstand, or a shrine to the Men of Honor in his closet, but when I walked out half an hour later, I knew what I needed to know.

So it was going through the list and finding ways to glimpse what they'd hidden successfully for years, or eliminating people who truly were as innocent as they looked.

Three hours later, Ivy and I walked out of class and went separate ways. She did sit next to me during the lecture, huffing and glaring at me as if being Cairo's oldest friend somehow gave me control over his actions. It barely gave me insight into them.

I couldn't begin to guess what he was doing bringing that woman into our house and flaunting her in front of Ivy. Somehow, he'd gone from wanting nothing to do with her to wanting to hurt her, and fuck knows what caused the switch.

I left the poli-sci building and crossed campus, coming up the back way to Psychology. A woman in an orange dress and matching shoes loitered by the steps.

"Ah, there you are. I've got what you asked for." The teaching assistant handed over a stack of papers. They disappeared into my shoulder bag. "You were right. I told the professor it was a quick, ten-minute quiz to test my thesis, and he waved me on without a fight. But I don't understand," she said, studying me. "What good are any of these answers to you? *What kind of animal are you? Are you an alarm clock or wake-up-on-your-own-time person? Who's your favorite* Doctor Who *villain?*"

"It was all totally random."

"I'm testing a thesis of my own. Studying law is also the study of human behavior. You've got to understand how people think to get twelve random jurors on your side. Having you ask your class to do this saved me tracking down twenty-five participants myself. For that"—I handed over her money—"two hundred as agreed."

"Thank you very much," she replied, pleased. "Next time you need a favor, don't hesitate to text me."

I left, taking the quizzes home. Not the Bedlam Boy house, but my mother's home. That time of day she'd be in court, and I needed peace and quiet while I put the last pieces of the puzzle together.

Mother's two-story French country-style home was as immaculate as ever. The lawn neatly trimmed. The rose bushes tended. The smell of fresh linen air freshener and bleach wafting over me when I stepped inside.

I passed into the marble-and-steel kitchen, and dumped every test other than two in the trash. My next stop was in the living room. I dropped on the couch, reading through the seemingly random answers.

Giving them the actual questions to test for sociopathy would've been a waste of time. If they were any kind of intelligent sociopath, they'd lie. No, the only way was to disguise the questions within other questions.

Are you aggressive? became *What kind of animal are you?*

Choosing a crocodile over a harmless little bunny answered that question.

Asking if they woke up when they wanted or set an alarm checked off another box too. We were college students with classes, internships, campus jobs, and interviews. We all had an alarm clock, and anyone who didn't wasn't too concerned with other people's time, or sticking to their commitments.

And you both wrote that you're wake-up-on-your-own-time people.

I moved on to the next question: *Who's your favorite* Doctor Who *villain?*

A risky one if they didn't watch the show, but both wrote an answer, so the risk paid off. Back when Ivy thought she was her sci-fi-loving sister, she went on about the show and the different creatures from the good guys to the bad. There were villains that didn't actually kill or hurt anyone. There were villains that only killed when they were under someone's control. There were villains that killed out of a warped belief they were doing good.

And then there were villains who slaughtered out of nothing but pure hate and enjoyment.

Their answers were the final two on that list: the villains without remorse.

I went through the rest of the answers to the sociopath test they didn't know they'd taken, and one test fluttered to the floor as I focused on the last one—*the* one.

Twelve for twelve, they answered every single one correctly, or incorrectly under the circumstances. I traveled back up to the name. A name that out of all nine, did not surprise me.

I couldn't yet be sure about the other eight but—

You, I thought, eyes narrowing. *You're in the Black Letter Crew.*

ARSENIO

I stopped to give Ivy a slice of mango, then continued my chopping. She was spread out on the kitchen table—naked and covered in my dinner. As I explained to her, since she broke a plate that morning, she had to be mine.

"Jacques hasn't come home," she said. "Shouldn't we be worried?"

"He usually takes off to get some space when he's thinking about something that actually taxes his genius, but he is cutting it close this time. He was supposed to give us a name hours ago. Whoever we need to interrogate, I'll give the Black Letter Crew some credit and assume they're not easy to break. We need to get Sharpe's location from them before the decision is made for us, and we leave tomorrow for the tournament."

"Do you really think their plan is to kill the sheriff whether or not you get rid of the Ellises?"

"Do *you* think that's their plan?" I finished prepping the avocado and lined the slices down her chest. I enjoyed cooking. Of all the activities my mother forced on me to channel my anger, this was the most effective. And with the addition of Ivy, I was finding a whole new interest in the culinary arts. "You know Cavendish. If anyone can guess how he taught his acolytes to think, it's you. What are the sheriff's odds of making it out of this if we don't get to him first?"

She turned away, gazing at the opposite wall. "Slim. If you don't get rid of Steven, Micah, and Jeremy, he won't live to the weekday, and I don't doubt that for a second. This is a test. A grim and gruesome test to see if they can use him to control their new Bedlam Boy action figures.

"If you disobey them, it's just proof Sheriff Jack isn't enough of an incentive. They'll kill him and grab someone you guys will do anything for. Which leaves you no better off than you are now, except Cairo loses a father.

"If you do follow their orders, they won't have a reason to kill Sheriff Sharpe now. He's useful. He can keep being useful while the Black Letter Crew needs you to do their dirty work. But the second they no longer need that..." She trailed off to eat a piece of avocado.

That was fine. I could fill in the rest myself. "They will kill him. Then they'll come after all of us. All of their enemies swept off the playing field."

"It's what Cavendish would do."

"If the suicidal bastard hadn't ordered you to set him on fire. Still no insight into why he decided to die?"

She shook her head. "Now that I have my memory back, I'm sure there was an ulterior motive. I just don't know what it could be."

"Perfect thing to ask Dante and his buddies once Jacques tracks them down."

"If he doesn't come through in time, will you really go through with your plan? Kidnapping the Ellises, faking their deaths, holding them hostage until you free the sheriff?"

"You just laid out our options. According to you, we don't have a choice."

"I'm still hoping it doesn't come to that."

I bent down, helping myself to a chunk of mango nestled on her right breast. She made a soft noise as I closed on her nipple and scraped it between my teeth.

"I have no idea what to say to Mr. Ellis to get him to speak to me alone," she continued when she recovered. "And his sons won't want anything to do with me." Ivy blew out a breath. "But I'll figure it out. As badly as I want to beat Jeremy and Micah for what they did to Roan, what I want more is to get us out from under Dante's hold. An unseen enemy has too much power."

"Enough about this. I'm fucking you now."

"Now? But I'm covered in fruit and avocado."

"And you taste delicious."

Naturally, Ivy had no more protests, and my plate became my sex toy.

We messed around in the kitchen for hours, then I took my meal upstairs and messed with her up there. It wasn't until she was softly breathing underneath me, wrapped around like a garland, that I recalled everyone came home and walked past us while we were having our fun on the table. Everyone except Jacques.

Untangling myself from Ivy, I crossed the hall to Jacques's room, shoved on the door, and peered at an empty bed. A glance at the clock read two in the morning.

Where the hell is he?

"YOU DON'T NEED TO TELL me he's missing. I've been after him since he blew me off yesterday morning." Cairo loaded his golf clubs in Legend's trunk.

The tournament started in two and a half hours. We were done waiting for Jacques. The decision had been made for us. We had to go to Hunter's Crest and turn Steven, Jeremy, and Micah's night into a bad one.

"He was looking for members of the Black Letter Crew," Legend said. He was the only one of us that didn't look idiotic in that polo-and-khakis getup. "I'm thinking he found them."

Silence pressed in on us.

"If they have him, we need to do something." Ivy slammed out of the house. "You're not going to know anything until the mail arrives, and that won't be today. We can't sit around doing nothing if they really have him."

"We can't sit around doing nothing because if we do, my old man is dead," Cairo replied.

Ivy shot him a withering look. She had not forgiven or forgotten.

"We go on with the plan, but Roan stays here," he continued. "Jacques was supposed to play while you caddied. They're not going to let you walk about with a bag of clubs doing nothing, so you'll stay, find him, then bring the bastard to the club when he finally decides to show up."

"I wasn't only going to hold a bag. I'm supposed to cause a distraction in the kitchen and pull as many guards away from the east door."

"We'll improvise," he barked. "But it won't matter because you'll find him before then. Let's go."

We split up—half going to Legend's car and half climbing into the gift I bought myself over the holidays. It wasn't my father's Chevrolet Corvette, and for that I was still tempted to hunt the Crows down and make Jeremy piss himself crying on a stake again.

We all made for the cars except for Roan... and Ivy.

"I should stay and help him look," she announced. "I don't play my part until tonight. Until then, I... I know what those guys do to people. If Jacques is with them right now, I have to get to him—"

"If I'm with who?"

Five necks twisted, landing on the cool and collected prodigy walking down the sidewalk. *Wait*— I squinted. *Not so cool and collected.*

Jacques was wearing the rumpled version of the clothes he'd worn the day before. Mud decorated his shoes, and red bled into his eyes telling of how much sleep he'd gotten the night before.

None.

"Where were you?" Cairo asked, shoving out of the car.

"Listen—"

"We're out of time. Did you find the five or not—?"

"Listen," Jacques growled. "I found three I'm uncertain of, and one I'm not. They're one of them, I know it, and I looked for them all day and all night. They're *nowhere*! If I didn't know better, I'd think they were on to me, but it's not possible. I was careful."

Boop. Boop.

"Who are you talking about?" Legend asked. "Their name, Jacques."

"You're not going to believe this. It's—"

Boop!

Sound blared in my ear, spinning me around. Bellowing, I jumped out of the way as the car rocketed up the curb.

"Arsenio Creed, Jacques Stone, Legend St. James, Roan Banks, and Cairo Sharpe." Davidson heaved out of his police car while two more rolled up, pinning us in on both sides. "Put your hands up and get on your knees slowly. You're under arrest."

"What?" Ivy screeched. "What the fuck are you talking about?"

Davidson didn't even look at her. He trained his gun between my eyes—the grin tugging his lips clear as day. "Don't make this difficult, mayor's boy. Get those hands up."

Moving only my eyes, I gazed around at the officers whipping their guns back and forth between Roan, Cairo, Legend, Jacques, and Ivy. We outnumbered them, but they'd squeeze off a few shots if we attacked, and then we wouldn't outnumber them at all.

Slowly, I raised my hands. "Officer Davidson, there seems to be some mistake. We haven't committed any crime."

He belly-laughed. "You said that with the best straight face, Creed. Very believable, but I'm afraid your mommies aren't getting you out of this one. We've got evidence, witnesses, video. The five of you will be breathing stale prison air for two life sentences."

"Evidence and witnesses to what?"

That tugging grin morphed into a full-blown, shit-eating smirk. "The murder of Scott Cavendish."

My brow cracked. I was not expecting that.

"Sheriff Sharpe should've never been in charge of that case, considering his son was the main suspect. I smelled a rat from the beginning. When I took over, I investigated properly and the evidence led exactly where I knew it would. It's over, boys. Your free rein in this town is over." His finger twitched on the trigger. "I said on your knees. Hands behind your head."

"No. Wait!" Ivy lurched forward, swinging three weapons to her.

"Stop! Don't move!" we shouted.

Jacques caught her, snapping her to his chest. He bent his head, whispering something in her ear. The officer grabbed and pulled him away, forcing him onto his knees.

We all dropped—folding our hands behind our heads and getting cuffed in front of a gathering crowd. One by one we were loaded into the car. Ivy's pale figure was the last thing we saw as we turned the corner.

It was a silent ride to the police station—for us. Davidson kept up a steady string of triumphant chatter about how he solved the town's most notorious case, and that the *acting* part in acting sheriff would be removed after everyone found out that Jack Sharpe hid evidence and tried to let his murderous son and his friends go free.

He kept up his bullshit all through fingerprinting, photographs, and shoving us into the small-town station's cramped cell.

I faced him as the bars slammed shut. "I don't understand this," I said, not letting my voice carry. "He gave us instructions we had every intention of carrying out. Why tell us to go to that party if he was just going to have you pull this? What was the point?"

Davidson laughed. "You really don't understand, do you?" He glanced over his shoulder, then turned his smile on all of us. "Nothing has changed. The plan is still for you to sacrifice the Ellises tonight, or the sheriff dies. Too bad the five of you never made it to Hunter's Crest. You got caught up in some legal trouble and the clock ran out on Jack Sharpe."

My eyes sharpened. "What the fuck are you doing?"

"You're supposed to be intelligent, Creed. Do you need me to spell it out for you? I don't give a shit about Steven Ellis or his sons. On the contrary, I'm quite fond of the man. He intends to see me live the life that I'm meant to. *I*"—he thumped his chest—"should've been the sheriff of this town. *I* should've been mayor. But you know what? I'll settle for stepping up in Jack's place until it's time for me to move to my obscenely large mansion on a private island with my wife and two mistresses."

"The mistresses are for her, yes? Because no way that woman can stand having your wrinkled one-inch dick anywhere near her."

His smirk flickered. "Reduced to penis jokes? Pathetic."

"Why not? You don't think I'm taking you seriously, do you? You arrested us on campus. It's all over school by now, which means your boss knows we didn't back out of the plan. You screwed it up."

Davidson shrugged. "Changes nothing. He can't get to either of us here, and once you five are transferred to the correction facility upstate, you'll be useless to him. As will the sheriff. I, on the other hand, am vital to him and his plans for Bedlam. I'm the fucking sheriff. I make his crimes go away. I bring his victims to him."

Confirming that it was you who lured Jack Sharpe into Dante's trap.

"He'll be pissed about this, but he'll get over it. Meanwhile, you'll still be in prison and Sharpe will still be dead."

My expression didn't change. "Dante doesn't seem like a think-ahead kind of guy, but he does seem like the kind who values loyalty and orders. You've proven today that you're a self-serving piece of shit that'll turn on him whenever it suits you. Be honest," I said, dropping to a whisper. "You're never making it to that island."

Something flashed in Davidson's eyes—too fast for me to read. "Get comfortable, boys. You're not getting out of here anytime soon."

"We'll see. I'll take that phone call now."

He walked off, laughter floating over his shoulder. "Did I forget to mention? The phone's broken."

I watched him go until he disappeared into *Jack Sharpe's* office. Cairo was a silent, shadowed figure in the corner.

"What did he say?" he asked when I sat next to him. His voice was entirely too calm.

"He said we're screwed, Sharpe. We're not getting out of this one."

"Maybe," Jacques said from where he shared the wall with the toilet. "Davidson didn't get all of us."

IVY

I stood there long after the sirens faded and the onlookers found something better to do.

Everything had changed. The tournament would start in a couple of hours. There was no point in me going up there by myself. I wasn't about to disable the cameras, knock out three grown men, and haul their bodies out a side door by myself without being seen.

Jacques knew that too, which is why he told me what to do.

But how? Helplessness paralyzed me, keeping me pinned to the sidewalk. *Jacques searched all day and night and couldn't find them. How am I supposed to?*

My phone buzzed. I scrambled for it, hoping it was one of the guys using their one phone call to tell me what the hell was going on.

I checked the screen. *Paris.*

"Rainey? Rainey," she cried. "Where are you? What's going on? Someone just texted me that my brother was arrested."

"He was," I croaked. "Officer Davidson arrested him— Arrested all the Bedlam Boys for the murder of Scott Cavendish."

"What?! That's insane. They were framed. Cops figured that out a long time ago. Did Davidson up and decide to stop doing actual police work and just take the easy way out to solve the big case?"

"I wouldn't put anything past that man," I said, lips twisting. "He didn't do any police work in solving my grandmother's murder either." *The corrupt piece of crap had other plans.*

"Oh my gosh. I'm sorry, I have to call my mom. We need to get Cairo a lawyer. Ugh, I wish I had Jack's number," she cried. "Why did he choose now of all times to take a vacation?"

"Paris, before you go, I'm looking for someone who might be able to help..."

I told her.

"Oh, I do know where they are. Amy's there too. It's some kind of sorority bonding thing to break in the new pledges. They kept it secret because they're all blowing off classes, and the sorority has already been busted once for a hazing gone wrong during one of these *bonding trips.*"

No wonder Jacques couldn't find her.

"I'll text you the address."

"Thank you, Paris," I said as the notification chime sounded in my ear. "This'll be over soon. I promise. The guys won't go down for something they didn't do."

"No, they won't. I'll see you later."

"Thanks." I hung up and went straight to Legend's car. The keys were in the ignition, waiting for the trip that wasn't happening. "No, but we've got somewhere else to be."

I plugged the address in the GPS and followed it out of town. My mind churned the whole way. I didn't fault Jacques's genius, but he said he eliminated five, was uncertain of three, and knew without a doubt the final one was in the Black Letter Crew.

How? What did he discover that made him so sure, and why did that stupid oaf Officer Mars have to pull him away before he could tell me more than a name?

What if he's wrong and I spend precious time my guys didn't have by interrogating an innocent?

What if he's right and it all falls on me to rescue the sheriff before the clock strikes seven on Steven Ellis's Bring Back Crystal Canyon party?

I glanced at the clock. Less than eleven hours to do what Cairo couldn't do in weeks. And if I fail and his father dies, leggy blondes won't be the only thing between us. Jack Sharpe's death would break us for good.

I slammed on the gas. If it ended between me and that cheating bastard, it damn sure wouldn't be because of the even bigger bastard that fathered him. This ends tonight.

The Black Letter Crew finally pays for what they've done.

I held on to that conviction as I turned off the main road. Between Bedlam and a town three hours to the east, a lake cut through the hills. Someone took advantage of that years ago and built luxury cabins along the piers and scenic views. It'd be nice for the pledges if they were coming to this spot to bond, but I severely doubted anything so tame was happening.

I turned the final corner, rumbling down to the cabin on the end where I parked at the end of the line of cars. The place was gorgeous—proving someone in this fraternity had money. A beautiful gray stone paradise with a wraparound porch, sloped roof, and three floors. I walked past the tree line and spotted something down by the lake.

Two rows of pledges doing jumping jacks outside on a chilly morning. If I was hearing what they were shouting correctly, they were on number eighty-two.

Bonding, my ass.

I squinted, but couldn't make out any faces. Certainly couldn't tell if who I was looking for was down there. Steeling myself, I approached the house. Climbing the steps, I saw a couple of sisters through the window—kicking back playing a card game and sipping beers in front of a fire. One of them was Amy.

I knocked on the window, waving when she looked up. Amy pulled a face—looking around like she was making sure she wasn't the one in the wrong place. She got off the couch and the door swung open.

"Rainey? What are you doing here?"

"Hey, Amy. Sorry to crash. Paris told me I could find you guys here."

She didn't move from her spot in the entrance—blocking the entrance. "Why did you need to find us? What's going on?"

"Cairo and the guys were arrested for the Ruckus night murder."

Her eyes bugged. "Wait, what? Arrested? Paris must be freaking out. And you," she cried. "Are you okay? What do we do?"

"Officer Davidson"—I would never call that man sheriff—"said they have evidence and witnesses, but it's not true, Amy. They didn't do anything. The murder went viral and threw a spotlight on the town and Ruckus Royale. We think Davidson is getting pressure from above him to solve the case and prove we're not a lawless outpost. Trouble is he's an idiot who'd rather snatch up the convenient suspects, and now Sheriff Sharpe isn't here to stop him."

She bobbed her head. "Yeah, yeah, of course. Anyone with sense knows they wouldn't kill a man in front of hundreds of witnesses and their camera phones. What is Davidson thinking?"

"I don't know, but I won't let them go down for this. I was thinking there was another witness that night who can tell the police what she saw, and what she didn't see—which is Cairo burying a gas tank under Scott Cavendish."

Amy caught on immediately. "Oooh, good idea. Come in, she's upstairs."

Just like that, I was in. *But that was the easy part. The part where I get her away from all the witnesses is where it gets hard.*

Amy took me up a grand staircase to the third floor. I skimmed the fancy sconces, plush runner rug, and expensive hardwood floors. Granted I didn't know anything about her past, but this bitch certainly wasn't living the hard life now. What reason did she have to run around with the Black Letter Crew? Was all this really about money? Did the last of my family have to die for a couple of shiny rocks in the dirt?

Amy pushed open a door on the end, surprising the person teasing her already perfect hair in the mirror. Quinn locked onto my reflection and scowled.

"What are you doing here? What are you both doing here?"

"Quinn, you're not going to believe—"

"Thanks, Amy," I cut in. "Do you mind giving us a minute?"

"Sure, no problem. I've got to call Paris anyway. See if she needs my dad."

Amy's dad was a lawyer, and would definitely come in handy right now, but—

He won't do as much as you.

Quinn cocked a brow when I closed us in. "What is this? What could you possibly have to say to me?"

"I need your help."

"My help?" She laughed. "What the fuck are you talking about? Why would I help you?"

"Quinn, I know we've gotten into it in the past, but I never had a problem with you." I dropped my voice, eyes growing big and pleading. "I only snapped back because you kept coming for me. I never stole the Bedlam Boys away from you. They stole me. After that whole thing with embarrassing Jacques in class, they gave me a choice between being their pet, or their target."

Rolling her eyes, she finally faced me. "Again. What does that have to do with me?"

Quinn Cunningham was beauty itself. Soft, pouty lips. Skin that never knew a blemish. Perfect figure and cute designer clothes to drape it in. It was hard to believe the outside was just a pretty wrapper for a dead, shriveled-up soul.

But if Jacques is right, you killed my sister.

I balled my fist behind my back, careful to keep the rage from bleeding onto my face.

"I knew they weren't good guys," I went on, "but over the last couple weeks, I... I've seen things. O-overheard things. Things that scared me, Quinn."

The nasty glare lessened around the edges. "What do you mean?"

"Intense stuff about doing whatever it takes to protect the town and stop Foundry. A few weeks ago, they didn't know I was in the kitchen. Cairo and Arsenio came downstairs saying they'd have to get rid of Adriel and the new Crows permanently because Foundry wasn't getting the hint. Then Cairo replied, *that'll be hard without my dad to cover our tracks.*

"I mean, I'm not crazy, right? Doesn't that sound like they're planning on doing something horrible to those guys, but they're worried what'll happen if Sheriff Jack isn't here to cover their crimes?"

She folded her arms, eyeing me with a strange expression. "Well, like you said, they're not good guys. But why are you coming to me?"

"Because it's no small thing to betray the Bedlam Boys. And because... I found something."

"Found something?"

"After that comment about the sheriff, I went looking through their rooms while they were in class. I found something at the back of Arsenio's closet and—and—" I tossed my head. "At this point, I'm spinning out and reading dark intention in everything they say and do. Look, I came because I can't spend another night in that house like this. I either need to figure out if they're lying to me, or let this go and trust them.

"You dated them for longer than me. You know them. Stayed with them. Am I imagining things? Everyone knows not to cross them, but they don't really go around hurting people, do they?"

Quinn stared at me for a beat, then her eyes narrowed to slits. "What's your game, de Souza? Why are you really here?"

"You know what? Fuck this," I cried, throwing my hands up. "I knew it was a mistake coming to you."

"Wait," she barked, pulling me up short with my hand on the knob. "Just wait a second. What did you find in Arsenio's closet?"

"You're going to think I'm crazy."

"Try me."

Sighing, I summoned my best performance. "I don't know how else to describe it other than... a box of trophies. It's all this weird, random stuff, Quinn, but I have to ask why he'd keep it, and more importantly, why he's hiding it." I clutched my forehead. "But if it is just a box of junk, how stupid am I confronting him with it? They'll dump me for spying on them, and then I'll be put back on the target list."

I pinned her with a look. "So, I ask you again, am I making something out of nothing, or are these guys dangerous? I have enough going on in my life and too many people I can't trust, to add my boyfriends to the list."

"No," she said after a spell. "You're not making something out of nothing."

Dropping my head, I slumped against the door. "So, that's it, then. I have to go. I have to leave them."

"That's not what I said. You don't break up with the Bedlam Boys, they break up with you. No exceptions. Unless you plan on leaving town—"

"I'm not going anywhere. This is my home. No one is driving me away."

She inclined her chin. "Well, then you need something to protect you. Where's this box? Is it still at the house?"

"No, it's in the car. I brought it to show you in case you didn't take me seriously."

"Show me," she said, a little too quickly. "If it is what you think, it's the perfect blackmail. It'll keep the Bedlam Boys off your back for the next hundred years they'll hold a grudge."

"I hope so." I made like I was going out. "Actually, we don't have to go all the way to the car. I can just tell you what's in it. There's a hair bow, and a—"

"No, it's better for you to show me. I might recognize something."

Yeah, like an opportunity to give your boss, Dante, more leverage over the Bedlam Boys. Maybe this wouldn't be the hard part.

"I parked out front."

I led the way, not saying any more lest I overplay my hand. I dangled a chance to make the Bedlam Boys suffer, and she followed me right out the door. If there really was a box, I had no doubt Quinn was scheming too... to take it from me.

Together we tromped past the jumping pledges and left the pretty lake house behind. I rounded the car, beeping the trunk open. "It's here."

Quinn came up next to me, again a little too quickly. "Where?"

I lifted out the golf clubs and pointed to the mahogany box waiting underneath. "Do you think you will recognize something? Will this box get me away from them?"

"Maybe," she said, snatching it out. "But you should leave it with me for a few days, so I can make sure—"

I swung, bringing the gold club down in a graceful arc on her head.

"Uh." Quinn wobbled on her feet and tipped, falling face-first into the trunk. I helped her the rest of the way, shoving her legs inside.

"Don't worry. This trunk comfortably fits two people." I dumped the clubs in after her. "You'll be fine."

LEGEND

"Hey. Hey! I know you can hear me," I shouted. "We get a phone call. You either hand over your fucking cell phone, or my lawyers will tie you up in so many civil rights suits, you'll burst into tears whenever you hear the word motion."

"Shut up," snapped one of the officers.

"You three are idiots. Everyone saw you arrest us. The lawyers are on the way. Do you want them to hear you were good to us, or that you beat us to shit and then refused our phone call?"

"Beat you? We didn't lay a hand—"

"Roan."

My love and boyfriend of five years punched me dead in the face. Blood burst in my mouth.

"Hey! What the hell are you doing!" Officer Mars scrabbled out of his seat.

"Oh shit, you broke my nose too."

Roan reared back.

"Stop! Fuck's sake," he cried, rushing the bars. "Get away from him. Grab the wall. All of you."

Smirking, Roan backed up and faced the wall as ordered. Arsenio, Cairo, and Jacques followed suit.

"Crazy, lunatic thugs." Mars muttered to himself as he fiddled with the keys. "You're going to an interrogation room where you can't cause any trouble. And yes, you'll get your damn phone call."

Mars hauled me out none too gently and dragged me across the station. He shoved me in a seat and tossed his phone at me.

"Thank you very much. I'll also take a bottled water and first aid kit. Wouldn't want my lawyer to hear you denied me medical treatment."

He rattled the two-way glass slamming the door.

I laughed, but only for a second. There was nothing funny about the situation we were in.

What now? How do we get out of this?

The person we called when we were in this kind of trouble was Jack Sharpe. Fat lot of good he'd do us now. Calling my father would get me the same lawyer who I knew had to be on their way. Calling Jacques's mom wouldn't help either. If we were at the point of needing a friendly judge, we already failed.

I have to call someone who can get us out of here tonight. Someone willing to go against an acting sheriff and his brain-dead deputies. Someone who owes us a favor?

I lifted my head, meeting my reflection's grim expression. *No, not a favor.*

Aware of the fact Mars was likely listening from the other side of the mirror, I chose my words carefully as I typed in the number and listened to it ring out.

"Hello? Who's this?"

"It's Legend St. James."

"What? No shit? What are you doing calling me?" Adriel Burton asked, snickering. "Heard you got into some legal trouble. No way you've got time for a chat."

"I don't have much time, so it's a good thing you already know why I'm calling."

Yeah, I had the guy's number. I had his home address, license plate, and the name of the bar he meets his Hunter's Crest girlfriend in every weekend. The bar for dates with his Bedlam girlfriend was local.

"You were sent here to do a job—"

"I'm not—"

"Save it," I growled. "I just said I don't have time. Here's the bottom line: help us out, and I'll double whatever he's paying you."

Adriel snorted. "Please. I've seen this movie before. Bluffs don't impress me."

"It's not a bluff. As soon as my lawyer gets here, she'll wire half into whatever bank account you tell her. You in or out, Burton? 'Cause I know a few other people who'd love to get rich today."

"Then why didn't you call them? I'm not doing a job for Ellis. I've said a hundred fucking times that I've got nothing to do with—"

"Okay, cool. We've got nothing to talk about, then."

"Hold up— Wait," he burst out, stopping my finger an inch above *end*.

"Yes?"

"I don't admit to any fucking job for Steven Ellis." Sounded like the words were pulled out of him. "But if you want to pay me two hundred grand, why the hell would I stop you? What do you need me to do?"

"My boys and I have plans tonight. We're supposed to be there by seven."

"And? Wait," he said. "Is this being recorded?"

"Only my end."

"Then cough when I'm close. You got somewhere to be and you're not waiting till you make bail."

I coughed.

"You need me and my boys to break you out."

Cough.

"How many officers?"

I coughed three times. "I told you to get me water," I called at the mirror.

"And in exchange for this, you're going to pay me two hundred grand, and owe me a favor that I can collect at any time. No questions asked."

I gritted my teeth, hesitating. This shit was working for Steven Ellis no matter what he said. This favor would hurt us—fatally. But so would going down for murder and Jack Sharpe ending up in the ground.

But is it worth it? Survive one threat just long enough to get taken down by the other.

"Hello?" Adriel sang. "I said to cough when I'm close, and I nailed that. This doesn't happen without my money and my favor. So, let's hear it, St. James."

Ivy was right. Sometimes the only allies you had were enemies.

I coughed.

Chapter Six

Ivy

I spun the club in my grip, leaning against the wall as I waited.

And waited.

And waited.

Quinn stirred. A soft groan escaped her mouth—the only part of her not bound. I secured her arms, legs, shoulders, and even her head to the chair. I wasn't taking any chances. She was a slippery bitch.

Squinting, Quinn grimaced at the glare coming through the broken window. She lifted her hand and found she couldn't. "Wha...? What's going on?"

I dropped the club on the wood, snapping her eyes up. "Take a wild guess."

"De Souza? What is this? What am I doing here?" She strained against the ropes. "Let— Let me out! Untie these right now."

"Uh, no," I drew out. "I don't think I will."

"You will, you crazy bitch! Right now while you still have a chance of me telling everyone this was all just a prank."

I drifted over her head, gazing out that broken window. My farmland swept out before me, holding all the memories of my childhood like mirages flitting out of the corner of my eye. "Do you remember the last time you were here, Cunningham?"

"The last time? I've never been to this shit heap." Quinn tugged, flinging her body back and lifting the front chair legs barely an inch. If she was hoping to tip back, break the chair, and get away, she'd have to think of something else. I used a few old tools in the barn to weigh them down. "Get these off."

"It was the night you killed my sister," I continued like she never interrupted. "You, Zoey, and four of your closest psychopathic friends came here to teach me a lesson, but it was Rainey who paid the price."

"What? You're talking about yourself in the third person now?" She raised her voice. "You're not making any sense, bitch. Untie these and go back on your meds."

I laughed. "You know, now that I think about it, I should've been suspicious of you from the beginning. When I returned to Bedlam U thinking I was Rainey, no one had a clue who I was. Everyone—Paris, her friends, Cairo—all assumed I was from out of state. I had to correct them all and say I was homeschooled. But you..." I pointed the club. "You called me farm trash from the start. How did you know I lived on a farm when no one else did?"

If I expected Quinn to break down and say, *aha, you caught me*, I was disappointed.

"This isn't funny anymore. Let me g-go," she said, thrashing. "My sisters saw me leave with you. You should've thought this through."

"I did think it through. They saw you leave with me willingly after I told Amy you were going to help me get the Bedlam Boys out of jail. They stopped thinking about you the minute you walked out the door."

"What do you want from me?!"

"I'll spell it out for you. You're one of the Black Letter Crew—the name we gave the monsters sending us black letters who were once the acolytes of Scott Cavendish. Two years ago, you killed my little sister and broke my mind."

I knew as I said the words, they were true. I didn't see her face that night, and I didn't remember her voice, but I did remember her figure. She dressed for the occasion then too. Cute in a tight sweater dress, jeans, and leather boots. I remembered she laughed when Rainey's blood got on them.

"Good thing it's leather. It'll wash right off."

I repeated her horrid comment, searching for a reaction.

Nothing.

"You really are insane."

I heaved a sigh. "As much fun as this back-and-forth is, I don't have time for it. You're going to tell me where Dante is holding Jack Sharpe, and you're going to tell me now."

"How in the hell would I know?" Amazing that someone tied to a chair in a falling-down farmhouse could possess so much attitude. She looked like all this was an irritating waste of a Friday. "Jack Sharpe has nothing to do with me. Forgot he existed after your boyfriends stopped fucking me. Oh, is that what this is about?" Quinn smirked. "You're coming after me because I was the Bedlam Boys' favorite ride.

"Let me guess. That whole thing about breaking up was true, but it's them breaking up with you. They want their Quinn back because just like I told them, I'm the only one who can give them what they need. Aww." She pushed out her lips, pouting in mock concern. "You're so desperate, you're taking out the competition before she knows she's in the game. Pathetic."

"Holy hell, you talk a lot of bullshit. The Bedlam Boys wouldn't touch you with a flea-bitten homeless man's dick, let alone their own." One step, then another, I ate the distance. "We're not here to play games, Quinn. You're going to tell me where the sheriff is. That's it. That's all you have to do right now.

"My first priority is to free him and get him to stop whatever Davidson is planning. After that's done, we'll have a deeper conversation about the Black Letter Crew, everything you guys have done, and everything you're planning."

Quinn looked from me... to the golf club striking my palm. "And if I don't, what are you going to do, de Souza? Beat me? Torture me?"

"Yes."

Her grin twitched. Unsurety flashed across her features for the briefest moment.

"Oh, please," she snorted. "You don't have the stomach."

"I don't? A year ago, sure, I didn't have the stomach. But then the girl I thought I was burned a man alive. And the girl I really am remembered that you killed my sister." I bent, latching my gaze onto hers. "Look in my eyes, Quinn. Do I have the stomach?"

She looked, and the grin melted away. "You won't kill me."

"You sound like you're asking me, not telling me. If you need me to repeat myself, here it is: you will not survive this, Cunningham. No matter what, I will beat you bloody and bury you in the dirt for what you did to Rainey."

"I didn't do anything!" She lurched forward, trying to bash in my nose. Again she didn't get far. "I have no idea about any of this. You have the wrong person!"

"Jacques assured me you're the right person. Now that I'm finally looking, I know it's true."

"You're wrong," she said, shaking her head under the ropes. "You're about to make a big mistake, de Souza. The worst you'll ever make. This is your last chance to let me go."

I straightened. "Where is Jack Sharpe?"

"You're deaf and stupid. I. Don't. Know," she yelled.

"This is your last chance," I said, voice flat. "Where is Jack Sharpe?"

She made a frustrated noise. "I swear when I get out of here, I'm going to make a sex tape with all of your boyfriends—at the same time—and make sure it's the only thing they let you watch in your jail cell."

"Kinky. I'm not too interested in the *you* part, but put me in the middle of that orgy, and I'll happily watch it in prison. But I did say that was your last chance to answer, and I don't want to start this off by lying to you." I lifted the club, making her shoulders tense, then set it down on the floor. "I'm fortunate now that so many things were left in the barn to rust."

I reached over her head, and picked something off the fireplace mantel. Quinn's eyes crossed on the shears I held before her nose.

"One thing that'll always bother me about that night, and about you, is that even though you were there to do what you did, you dressed up like you were going on a date. It was that important to you to look pretty." I took a hank of her hair, and cut it off without pause or warning.

Quinn's scream echoed throughout the acres.

"It does bring me some peace to know after today, you'll never look pretty again."

"You bitch! You evil, twisted bitch!" Spittle showered my arm. "You'll pay for that. I fucking swear, you'll regret this!"

"Where is Jack Sharpe?"

"I don't know! I'm not who you think I am. You've got everything ass-backwards like the stupid farm hick you are."

I grabbed another hank.

"No, no, no—"

It separated in my hand. I let go, letting the strands fall on her lap.

"Where is Jack Sharpe?"

Quinn snarled, furious tears gathering on her lids. "You're going to wish you burned Ruckus night, de Souza. I'll never forget this."

"But I forgot. I locked away the truth of what happened to Rainey and you got to live two years on borrowed time. You had to know there was a chance I'd get my memory back," I said. "You had to know one day we'd end up here. At least quit the act and face me as your true self, because you're not getting away from me."

"I have no idea what you're talking about. Why won't you listen to me?"

I grasped her ends. She tensed, sucking in a breath. "Are you sure that's what you want to say? I'll give you three seconds to come up with a better response."

Quinn looked at me, jaw grinding, and said nothing.

Her hair joined the rest on the floor. So it went with each question about Sheriff Sharpe. Quinn refused to answer, either by claiming innocence, insulting me, or detailing all the things my guys did to her and would do again when she got them back.

My shears snipped for the last time. Stepping back, I admired Quinn's new look. An uneven mess that gave the vibe she got her head caught in a lawn mower. The wild thing was, she still looked beautiful.

I picked up the club. *I'll fix that.*

"You understand there's only one way for us to go from here. I don't have a lot of time, so if your hair wasn't enough to get you to speak, I'll see if your kneecaps are."

Her glare could've turned my blood to acid.

"Don't let it get that far, Quinn."

I couldn't help a glance at my watch. I was running out of time. Dante has to know what his pet cop has done by now. He'll probably put some effort into getting Davidson to let them go, so they can carry out the job he's too lazy to do, but when that didn't work, he'd have no reason to keep the sheriff alive.

I bet that's why Davidson made a scene and arrested them on campus. He wanted the whole town to know they were going down for murder, so it wouldn't be easy to make it go away.

If they were suddenly released from their holding cell without charges, there'd be questions. Too many questions.

That's why I needed Jack Sharpe to reappear, tell the world he was kidnapped, and wrestle control away from that shit-covered slime Davidson. See? Cairo didn't need to worry about me killing his father. Not while I still had need of him.

I stepped to the side, leveling the club with her knee. "Tell me where he is, Quinn."

"I don't know where he is. I didn't even know he was missing. I'm telling you that you have the wrong person. Whatever you do to me, you can't make me admit to being a part of your deluded fantasies."

"Just couldn't resist getting an insult in. Hope it was worth it." Angling my swing, I drew back and—

"Ahhh!"

I winced at her scream. Couldn't blame her. I think I heard something crunch.

"Where is Jack Sharpe?"

"I'm not who you think I am. I can't—"

I smashed the other knee. Quinn screamed herself hoarse.

"The next one is in the face. You'll black out and we'll lose some time, but it'll be worth it to break your teeth and rearrange that button nose."

"Evil... crazy bitch," she rasped, chest heaving. "You have no idea... the pain you have coming. It'll make your weak hits feel like love taps."

"I'll take that as your answer." I swung the club at her face.

"Stop. Stop!" she screeched. "Just stop."

I did, pulling back at the last second.

I waited.

"All right, de Souza." Quinn's voice was barely above a rasp, but it laced with menace. "If this is how you want to do this, let's stop playing games."

"Oh, let's, please."

"Yes, I'm one of what you call the Black Letter Crew, and what of it? Doesn't mean I was there the night they put down your sister, *Ivy*. Doesn't mean I know where Jack Sharpe is."

My jaw clenched. I fought to relax it. I wouldn't let her think her poison got to me.

"You were there that night. The games are done, Quinn. You can stop lying now." I moved in front of her. "The part about not know-ing where Jack Sharpe is could be true, but you understand I'm going to make *extra* sure, and keep questioning you until your busted jaw and broken teeth leave you unable to answer."

She hardened. Somehow tied to that chair, she lifted her chin and looked her nose down at me. "You don't scare me. Who do you think you're dealing with? I can handle a little pain. I'm not the weak little girl whose mind shattered into pieces that you see in the mirror every morning.

"Bring. It. On."

I hefted the club. "If that's what you want."

Metal struck bone.

"Ahhh!"

ARSENIO

"What time is it?"

I pressed against the bars. "Can't see the clock from here, but I can see the window. The sun's set."

"Then that's it," Roan said. "The tournament is over and the par-ty starts soon. We'll never make it to Hunter's Crest in time. It's over."

"I've accepted that and moved on to our new problem." Cairo paced the length of the cell. "The lawyer Paris sent said he can't get us in front of a judge until Monday morning, and that judge won't be Judge Stone. Davidson can keep us here all weekend. By then my father's dead."

"We don't know that," Roan tried. "They could hold on to him to force us to take another shot at the Ellises."

"You're assuming the judge grants us bail," I said quietly. "Or that the video of us admitting we kidnapped and tied to a stake the man that Cairo set on fire, won't be more than convincing to a jury of our peers. You're assuming we're ever getting out of this cell."

"I didn't set him on fire."

"But we can't say who did," Jacques replied.

Cairo didn't argue that. He could be pissed at her, and even have himself convinced they broke up, but he knew what belonged to the Bedlam Boys, belonged to the Bedlam Boys. She'd leave us when we allowed it.

Roan crossed to the bars. "Why haven't they brought Legend back?"

"Because they think you'll continue kicking his ass," Cairo shot back. "Wherever he is, he better be thinking of a way out of this. We've got to get to my father tonight."

"I've taken care of that."

Three heads swung to the guy in the corner.

"What do you mean you took care of it?" I said.

"I told de Souza the name. One of the Black Letter Crew. She knows what that means she has to do."

"Yeah," Cairo scoffed. "It means she kicks back in our bed, sipping smoothies, watching the clock run down. She hates Jack Sharpe. She's not lifting a finger to help him."

"She'd do it for you." Roan leaned on the bars—a rare, serious look on his face. "She loves you, despite you doing everything you can to turn that love into hate. She won't sit back and do nothing when she knows you need her."

"I don't need her," he snapped. "And if that's what she's been doing all this time, what's taking so long? Huh? Where are they?"

Roan, Jacques, and I shared a look. That was a good question.

"I couldn't find her," Jacques admitted. "Maybe she can't either."

Roan held up a hand. "First, who is her?"

"You won't believe this but it's—" Jacques gestured with his chin.

I shook my head no. No one was listening to us.

"It's Quinn Cunningham."

Pure shock slackened my jaw. "What? No. It can't be."

"It is. I tested her and she was twelve for twelve on the sociopath scale."

"Yeah, but what does that prove?" Cairo said. "That's one of the things we like in our girlfriends. Or else they'd run screaming."

"You're a psych major, Cairo. You know what that proves. Even you wouldn't pass that test with flying colors." Jacques got to his feet. "But that wasn't the only thing. Unlike the others, I spent time with Quinn. Lived with her. I had hundreds of memories to access," he said, tapping his skull. "The night of the party when her sister was killed, Quinn left to drive a drunk friend home. She never came back.

"Then there were things that she said. Stuff that she did. We know Quinn has a mean streak. There was all that shit with the sorority hazing, but we can't forget what she did during the Dallas away game.

"She and her friends shoved alcohol down a freshman's throat, then Quinn took her up to the roof. She told her she'd get in with the sorority and with her friends if she walked across the hotel's roof ledge five stories up. The girl was drunk off her ass. There was only one way that story was going to end."

Cairo nodded, eyes glazed. "She's still in a coma. We only know Quinn did it because we saw her running from the roof staircase that night. She still lies with a straight face and says she doesn't have a clue what happened to that girl."

"Exactly," Jacques said. "And if all that wasn't enough to convince me, hooking up with Jeremy Ellis did. We thought he went after her to get dirt on us—and he probably did—but Quinn isn't an idiot. She would've known he was using her, and that using him to make us jealous was a waste of time. It wasn't about us—"

"Dante wanted her to snuggle up to the sons of Foundry," Cairo finished.

"Exactly."

I swore. "How did we miss that! We fucking shared a bed with this woman."

"We didn't know the Black Letter Crew existed then," Roan reminded. "Like he said, the things off about Quinn just turned us on. But now I'm wondering did we pick her... or did she pick us?"

Silence spread through the cell.

"And you sent de Souza to question her," Cairo said. "Our ex and one of the people who killed her sister. No wonder it's taking so long."

He didn't need to explain that. Naturally, Ivy was taking a while because burying a body six feet under wasn't as easy or quick as people thought. I could only hope she got Cairo's dad's location before—

The lights winked out, plunging us in darkness.

"Hey," Mars called. "Peters, what happened? Did you trip the breaker again?"

"Just walked into the kitchen. Didn't even get the chance," she said. "Relax. It's an old building. Faulty wiring. The backup generator should kick on in a minute."

She no sooner ended her sentence than light returned to our cell.

"See? Told you it was—?"

The lights went out again.

"Now what?" Mars cried.

"I bet you can answer that. Did you forget to put gas in the generator even though I reminded you? Twice."

"Uhh, yeah. Sorry about that. I'll run out and get some." A chair scraped back, then boots shuffled across the floor. "We've got extra flashlights and batteries with the hurricane supplies. I won't be long."

We listened to him walk out, then the faint hum of an engine started and faded down the street.

"Mars," Davidson called. "Peters. Get these lights back on."

"Mars is taking care of it, sir. He went out for gas." I tracked her faint outline as she passed us, heading for the spare flashlights.

Door hinges squeaked, drawing my attention to the entrance. Two— No, three figures crossed the threshold.

"Hello? Wait at the front desk," Peters said. "I'll be with you in a minute."

One of them broke off and sprinted, streaking past me.

"Hey—!"

There was a smack of flesh on flesh. Running to the other side, I strained to see past the limits of my cell. Who is that? What's going on?"

Electricity sparked the air. The flash from the stun gun illuminated their faces for a blink, letting me see Peters red-faced and panicking with a hand clamped on her mouth, and her attacker's beady eyes glaring through the holes in the ski mask.

The stunner went off again, and a body hit the floor.

"You're welcome," said a dry voice I didn't recognize.

"You." Seems Roan did. "Why are you here?"

"You and your boyfriend need to talk more. Especially since you're paying handsomely for this jailbreak."

"Who are you?" I demanded.

"No names until we're out of the police station, yeah?" Amusement laced his voice. "I was told three. Where's the last one?"

"In his office. Through the door you passed," Roan said. "If he heard Peters go down, he's ducked behind his desk with a gun pointed at the door."

"No less than we figured. Nathan," he called.

A scream ripped through the dark, stiffening me to attention.

"Peters?! What's going on out there? Did those little shits get out of their cell?" His door banged open. "If they try to run, shoot them— Ugh."

Thud!

"He's down, A."

"Hmm. That was easier than I thought," said our new friend. "I almost feel bad taking your money now. We didn't break a sweat."

"Want to continue the self-celebration after you get us out of here?" I remarked.

He chuckled. The guy went to the closet Peters was shuffling through, snagged a flashlight, and got the key off her belt. We filed out and Roan claimed the keys. He went through to the interrogation rooms.

"Go," I stated. "We've got it from here."

"Not even a thank-you." A faint *tsk* reached my ear. "Not very nice, but at least I've got a couple thousand to ease the sting. I'll be calling you about that favor, Bedlam Boys."

Favor? My eyes narrowed to slits. *What favor?*

"Real soon."

They left as easily as they came, leaving us with two unconscious bodies and an unsuspecting cop on the way back.

"We need to get out of here before Mars comes back," Jacques said. But he wasn't moving either.

The three of us, then five as Roan and Legend returned, made a still and watchful circle around Davidson.

"He'd know where my father is." Cairo spoke in a thin, low hiss.

"It's six fifteen," Legend said. "He'll tell us, but not quickly. And not before Mars sends out a statewide alert for a missing acting sheriff."

"Won't know until we try." Cairo knelt and secured the man in his own handcuffs. "I don't know about you, but I'm highly motivated to make this a quick conversation. Forty-five minutes is plenty of time."

"You... think so?" Davidson's laugh ground my teeth. "Let's find out, shall we?"

"Get him up."

We lifted him, dragging his dead weight out the door. Davidson's head lolled to my side. "This will be fun."

He smiled. "For me too."

DANTE

We watched through the window as the Bedlam Boys strolled out of the station, and loaded Davidson into the trunk of his own car.

"Shouldn't we do something? Stop them?"

I shook my head. "We came here to pick Davidson up and teach him the error of his ways. Whatever they're going to do to him, he's got coming for messing up the plan. The Bedlam Boys are supposed to end up on trial for murder, but not for Scott's. Stupid, shortsighted fuck set us back so far, I'm wondering if he's double-dealing for Cavendish."

"I wouldn't be surprised," my companion replied. "Scott always said he wasn't really one of us. He was just too useful to get rid of."

"While Sheriff Sharpe is not." I started the car. "The Bedlam Boys can have him, but they don't get Jack Sharpe. I promised to kill him if Steven Ellis lived to stand up before the crowd and make his speech. Unlike everyone else in this town, I keep my word."

Steering away from the curb, I headed off in the opposite direction... to Sheriff Sharpe.

"We still need the Ellises dead. What's the plan now?"

"The Bedlam Boys can figure out the how and where. The only thing I need to do is provide the motivation." I dipped my chin. "Paris. We grab her next. Cairo endured Riot Royale to protect her from the Crows. He cares about her, even if he pretends he doesn't."

"Wish we could grab one of the Sisters. The judge or the dean."

"Me too, but they don't make it easy like the partying Paris, or the alcoholic cop. As long as we can get the Bedlam Boys to do what we want with just the girl, we don't overplay our hand."

They shrugged. "Where are we putting the sheriff's body? We don't need him to be found when he's conveniently on *vacation*. When he goes missing, the cops will spend all their time looking in the wrong place."

"That would be convenient, but as I said, I'm a man of my word. The town will wake up tomorrow and find Sheriff Sharpe's mangled body in the town square, surrounded by a ring of fire."

IVY

One eye swollen shut, but Quinn managed to glare at me just fine through the other one. I'd give this monster something, she didn't go down easily.

"Where is Sheriff Sharpe!"

"I'm not... telling you... shit," she wheezed. "But you can go back... and tell Cairo... how you failed."

Her laugh rattled in her chest. "He'll die... and it'll be all your fault. Cairo will never forgive you."

I shook—the bloody club trembling in my hold. It killed me that she was right. Cairo would never forgive me, because I was too late.

It was seven o'clock.

The party had started. Steven Ellis was stepping up to a podium at that moment to grandstand, and wax on about destroying our town for his profit being the best thing for everybody.

Anger corroded my veins. I wasn't done with that cheating bastard yet. First I lose my sister for protecting Cairo. Now I lose Cairo because this bald shit stain was protecting her buddies. The Men of Honor had taken so much from me. When would it end?

"Hours of questioning and you didn't crack."

"Fucking right I didn't." She spat blood in my direction. "Never will."

"Then, there's no point asking you about the Black Letter Crew. Who is in it or what you're planning?"

"None at all."

I bobbed my head, lips pushed out. "That makes things simple. If I've got nothing to lose, Cunningham, I've got nothing holding me back. You might as well die now."

Quinn's bloody smile slipped. "What? You're not—"

"I hope you and Zoey enjoy your *victory* over me in hell."

"Don't you dare—"

"Goodbye, Quinn."

I swung, striking her chest dead center. The hit knocked the air out of her, trapping her scream in her throat. She got no chance to recover before I hit her again. Then again. And again.

I didn't stop until she did—her screams fading in the night.

DANTE

My car rumbled down the dirt drive. Ten years ago, this place was a charming bed-and-breakfast that didn't get a lot of visitors, but those that did came back every year on holidays and anniversaries. That is until Foundry came in and offered the elderly couple who owned the place to sell for far more than they thought it worth.

Foundry and Steven Ellis were a leech on this town. They were plague. Poison. But the blame could not be shifted away from the fools who chose to drink. Why did no one else see what we had in

Bedlam? This town we built on blood-soaked soil was worth fighting for.

If no one else would do it, we would.

We climbed out of the car, taking rickety, rotting steps to the busted front door. There was no good reason Sheriff Sharpe should enjoy his accommodations. Not after all the trouble this man caused Cavendish and now me.

But now he neared the end of his usefulness, which was why I finally sent that letter to the Bedlam Boys. I thought the man had information I needed, but after weeks of questioning, I could be sure that he'd have given it up if he knew. His only use now was to keep the Bedlam Boys in line, and I had other options for that. At least Paris Keller would be nice to look at.

Together we crossed the threshold, stepping into a long hallway that still held the memory of the faded floral wallpaper, cobweb-covered lamps, and green carpet that had long since turned black and brown from grime.

The filthy carpet muffled our footfalls, and the bag of tools and trash bags my companion dragged behind them. We made sure to stop and get the best for Sheriff Sharpe. His mangled body would haunt his son's nightmares until he finally blew his brains out. Out of respect, we had to put the effort in.

I shoved into Sharpe's bare, filthy room, and my grin melted away. Sitting on the chair in the middle of the room, was a pile of cut rope and a gag.

He was gone.

"What? How!" I stormed in, craning my neck around as if the fat, drunk slob was hiding in a corner. "This isn't possible. Where is he?"

"Davidson must've cracked."

"He wouldn't crack," I barked. "Especially not that quickly. Fuck!"

Heaving the chair, I threw it at the wall—busting through the falling-down wood into the other room.

My roar echoed through the forest.

JACQUES

I walked a ways down the forest path until Davidson's grunts and maniacal laughs were as loud as the owl hooting overhead. Cairo was motivated to get that man talking. Unfortunately, Davidson was just as motivated to see Cairo desperate and suffering. He wasn't giving anything up.

He was enjoying this too much.

Ivy must have something.

I typed her number in Davidson's phone. We had to get out of the station fast since Mars was due back at any second. That left no chance to retrieve the phones, wallets, belts, and everything else they took from us during processing.

Davidson's cell was the only way to reach her once we beat it out of town and took him to the one wooded spot we knew well, Buller's Den. Though, also unfortunately for us, Davidson wouldn't give up the code to get into his phone either. I wasted time we didn't have breaking into it to finally—

"Hello? Who's this?"

"Ivy, it's me."

"Whose phone are you calling me from? Are you at the police station?"

"No. We left and took Davidson with us. We've been questioning him for a while, but I can read the time. It's long past seven o'clock. Tell me if there's any point in continuing," I said. "Did you find Quinn? Did she tell you what you needed to know?"

"Of course she did, baby." Ivy dropped this like someone says they made meatloaf for dinner. "You told me to find her and I did."

"And... she told you where the sheriff was," I said slowly.

"She didn't want to at first, but it turned out repeated blows to her broken ribs was pain even she couldn't bluff her way through. I've got her and the sheriff. Whenever you feel like joining us, love."

I didn't speak as she told us where she was, blew a kiss over the phone, and hung up.

All that effort, time, money, and the *favor* it cost us to get out, and Ivy had the situation in hand.

Cairo kept saying she was colder, smarter, and more manipulative than us. Make that the last day I underestimated her.

Chapter Seven

*C*airo

I slammed into my father's house, leaving the rest of them to haul an unconscious piece of uniformed trash.

"De Souza? Dad?"

Thud.

My head snapped up. Taking off, I bounded up the steps two at a time. My father's door banged into the opposite wall with a splintering crack that assured I broke something.

Ivy leaned over my father, holding a pair of scissors to his throat.

"Get the fuck off him!" I raced across the room and heaved her up, smothering her soft cry in my chest. Quickly I pulled her back and away from him.

"Son?" The thin rasp came from the broken wreck on the bed who I assumed was my father.

He looked terrible. His face was a mottle of bruises in various stages of healing. His left arm was in a sling while the right wrist was encased in a bandage, and that was just the parts of him that were visible. Dad was covered in blankets, but they weren't covering the hefty, sturdy lump they should be. My father was starved. Beaten. Broken.

"Let... her go..."

"Let her go? She was trying to slit your fucking throat."

"I had plenty of time to do that before you got here," said a dry voice. Ivy tried to untangle from me. "I'm the one doing the fixing."

"She's... telling the truth," he rasped. "She's helping me, Cairo. Let her go."

What he said made no sense, but then, neither did another, closer look at him. My father was bandaged and in bed with a glass of water and painkillers next to him. Dante sure as hell didn't do all of that, so—

Ivy's caring for the man she wants dead as badly as anyone in the Black Letter Crew.

As if to drive that thought home, Ivy got free of me and rescued the scissors from where she dropped it. She bent over my father and I bent over her, watching her closely.

Dad had a nasty, shallow cut on his neck. Looked like Ivy sewed it closed and was now snipping off the extra thread. She was gentle applying clean gauze and wound tape.

"Where did you learn to do this?" I asked as footsteps sounded on the landing.

"Once again, I must credit my farm education. When the animals get hurt, you can either keep shelling out for an expensive vet bill, or pay attention when they fix them up the first time."

"Well, I have been... called an old goat," Dad croaked.

They both laughed. Though my father's was more a rattling wheeze. I narrowed on the both of them.

"What the fuck is going on in here?"

Ivy shot me a knowing smile. "Relax, Cairo. You can stop looking at me like I'm going to go crazed killer at any second. Your father and I were waiting for you guys for quite a while. We had a long talk," she said. "I understand what happened all those years ago much better now."

"Care to share?" Arsenio spoke up. "We could use a little understanding right now."

"Okay, but is it a good idea for us all to be here? I drove by the police station, and I could tell something had gone wrong. I'm guessing you didn't get bail."

Arsenio just shook his head.

"Then, won't your houses be the first places they'll look for you? We should get out of here and go somewhere safe."

"Yes, we should," I ground out. "So talk fast."

She gestured with her chin. "It's better if you hear it from him." Ivy made to leave. "I've got Quinn in the other room. I should check to make sure she hasn't succumbed to her injuries—"

I grasped her wrist and tugged her back where she was. "Stay."

Arsenio, Jacques, Legend, and Roan piled in. I didn't know what they did with Davidson, but I was sure they had him locked up and secure somewhere uncomfortable. Dad had our full attention.

"I'm not sure where to begin." Dad tried to sit up and quickly changed his mind. Sighing, he just eased back onto the pillows, gazing at the ceiling through black, swollen eyes. After a time, he began in slow, halting speech. "All I've ever tried to do is be a good man and father. It's been a source of unending pain and shame for me that I'm neither."

I didn't correct him. Why do that when someone speaks the truth?

"Why do you think I d-drink?" Dad burst into a coughing fit.

Ivy helped him sip some water. The act so disturbed me, I pulled her away from him—taking her place by his side. These two would stop confusing the fuck out of me until I heard this story.

"I started out wanting to do what was best for the town, but along the way, I ended up doing what I was *told* was best for the town. For a long time, that was okay. It was enough... until I was asked to do something I couldn't justify in my deepest drunken stupor."

I frowned. "What were you asked to do?"

Dad lowered his gaze. It wasn't my eyes he met. It was Ivy's.

"You boys think you know all the secrets of this town, but you don't. There's one left. The biggest one. The oldest one," he rasped. "That makes all the rest insignificant."

"Stop talking in riddles, Dad. What are you trying to say? What secret?"

"What I'm trying to say is... Bedlam is not a town. It never was," he said. "It's an estate."

"An estate? What's that supposed to mean?"

He still wasn't looking at me. "Everything from the university to the Roadhouse sits on private land, Cairo. Long ago before Bedlam. Before Crystal Canyon. A wealthy family bought this plot of land and built the weapons factory on top of it.

"Workers used to ride in from the surrounding towns, but this became inconvenient, and the family became even more wealthy from weapons sales. They could afford to build bunkhouses. Then an eatery for the workers. Then a bar.

"The next thing they knew, they had an entire live-in operation. Got to the point that workers were living in the bunkhouses through the workweek, then visiting home on their day off. They wanted to come home to their families every night, so—"

"Down came the bunkhouses and up went the cabins and two bedrooms," I finished. "Nice racket. The owner pays their wages, and then gets it all back as their landlord."

Dad made to nod and winced. He settled for resting his head back on the pillow. "Likely why he gave in to their requests. It was just more ways to make money, and keep his employees working efficiently. And what was losing a few plots of land?" Dad swept out a shaky arm. "He had plenty."

"All right," Roan said. "Bedlam wasn't a town. It was a wealthy man's plot of land. What does that have to do with anything?"

"It has to do with everything, Roan," Ivy said softly. "It's how this all began."

"Explain," said Jacques.

"The owner suddenly found himself a de facto mayor. From dealing with his employees' demands to the demands of their families. They needed more land for farming. They needed shops. They needed schools. They needed wells. On and on," Ivy said. "The owner accommodated. He built schools. He built shops. And he dug wells."

My spine stiffened. I knew where this was going.

"While the well workers were digging, they found diamonds," my dad continued. "They didn't know what they had. No education. Most of them didn't know how to read. They just found these shiny rocks that kept getting in the way of the digging, and brought them to the boss. Asked him what he wanted to do with them."

"And," Legend pressed when he stopped. "What did he do?"

"He shut down his factory and fired half his workforce. Those that remained had a new job."

"Mining for diamonds," I finished.

"Yes."

Ivy picked up the thread. "The owner didn't want anyone to know. Everywhere they dug, they just kept finding more, and more, and more. He was the wealthiest man in the entire United fucking States, and he wasn't sharing. Why should he? It was all his free, clear, and legal. He owned the land. He could do what he wanted with it.

"But his miners," she said. "They may have been illiterate, but they weren't stupid. They figured out pretty quickly they wouldn't be doing this backbreaking work if they were just digging up some shiny rocks. One night, a couple of the men snuck out of the bunkhouses, rode to the next town, and asked around. *What is this thing? How much is it worth?*

"The minute they got their answer, the tide turned for the owner."

"They killed him," I stated. "Made off with as much as they could get."

She shook her head. "I'm sure a few did run off, but remember, illiterate. Not stupid. A group banded together and came up with another idea. They informed the owner the secret was out, and things would be done a little differently from then on.

"If he didn't want the whole world finding out what he was sitting on, he had to promote them and give them a cut of the haul. If word ever got out, every fortune-seeker in the country would descend on this part of the world like locusts. It'd be the gold rush all over again, except he and his sweet little family would become targets. Couldn't claim the land and everything from it was his... if he was dead."

"What deal did they propose?" Jacques asked.

"They'd help him. They would oversee the workers—keep them mining and keep them quiet. Anyone who stepped out of line or even had the thought of slipping a little extra into his pocket, would be caught and subjected to their swift and quiet justice. It wasn't like they could bring the thieves before a real judge and have them admit what they stole."

Roan's eyes widened. "Oh, shit. Are you saying...?"

Ivy nodded. A connection was just made that I was clearly missing.

"What? What is it?" I demanded.

"That group of men," Roan said, eyes unfocusing. "That said they'd oversee the workers. Watch them. Punish them. Run the unofficial, private town under their own brand of justice.

"They were the Men of Honor."

"Yes," Dad whispered. "Yes."

"No wonder they gave themselves that name." The mattress dipped under Ivy's weight. "They probably did see themselves as honorable, because they didn't do what they could've done, and run off in the night with a cart of this man's diamonds. They stayed to work with him. Help him protect his land and secret.

"For a time, Crystal Canyon prospered. The weapons factory re-opened. Families returned to live in the area. They went to school. They worked in their shops where they were paid well and lived well. If the trade-off was steering clear of the Men of Honor, and not asking questions about what went on in the mines—fine with them. At first. Of course we all know how the story ultimately ended."

"The power and wealth went straight to their empty heads," I said. "They started terrorizing the people, believing they could do whatever they wanted to the serfs within their kingdom."

Dad glanced at the water. Ivy reached for it, but I was there first, helping him drink. She wasn't going near the guy again until this story was finished.

"We know the story, so I won't repeat it," Dad went on. "The townspeople rose up. They slaughtered the Men, their families, and the owner, Amadeo de Souza."

Our heads swung to Ivy—the calm and silent figure at the end of the bed. She gave us what would've passed for a smile, if it reached her eyes. "Surprise, boys. I'm the direct descendant of the owner of Bedlam."

"And that," Dad said, "is how we got here."

"I don't understand." I backed away, eyeing her through slitted lids. "Her great-great-great-grandpa owned the land. What's that matter? Bedlam is a town now. Our mothers run it."

"But it isn't," she said, "and they don't."

Arsenio came in, moving in front of her. "What the fuck does that mean?"

"Bedlam is unincorporated." Dad tried again to sit up. "It never became a real town because the threat of ripping up the land, and throwing off the people that had come to live on its back, was a threat that always hung over the Society of Sisters' heads."

"Amadeo was no fool," Ivy continued. "The Men were out of control, and it was only a matter of time before they turned on him. Even though he supported them and looked the other way—the greedy, evil bastard that he was—he figured the night was coming that his wife and daughters would be chosen for the Hunt. He and his sons would be killed so the Men could have everything. Amadeo sent his family away somewhere safe long before the revolt ever happened."

"Wait," Jacques said, holding up a hand. "Ivy, you told us all your family owned back then was the farm. The farm that was taken over by your many-great-grandmother who joined the fight to kill her uncle, Jonathan de Souza. You said he beat his wife and children to death, and the other Men didn't do a thing to stop him."

The line of her shoulders tensed. "I did say that, because that's what I was told by Scott Cavendish. Fiction," she spat. "All of it lies to prevent me from knowing my true history. I wasn't a direct descendant. I came from a niece that turned on him and stole some farmland. And of course he didn't tell me his real name. He wouldn't have wanted me to look up Amadeo de Souza for myself.

"Cavendish couldn't have me know that his wife and children didn't die before their time. They lived safe and sound with the deed to *their* land, and a deal with the Sisters. Everyone can go about their lives if the Sisters filled up the mines, and forgot the diamonds ever existed. Amadeo's wife, her children, their children, and so on would let them keep Bedlam. It was a family secret, and a promise."

Roan pulled a face. "Why would they do that? Just give up their land and money?"

"They had land and money," Ivy explained. "Amadeo didn't send them away with nothing. Crates and crates of uncut diamonds. They were filthy rich and would be for generations to come. And if that changed, the land and the wealth beneath it were always right there. They had the deed."

"But why did the Sisters agree to leave the fortune alone?"

"Because they had something that was more valuable than diamonds," my father said. "Almost every land-owning man was dead. Law enforcement—dead. Corrupt magistrate—dead. Abusive husbands that ruled with an iron fist—dead. Racists and segregators that made the impossible lives of Black families even harder—dead.

"In thirty days and nights, they wiped out their oppressors. They were free."

"And if the de Souzas reclaimed the land and forced them off, all of that was waiting for them in another town," Arsenio said slowly. "Bedlam was one of the first towns with equality. Yeah... that was definitely worth more than diamonds."

"Not one of them," Ivy amended. "It was the first. Here, every child was educated. Wages were equal and fair. Women ran their homes and businesses. Segregation was dismissed as the idiotic nonsense it was. The revolt happened because Mayam Westchester fought back when no one else did.

"It was Mayam who formed the Society of Sisters. She became their first leader," she said. "But her power was here. Her freedom only existed on this soil. So yes, Roan, she and the Sisters took whatever deal the de Souzas offered, and they were thankful it was so generous."

"All these years later," Legend said, "they're still holding up their end of the deal."

"Not quite."

We looked to my father, whose expression shifted into something harder—darker.

"What do you mean not quite?"

He gestured at Ivy. "The young woman before you is not covered in jewelry and designer labels. She did not grow up in a mansion by the sea. The de Souza family fortunes changed, son. Drastically."

My gaze locked with Ivy. "How?"

"The way it always happens," Ivy said, smiling mirthlessly. "One lousy businessman and degenerate gambler, and suddenly your bank account is empty, your furniture is repossessed, and you're thrown out onto the street with nothing because the same lousy businessman was your husband, and he was beaten to death by men he couldn't pay back.

"My great-grandmother, Sabrina, didn't know what to do. Her husband told her his family had a deed to land in this area, but that was all. He didn't tell her how much it was worth, or that it could make their fortune again ten times over." She threw up her hands. "Why would he? Christopher de Souza didn't think much of his trophy wife. She made his meals and raised his children. Why would he discuss finances with her—let alone tell her he was flushing their lives down the toilet?

"I can only guess that having the deed to fall back on fueled his recklessness. Too bad he was killed before Bedlam could save them."

The guys were all the way in the room now—pulling up the desk chair, claiming my armchair, sitting on the bed.

"So, Sabrina de Souza had the deed but no clue of its value," Legend clarified. "The family secret died with her husband."

"But not the Sisters," Ivy said. "Sabrina had three children and no home or money. She was desperate, so she packed up her kids and came out here where her husband told her they had land."

"She took her deed to a judge," said Dad, bringing our attention to him. "My grandmother, Cairo. Your great-grandmother. A Sister."

I stiffened. Ivy noticed immediately.

"I know, right," she said. "And to think, you were worried about what *I* would do to *your* family when it turns out the Sharpes have a family tradition of screwing over de Souzas. I should've stayed away from you."

Her tone was teasing, but I had a heavy feeling there was no trace of a lie. "What did Granny Sharpe do?"

My father answered. "She told Sabrina, 'oh, yes, there is a plot of land in your name. It's been sitting barren for a while, but it's yours to claim at any time.' Sabrina was so happy with those overgrown acres and the rickety barn and farmhouse on top, she didn't do a thing other than hug, kiss, and thank her. She moved her family into what became de Souza Farm."

"She had no idea she owned everything around her," Roan breathed. "Neither did your grandmother, your father... or you."

"No." Emotion leaked into Ivy's voice. "None of us knew. The Sisters wanted it that way. Caution for her family's last hope drove Sabrina de Souza to protect that old deed. She brought a copy to her meeting with the judge, where she was told even though it said eight thousand acres, Bedlam was now an official town. She couldn't own it, but that twelve-acre farm was all hers.

"Matter of fact, why didn't Sabrina bring her that crusty old piece of paper? She'd destroy it, and write up a new one that listed their actual property." Her gaze drifted over his shoulder. "I don't know where we'd be today if Sabrina had fallen for that trick, but she didn't. Sabrina kept it locked in a safe-deposit box, and didn't tell anyone about it or where it was."

"Why did your grandmother try to trick her out of the deed?" Roan asked Dad. "She didn't even know what she had."

"That's exactly why. Things have changed in the last hundred years," Jack said. "The Sisters have the vote. They have land, businesses, money, choices. Everything they'd lose back then if they didn't accept Amadeo's wife's deal. Now they have a town they control absolutely. They have the power, and they can have the money. Why should they be held back by a clueless farmer?

"Ever since Sabrina de Souza returned to town, the Society of Sisters has had a new goal. Destroy that deed."

Legend half rose from the armchair. "But... not our mothers, right? They're not after—"

"Yes, your mothers," Dad snapped. "Are you kidding? People whisper around town that it's a mother's blindness that explains why Josephine, Marjorie, and Eileen don't rein you boys in or see how you behave. But it's your blindness that didn't let you look past what your mothers have told you.

"Boys, by the time my grandmother's generation took over the Sisters, they reneged on the deal. There were millions beneath their shoes and no de Souzas around to stop them. They've been secretly mining the land for decades.

"Started by your great-grandmother," Dad said to Roan, blowing his brows up his forehead. "Continued by your grandmothers and now your mothers. They are the wealthiest women in this region, boys. By so much more than you could imagine."

I opened my mouth, but not a damn word came out. For the first time since we came screaming out of the womb, we were speechless.

"Naturally, they were careful. They had the same issue as Amadeo, but no right of ownership to back them up. If people found out why Crystal Canyon got its name, it'd be overrun by fortune hunters. And if the de Souzas found out, that'd be even worse.

"They amassed their wealth, but were cautious in explaining it. Josephine Banks lives in a mansion provided by the university. She didn't buy it. The mayor's son rides around in a 1957 Corvette worth one hundred and thirty thousand dollars, because her husband bought it for a steal in some romantic tale."

Arsenio crushed the sheets in his fist. He was told the same romantic tale.

"Eileen was under more scrutiny as a judge, but I'm sure you enjoyed all those vacations in your childhood, Jacques. Especially your summers in France."

Jacques could've been chipped from stone. And Ivy... Ivy didn't look at either of us, and I couldn't blame her. Our mothers made themselves rich while she scrubbed chicken shit from her boots and watched her grandmother toil from sunup to sundown. Framing us for murder wasn't a betrayal. It was years' worth of karma falling on our heads.

"But your mother wasn't happy with our cover story." I knew Dad was talking to me, though I didn't look away from Ivy. "I was the descendant of the Sister. The money was mine, and when I was trying to win her heart, I used it to take her all over the world.

"But then we had kids," Dad said, voice heavy. "And we had to settle down while I fulfilled my duty to the hand that fed me—serving as sheriff and making every threat to the Sisters go away. Nora wasn't pleased. Not with this house. Not with this life of wearing jeans and bargain threads while she pretended to live on a sheriff's wife's salary."

My voice was dead. "That's why she dropped us like hot shit and ran to Isaac."

"There were many reasons why she left, son." Dad lifted his hand as if searching for mine. I didn't reach back. It dropped by his side. "Yes, that was part of it. With a wealthy husband, she didn't have to hide her money anymore. I hate to say this, because I know she loves Paris, but getting pregnant by Isaac was by design. Once he finally left his first wife, playing pretend with me was over.

"She ran off with the sweet little girl I thought was my daughter, and my secret. Nora used her knowledge of the Society to get all my money in the divorce, then she blackmailed Marjorie, Eileen, Josephine, and Cynthia St. James for a place among the Sisters. If she wasn't getting a cut of the money and their power, the whole world would find out the truth."

I chuckled. "No wonder you were always sending me to shrinks, testing me for psychopathy. I come by my dead soul honest."

"No, Cairo. There's nothing wrong with you, son. You're just... garden variety screwed up by your parents like the rest."

That was the same thing I said to Dad all those months ago in an interrogation room.

"So our moms have us risking everything to protect Bedlam from being exploited, because they want to be the only ones exploiting it," Legend said, voice deadened. "And because of that, several generations of our families have been trying to get their hands on that deed. But what are we saying? That old scrap of paper is still valid?"

"Of course it is." Jacques stood and started pacing. "Deeds don't expire. A de Souza never sold the land. They never signed it away. The owner of Bedlam is Amadeo de Souza's last descendant."

The truth hit me hard and fast in the face. "That's why Steven Ellis had you sign that contract."

"Yes," she replied, shaking her head. "It really does all make sense now. The contract said all the land I owned would go to Steven Ellis if it wasn't inherited by a blood relative. The land wasn't the farm. It was Bedlam."

"So he knows about the deed," Legend said.

Ivy made a harsh noise. "He knows about the deed. The Sisters know about the deed. The Black Letter Crew knows about the deed. Everyone fucking knew but me."

"It had to be that way, Ivy." Dad reached for her hand, and she took it. "Your grandmother did have a will. In it she left you and your sister everything, including the deed and its location. Eileen sent me to retrieve the deed, and destroy it."

"Destroy it?" Jacques repeated. "Did you?"

Jack dropped his gaze. "No, I didn't. I knew I had done too much wrong to ever call myself a good man again, but as I stood in that bank holding the last thing an old woman had to give her orphaned granddaughters. A woman who had suffered because of tricks and lies told by my family. I just couldn't do it.

"Instead, I kept the deed and lied to your mothers, saying I destroyed it."

My brow scrunched. "Why? You didn't give the deed to Ivy and Rainey. You kept up the lie that there was no will, so why bother keeping the deed?"

"I didn't plan to keep the deed, or back the lie," he explained. "It was the day after I retrieved the contents of the safe-deposit box that I found a black letter on my doorstep."

"Cavendish," Ivy hissed. "He did the farm's taxes for free. How easy is it to imagine that Gran asked the *kind* young man she thought was her friend, to help her draft her will too. I know now that it was no coincidence that Cavendish was so near my grandmother when all of this happened. He didn't offer his services for free because Gran was nice to his mother.

"Steven Ellis must've dug up Bedlam's true history while he was looking into his own. He found out a de Souza owned it and still did. He had backup plans on backup plans. First, get Gran to sign over everything legitimately to AgriProspects. That wasn't working, so... he sent Scott to get close to her, and he killed her."

"Scott did?" I asked.

She pressed her lips tight. "Who convinced me Andrew Clein had to be responsible after I got that autopsy report back? He'd been in my ear from the beginning—manipulating me. I didn't even think about the fact that Scott had access to Gran too. Why would I? I didn't know he had anything to gain."

"Cavendish killed her." As I said it, I knew it was true. "Triggering the release of her estate and a chance for him to get his hands on that deed. I bet that was too far for Ellis. If he was willing to resort to murder, we'd all be dead already. He wasn't interested in getting in bed with a murderer, so he backed off and continued his plan through Foundry—without Cavendish."

"Wasn't like Cavendish needed him anymore," Jacques admitted. "Once Ellis told him about Amadeo, Scott had all the information he needed. He set to work manipulating Ivy and his band of psychopaths. Anything Ellis tried to take, he would get back."

Ivy scrubbed her face, suddenly looking bone tired. "That was his plan. Jack told me the letter said to hand the deed over. A new will was about to appear that said Rainey and I inherited, but Cavendish was our executor. He'd run my estate until I turned twenty-five, and if Rainey and I died before then, it would all go to him.

"I was never going to make it to twenty-five. When that will appeared, we wouldn't have lived past Tuesday."

"But that was another thing that never happened." I cut to Dad. "Why?"

"Because there were three forces at play. One of them I now know to be Steven Ellis. At the time, all I knew was that I received an anonymous phone call stating Scott Cavendish killed Abigail de Souza. I accepted this right away. Between the letter, the forged will, and the way Scott Cavendish seemed to hover around Ivy, it had to be the truth."

"You didn't arrest him," Roan accused.

"There was no proof. I thought she died of natural causes, so I closed the case pretty quickly. It was Ivy that suspected more. I suspected nothing until I got that letter and phone call. By the time she came to me with the autopsy report, I had already worked out a deal to protect her"—he flicked to me—"and you."

"Protect me?"

"I arrested Scott Cavendish. Brought him into an interrogation room and said the case would be reopened, and he'd go down for what he did. Cavendish sat in that chair... and laughed," Dad spat. "The twisted little shit laughed himself sick, saying unless I planned to bury my son, he wasn't going anywhere other than home.

"I served a new master now, and while the Sisters wouldn't kill Cairo for my disobedience—any refusal to do what he said, and he would. The next time he came back, holding that fake will, I was ready for him.

"I told Cavendish I entrusted everything to a friend. The deed, the true will, the town's history, the Sisters, the Men of Honor, Abigail de Souza's death, and who killed her. If anything happened to me, Cairo, Rainey, or Ivy, he was to send it to the news station. Cavendish walked away, shouting his threats, but I honestly thought it was over. He was beaten."

"He wasn't," Ivy croaked. "Cavendish kept his word. When you refused him, he tried to get me to kill Cairo. I wouldn't do it, and my sister paid the price."

"I didn't know this, Ivy. I swear I didn't."

"Dad, you didn't think it was weird when she suddenly lost her memory and started going by her sister's name?"

"Of course I did," he cried. "But it wasn't as though she came to me saying there'd been another death. She kept saying her sister took off to Chicago and wasn't coming back. That she was calling her sister by her own name worried me. But I went out to the farm and there was no sign of foul play. One room was empty as if someone packed. Plus, Ivy seemed fine other than whatever delusion gripped her.

"I concluded that *Rainey* left, and in her grief at being abandoned by the last of her family, *Ivy* had a mental breakdown and tried to keep her sister around the only way she knew how."

Very close to what actually happened.

"Rainey was eighteen and, to be frank, safer away from Cavendish and Bedlam. I thought I was doing the right thing by not tracking her down, and turning Ivy over to Doc Nash's care."

"You could've told her the truth of who she was." *You could've told me*, went unsaid.

Dad was shaking his head. "Doc Nash said not to. It could do more harm than good to try and force someone out of a delusion.

I'd either be wasting my time, or cause their mind to react violently against me reintroducing the trauma it's trying to protect her from."

Again, I couldn't object. Ivy found out the truth and immediately jumped off a bridge. Doc Nash wasn't spinning bullshit.

"Cavendish backed off after that and I didn't receive another letter, so I assumed— I hoped," he corrected, "that it was over."

"Still don't understand why Cavendish backed off," Roan said.

Ivy pushed up, moving to the window. "My guess is after Jack made it clear that fake will would never see the light of day, he gave up any idea of controlling my inheritance through me. That's why it didn't matter if I went down for Cairo's murder. Or why he didn't care if I knew he ordered Rainey's death. He was done with the de Souza sisters, and on to something else."

"Suicide?" Arsenio scoffed. "The afterlife? That was his grand plan?"

"We'll never know," I said, steering the full truth of Cavendish's death away from my father's ears. "But he gave up on that plan, and now his devoted lunatics have one of their own. We know it starts with the Ellises, not Ivy."

"And there it is," Ivy said. "That's how we got here."

"I'm sorry we did, Ivy. You'll never know how sorry." Tears collected in the corner of Jack's eyes. "I thought I was protecting you from the Sisters who couldn't know the deed survived, and that monster Cavendish who knew it did. I hated that your grandmother's killer lived free all that time but all I had was a lack of evidence and a threat hanging over my head that his friends would carry on in his place if anything happened to him."

He wasn't lying. Cavendish did keep his word.

"I got it all w-wrong," he cried, voice cracking. "I made life so much worse for you."

"You didn't, Jack. It wasn't you. Amazingly, the man I hated most of all was the only one who tried to help me. No, the people who ruined my life are Scott Cavendish, Steven Ellis, the Black Letter Crew, Eileen Stone—"

Jacques snapped his head up.

"—Marjorie Creed, Cynthia St. James, Josephine Banks, and Nora Keller." A suffocating, pressing silence blanketed us as Ivy turned... and smiled. "It's them who'll pay."

I was too numb to stop her walking past me. Arsenio recovered quicker. Sliding into her path, he blocked the door and grasped her chin. Tipping her up, he placed a slow, thorough kiss on her lips. Ivy responded easily.

"Where exactly are you going?" Arsenio murmured, tracing her lips. Only someone who knew them both would sense the growing air of danger.

She smiled sweet. "To get the deed, of course. Where else would I be going, baby?"

Roan half rose. "You know where it is?"

"Jack told me before you got here. I won't be long." Ivy made to go around him. Arsenio sidestepped in her way.

"We'll go with you."

"That's very sweet." That smile didn't fade. "But the five of you are currently on the run from the police, who happen to be on their way here right now."

I shot to the window. Two police cars came straight at the bungalow, their sirens lighting the way.

"Sheriff Jack will be easy to explain, but not the two hostages. You guys have to get them and yourselves out of here. Quick. Text me where you are and we'll meet up there.

"I love you guys. Stay safe."

Ivy tried again to leave and was promptly tossed over his shoulder. "Let's move," Arsenio barked. "Roan and Legend, grab Quinn. Cairo and Jacques, get Davidson. We're parked out back." Arsenio bolted carrying a suspiciously docile Ivy.

"Dad, tell them what Davidson did to you. He's corrupt and our arrest was an abuse of power. Make them believe it. We don't have time for this on-the-run shit."

"I'll take care of it, son." Dad never looked weaker or less able to take care of anything. "I'll make it right."

There wasn't time for more. I hauled ass down the stairs where Jacques hefted Davidson. Taking his other side, we dragged him out the back to the waiting car, and Ivy.

She sat in the passenger seat, looking wholly content as Arsenio leaned on her car door and prevented any chance of escape. Locking eyes with me through the windshield, she winked.

Chapter Eight

R*oan*

Ivy burrowed into Legend's side, the picture of content-ment with her head on his shoulder and fingers running up and down his chest. His tight arm around her looked less like a lover's embrace, and more like a precaution to keep her from jumping out of the car at the next red light. If that's what she was thinking, her face gave no sign. I couldn't tell what was going on in her head.

"Are you going to kill our mothers?"

The car jolted forward, rocked by Jacques's sudden jolt to the gas. We got away with two hostages in the trunk, but only barely. Right then, we were circling the back roads while we figured out where to lie low until our names were cleared. A heavy silence choked the car the entire time.

Jacques, Arsenio, Cairo, and Legend glared at me.

"What?" I said, unrepentant. "We all want to know. Won't find out until we ask."

Ivy laughed. "That's what you're all thinking right now? Oh my goodness, you five are ridiculous. Of course I'm not going to kill your moms. You'd break up with me."

She genuinely sounded like that was her only problem with that option.

"That's the only reason?" Jacques asked, echoing my thought.

She shrugged. "I have no loyalty to them, but I am loyal to you. I'm not going to harm them. I'm just going to take back what's mine." Hooded eyes met ours in turn. "That won't be a problem... will it?"

"No problem for us." I didn't have to think about it. "Whether you run the town or they own the town, the job's the same. We protect what's ours—Bedlam and you."

Ivy moved from me to the others.

"That's right," Jacques said.

"You will never not belong to me," Arsenio added.

"I'm a rich man either way," Legend said. "What do I care if there's a little less from her half of the inheritance?"

Everyone spoke up except for Cairo. He stared at the window—no longer acknowledging us or the conversation. Ivy visibly tensed.

I changed the subject. This required a deeper conversation, and industrial tools to remove Cairo's head from his ass. None of that was happening in that cramped car with a full trunk.

"Where are we going to go? Hunter's Crest? They have vacation cabins on the outskirts," I said. "We can rent one under fake names."

"Too risky," said Jacques. "You have to show ID to get a cone from an ice cream truck these days. We don't have fakes, or enough money to bribe a receptionist not to care."

"What about our guests in the trunk?" Legend asked. "I'm not hauling two counts of twenty to life around with us. We need to figure out something to do with them. Now."

"While we're talking about the Black Letter Crew, there's something you need to know," Ivy began.

"What is it?"

"It was a tight thing getting Jack out of there. Quinn waited until past time to tell me where he was. I had to speed the whole way. I ended up at an old bed-and-breakfast at the end of town, and I wasted more time searching all the rooms for him. I finally found him when I heard a car pull up."

I bolted up. "Did they see you?"

"No. It wasn't easy with two busted arms, but I got Jack out through the broken window. It's how he cut his neck," she said. "But it's when they came into the room. I looked back for a split second and, guys, I saw their faces."

She had all our attention—including Cairo.

"It was two men. Our age. Got to be university students." Ivy tried withdrawing from Legend and didn't get anywhere. "Jacques, love, I appreciate your commitment to privacy, but I didn't go to school with these people my whole life. I didn't recognize them. You need to tell me about the nine we picked so I can tell if it's one of them."

"Describe them."

"One of them had long, dark hair pulled back into a ponytail. Thin. Small eyes, small mouth, and large nose—"

"Jackson Hyde."

"Hyde," I sputtered, recalling the anime-loving nerd from high school who always sat alone at a lunch table, scribbling in his notebook. "He's in the Black Letter Crew?"

"I'm not surprised," Jacques said. "I took a look in his room this week and it was an altar to death. Serial killer books and movies. Posters for true crime podcasts. He was one of the three I couldn't prove was in the Crew, but highly suspected he was."

"Describe the other one," Cairo demanded.

"Short dark hair. Attractive. Square jaw and light-brown eyes. Taller than Hyde, and in good shape." She flicked between us. "Anything?"

Sharing looks, we shook our heads one after the other.

"I know too many guys that fit that description," I said.

"A description that doesn't match any of the nine," Jacques added. "Was there anything else about him? Tattoo? Piercing? Expensive clothes?"

"No, sorry. No tattoos or piercings, and his clothes just looked normal to me."

"Don't worry about it." I jerked a thumb behind me. "We've got two people who can help us fill in the blanks. Jacques, make a U-turn, I know where to go. It's time we end this shit."

QUINN

"Wake up. Wake up!"

I peeled my eyes open and fucking sunbeams assaulted them. I winced, snapping them shut.

"Not again, Cunningham. If you slip back into your coma, this is going to end early for you."

Coma? That sounded nice right about now.

My body was the living definition of agony. Each breath was a hot poker through my chest. Fractured and broken bones. Bleeding nose. Busted lip. And my hair.

That bitch cut my hair.

Fury surged through me, burning through the pain and sluggishness. I forced my eyes open, focusing past the flashlights in my face to... *her.*

Fixed on Ivy, I almost didn't notice the Bedlam Boys fanned around her, or the forest behind them.

Cool night air tickled my swollen lips, providing the only sweet, soothing mercy I'd received since Amy walked that slut into my room. Grass teased my thigh where the skin hadn't gone numb, and my wrists...

I carefully bent my neck. I was still bound, though now the other end of the rope was in Jacques's hand. Another careful turn of the neck and I saw why.

I wasn't at Black Widow Hill. I was sitting on the edge of it.

"Do you think this scares me?" Davidson perched next to me, his rope held by Roan. He had received a beating too, but not as bad as mine. He was able to sit up. As for me, only the rope and Jacques were keeping me upright.

Does bring me some satisfaction to know I made that stuck-up farm princess lose control.

"You don't have the balls." Davidson laughed. "We're not on the playground anymore, boys. A few taps to the jaw and a roll on the dirt won't send me off crying. From here on if you make a threat, you better be ready to carry it out, and it's written all over your faces"—he spat at Roan's feet—"weak, weak, weak, weak, weak, and weak."

"You finished?" Cairo asked, amused. "Good. Now we can get started. I'm going to make this simple. One of you is going to tell me the names of everyone in the Black Letter Crew, and what you're planning. Whoever speaks first, lives. Whoever speaks last will have the last thing they see be my boot in their face before the long drop down. Understood?" He swept out his arms, turning to both of us. "Simple, right? Now, who is going first?"

My lips sealed shut. I reduced this man to a quivering bowl of cum with one good ball fondle and blowjob. He didn't scare me.

"Cairo, you forgot to mention," Roan chimed in.

He clapped. "Of course. I should mention there's a time limit on this offer. If ten minutes pass and neither of you give it up, it'll be up to me to pick." His handsome, wide smile beamed on me. "I will kick you off this cliff and your friend will have until your screams fade to give it up, or go sailing off too. It's been a long day and I'm not interested in being out here with you two for a second longer than I have to be."

I rolled my eyes. I'd give it to the Bedlam Boys. They could talk a good game, throw a good punch, and that was enough to cow everyone else in this stupid town, but it didn't impress me. I knew real pain. True sacrifice. That was something these pretty boys playing pretend would never understand.

"Legend, start the timer."

My handsome former lover who licked my pussy so good it curled my toes, pulled out a phone and did as requested. I smirked when he showed me the countdown. "Wow. You really think I'm buying this? You're not getting anything out of me, except an orgasm." I blew him a kiss through busted lips. "I know the hick trash hasn't been giving you what you need. How about we skip this foreplay and go straight to you pumping my throat while Roan does me from behind?"

"Gonna have to pass." Legend winked. "I don't screw bald chicks."

I bared my teeth as Ivy howled.

"Wasted a whole minute on that," Cairo remarked. "I'll repeat the question. Who is in the Black Letter Crew, and what are you planning?"

"Consider my time up," Davidson sang. "I'm not telling you shit, so do it. Do it, Sharpe. Kick me off the cliff. Murder a bound, weaponless man in cold blood. Make your drunk daddy proud.

"Go on," he pushed when Cairo didn't move. "What are you waiting for? I want you to do it, Cairo. I want to see you become... me."

Cairo's eyes flashed.

"That's right. You think you're so above us. Believe you're protecting the town with everything you do. Every law you break. Every person you hurt is for the greater good. You know who else thought the same? The Men of Honor.

"You and the precious Society of Sisters have become exactly what you hate." He cracked up. "Is it any wonder I can't stop laughing? You're no different from us. Actually, you're worse. At least the new and reforged Men of Honor are honest about who we are. We don't pretend to be Bedlam's saviors while we sink the boot in its throat. We are what we have always been—its rightful owners."

Roan cracked a jaw yawning. "Wow. How much time did he waste on that speech?"

"Three minutes," Legend replied. "Should we let him waste the final six with more hypocritical ramblings about his crew's *honesty* while they hide behind black letters and wear masks when they attack innocent girls?"

"Would love to hear him spin that, but we're short on time, and the lady should get a chance to go." They turned to me. "Quinn, got something you want to say?"

I pushed out my lips, rolling my eyes skyward. "Mmm... no? That's right, no. I've got nothing. Come back to me."

"Rethink this," Cairo warned. "This isn't a bluff."

"If you've got to say it's not a bluff, then it is a bluff. Real men don't waste time threatening to do something. They just do it."

Cairo cocked his head. "Is that why you joined the Men of Honor? You wanted to be surrounded by real men who say they're going to gang up and murder innocent women, then keep their word?"

My jaw clenched. "This is about Rainey de Souza again? Oh, please." I curled my lips at Ivy. "None of that would've happened if *she* had the balls to follow through. Sacrifice one guy she didn't even know, but no. She refused and was stupid enough to think she wouldn't pay the consequences for it. That's her own fault. Don't blame me."

"What do you get out of this, Quinn?" Roan asked. "You're gorgeous. Upper middle class. About to graduate with a business degree and go anywhere you want. But instead you're here, dangling on a ledge because... what? You couldn't help it? You had to let your dark side come out to play?"

A grin teased my lips. "Don't we all?"

"Come on, Quinn," Legend said. "I know you're dying to monologue. Get it off your chest."

"Nice try, but I won't tell you anything about them. You can find out who they are when we pay you a visit in the middle of the night."

Blank-faced, Cairo drifted off me to Legend.

"Two minutes."

"Two minutes," Cairo repeated. "Who talks first?"

I didn't speak, but Davidson did. The Bedlam Boys were treated to all the ways they were exactly like the Men of Honor—if we were as gutless and pathetic. He explained in detail that Cairo's father was a lousy, useless drunk, and his mother was a gold-digging whore. Josephine Banks was a man-eating, dry-cunt bitch who dropped Roan out of her womb like a sow in a field, then continued climbing the ambitions ladder without giving him another thought.

Marjorie Creed, the fake mayor of a town that wasn't a town, was even more corrupt than Davidson said he could ever be. And she was a good lay.

"—no wonder your father crossed an ocean to get back to that pussy," Davidson taunted. "And don't get me started on Eileen Stone. She puts on a good show—the prim and proper judge. But the lady has a nasty kink for outdoor sex. I've caught her and Jack—"

The phone chimed. "Time's up," Jacques announced.

Roan dropped the rope. Without pause, breath, or hesitation, Cairo kicked Davidson square in the chest.

"Ooof!" Davidson flew back... and plummeted.

"Ahhhh!"

Davidson's and my screams echoed through the canyon.

"What the fuck did you do?!"

"I said you had until his screams faded to talk," Cairo snarled. He bore down on me. "Want to test if I'm bluffing again?"

"No, no, no." I thrashed, flinging my body away from him. Bruised and broken, I flopped helplessly on the ground—getting nowhere. He wasn't supposed to kill him. He wasn't supposed to! Who were these guys? We thought we had to kidnap his father to force them to kill, but no. They weren't just enforcers and thugs.

Looked like they too let their dark side out to play a long time ago.

"No! Stay away from me!"

"Names, Quinn." His boot dropped on my hip. "Or down you go."

White blotted out my mind. The words flew so quickly from my mouth, they tumbled over each other. "Ja-Jackson Hyde! Thea W-Wood! Lincoln Roberts! Everett Cooper! Including me, that's every-one, I swear. I swear!"

Cairo crouched next to me. I curled in on myself, trembling. I joined the Men of Honor to be around people like me. Have a little fun. Make a lot of money. Take back what once belonged to my fam-ily. I did not join to die.

Every other sheep in this cow-dung town could be sacrificed, but not me.

He reached for me.

"No. No!"

"Shh," Cairo crooned. "I believe you, Quinn. Hyde, Wood, Roberts, and Cooper. Which one of them goes by Dante?"

"It's Lincoln. He took over after he killed Zoey. She was chang-ing our purpose," I rushed. "Said why not make a little money on the side by selling our services? But then she took a job from the Crows to kill the Bedlam Boys, even though we still needed you. She had to go."

"Do you still need us? To kill Steven Ellis and his sons?"

I tossed my head against the dirt. "We could do that whenever. No, we need you because you are your mothers' only vulnerability, and hers," I said, glaring at Ivy. "It always comes back to *her*."

Cairo just nodded, accepting this. "How exactly are they going to use us to make our mothers vulnerable? Are they going to get a black letter on their doorstep like my father did?"

"How else? Everett was supposed to be at the party tonight. We planned for him to follow you and get evidence of whatever you were going to do to Steven, Jeremy, and Micah. With that, we'd have all of you in a vise. You'd do what we say to keep out of prison for murder. Your moms would do what we say to protect their violent little boys. And best of all, the Ellises would be dead. Win-win-win."

"Not a bad plan," Arsenio mused. "I mean, we guessed it, but it's still elegant. The only faction left with any power in this town would be the Men of Honor."

"Exactly," I croaked. "That's all I know. I promise. If you didn't get to the Ellises tonight, Dante just would've killed Jack Sharpe, grabbed someone else you care about, and started this all over again. There was no plan *B*."

He hummed. "Once again, Quinn, I believe you. I'm glad we've finally gotten to this point in our relationship where we can trust each other."

I gasped deep lungfuls of air—each one shredding my chest in agony. "So... I can go? I talked," I cried. "I told you everything. You promised to spare me."

"That I did." Cairo nodded at Jacques. He dropped my rope. "While you're crawling through the woods back to town, memorize this message for your friends: We're going to keep a promise to you too. You six will live up to the Men of Honor's legacy, and die in pain and fire."

Getting to his feet, Cairo turned his back on me. The men who once considered me their toy, paid me the same amount of humanity as they walked off without a second look.

"Hey, guys, wait," Ivy called. "There's just one more thing I want to say to her."

Ivy jogged back, planting in front of me. Meeting my eyes, she whispered five words that unhinged my jaw.

"No! Please! Noooo!"

She viciously kicked my thigh, sending me flying off the edge. Wind cradled me—rushing to hold me on my long, dark descent, carrying her final words in my soul.

"This is for my sister."

IVY

I picked through the cabin's selection of mini soaps and shampoos.

Apple harvest and jasmine? Or maybe lavender and chamomile? I picked the last two out of the wicker basket. *That would be soothing.*

Making my choice, I carried the bottles past five pairs of watchful eyes, and closed the bathroom door on them.

The guys had been watching me closely since I announced the Sisters' free ride profiting from my family's land, pain, and suffering was over. I said I wasn't going to kill them and I meant it. What more did they want from me?

My toes sank into the memory foam rug as I shed my dirty, bloodstained clothes. Impossible to believe that just that morning, we were standing in front of our home discussing golf tournaments. Less than twenty-four hours later, two of the Black Letter Crew were dead. Sheriff Jack was hopefully under the tender care of Doc Nash. We had all the names of the people coming after us.

I finally knew the truth of my history.

Around and around it went in my head, and as much as it shocked me, that's how much it made sense. Gran left a will. Jack was just too afraid of what would happen to me and Rainey if we inherited. Nora Keller dumped her husband and child to live the high life with my money. A woman like that didn't seem the type to sit back while I took it all away from her, and put her ass in jail for good measure.

Then there was the lurking, sneaking psychopath who did want me to inherit, so he could snatch it away, then put me and my sister in the ground next to our grandmother.

My whole life, people have been pulling my strings. Lying to me. Manipulating me. Using me. And they've all but won.

I'm the very last de Souza. Once I'm gone, the Sisters, the Black Letter Crew, and the Ellises will have no one to challenge them.

Those bitches will be sorry that now I know that. They thought they could avoid the fight and keep the little farm girl stupid. Not—

The door creaked open, spinning me around. Legend stepped inside.

Roan mentioned the cabin rentals on the outskirts of Hunter's Crest, and we decided that would be good right about now. We simply skipped the part about checking in, broke one of the locks, and let ourselves inside the three-bedroom luxury space filled with a big screen, full kitchen, plush living room carpet, queen-size beds in every room, and a rain shower that I turned to the highest temperature.

Legend didn't stop me climbing in. Through the steam, I watched him undress.

"What is it, Legend? Come to plan our next date?" I shot him a grim smile underneath the spray. "Or am I done proving that I'm worthy of you?"

"You're done."

I froze, not expecting that measured reply. "I see. Well then, you're going the wrong way, aren't you?" He slowly approached. "Go, Legend."

He climbed into the tub.

"I said go!" The shout ripped out of me. "I am so sick of dancing on the end of everyone's strings. You guys act like I betrayed you by holding on to my sister the only way my broken mind knew how, when it was everyone else who betrayed me!

"I'm done apologizing for being broken. For being lost, alone, and angry!" I shoved him. "If you can't accept that I love you and all I'll ever be is true to all of you in every way I know how, then *fuck you*! Let me go now."

Legend weathered my berating without reaction. "Goodness, woman. Why are you yelling? I just told you you're done proving yourself worthy... because you never needed to."

My lips parted, but nothing came out.

Taking the tiny bottle from me, Legend poured the body wash on his palm and brought me toward him. My flesh rippled under his touch as he lathered me up.

"I've spent my whole life fighting for the wrong thing, Ivy. I lived in my own delusion—pretending that the Sisters were honorable, and every order I followed was to protect what's ours." His grip tightened on my hips. "This place was never ours, and they were never fucking honorable. Even though I didn't know it, I helped them cheat and steal from you... and you don't blame me, do you?"

It took me a minute, but as he rubbed soft circles on my back, I shook my head.

"I don't understand why. I really don't," he said with a half-laugh. "When I found out you lied to me without knowing it, I acted like a complete shitbag. I blamed you. Said we were done. Made you jump through hoops to get me back. And all you did was forgive me."

My pants picked up speed, heating my chest with the steam soaking into my warming cheeks. Legend had never talked like this to me before. I didn't know what to say, how to react, or know if I should do either, and risk him stopping.

"I've only done this once," Legend whispered—rubbing kneading, soapy hands over the knots in my shoulder.

"Done what?" I asked, voice small. "Give a massage?"

"Fall in love with someone." Legend drew me in, tracing my lips with his. "You'll have to help me when I mess up. Tie my stubborn ass to the bed. Take me to see the hummingbirds. But if you still love me, Ivy, I want to prove I'm worthy of you."

I crumbled—breaking into pieces that swirled down the drain, never to be seen again.

This wasn't real. It couldn't be happening. On the worst day of my life—the day I discovered why all the other horrible days happened—my vicious, paddling, closed-off Legend couldn't be saying he loved me.

Grasping my chin between two fingers, the sweet smell of lavender and chamomile danced over us, sweetening his kiss.

I crumbled again, but this time into him—letting him hold me up under tangling tongues and fevered moans. No one kissed me like Legend St. James.

All of my guys were delicious and addictive in their own way, but Legend was wild and rough. He kissed me like he wanted the sensation to penetrate deeper than my lips. Spread through my whole body and put me under an intense high that I'd chase for the rest of my life.

"I love you," I whispered.

"I love your blowjobs."

I burst into giggles, soaring on that high.

He lifted a shoulder, side-smirking. "You know, while we're being honest. I have to admit I lied about you being crap at them. You've got the hottest, tastiest little mouth, and I'd love you for that alone."

"Good thing you've got a great ass too."

I threw my head back, laughing louder and freer than I had... in years.

"Well," I teased, smile playing at my lips. "It's a good thing I'm willing to take you back, and let you prove how much you love me until time takes us, and after."

"Let's keep being honest." Legend scraped my bottom lip between his teeth, making me squeal as he lifted and wrapped my legs around his waist. "I wasn't really giving you a choice."

Legend pressed me against the tile, flattening his muscled, dripping-wet body against me. I heard the door open and close again, but paid it little mind. Someone climbed in.

"You're going to share, aren't you, love?"

"Always." Legend spun me, and then I was pressing against a hard, lithe body.

Roan took my weight, wrapping around my thighs and holding me up. I didn't know why until Legend dropped to his knees.

"How is it with all things the five of us have done to you, you still blush?"

Saying that only made me blush harder. My brain tried to form a comeback in the midst of him dropping kisses on my inner thigh. "That's from the shower steam."

"What was your excuse when I had you ass up in the trunk?" The teasing monster that he was, Legend skipped my middle and continued his journey on the other side, kissing farther and farther away from where I wanted him to be.

"Sex in a trunk?" Roan repeated. "Oooh, fun. How come you've never had me ass up in a trunk?"

"Ivy seduced me in a zoo. Didn't have many options. Had to improvise."

I giggled. "If that's all it takes to seduce you, that explains so—"

Legend dove between my legs, catching my reply on a gasp. My eyes widened as he tasted me, tongue up, down, and around my clit like an Olympic event.

The guys only had me ass up or flat-backed. I'd never received head at this angle before, and making me wait this long was the cruelest thing they'd ever done to me.

Legend was a Greek god. Adonis kneeling before the throne of Olympus—come to bring a gift to the goddess, and she was very appreciative. From this angle, I saw everything. His delicious pink tongue darting in and out of me. The smirk on his lips as I moaned like a wanton trollop. The glint in his eyes as ours connected.

"Holy shit," I breathed, melting into liquid honey in Roan's arms. I dropped my head on his shoulder, and he dropped his—licking my lavender and chamomile skin.

His nips danced along my throat, sending shivers down my spine while Legend sent convulsions up my core. They were already undoing me, and we were still just dabbling in the foreplay.

Legend wrapped my legs around his neck, indulging his treat with rough and reckless abandon.

"Ahh," I cried, arching off Roan.

My red-haired devil imp took advantage. Moving to my side, he held me in his arms—encircling me like he dipped me in the middle of a dance. Roan closed over my nipple and I shuddered, releasing a soft squeak.

Everything about this was new for us. I didn't want to say my guys were selfish in bed... because doing so would get me spanked.

When I was in the bed, car, trunk, woods, kitchen with the Bedlam Boys, they took what they wanted from me without permission or mercy. I fucking loved it and wouldn't change a thing about the many screaming orgasms I've added up.

But giving me head? Teasing my nipples? Running rough, calloused hands up and down my thigh while Roan squeezed and teased my nub? That didn't happen before I sucked their cocks dry or stained them with my juices. Beyond all comprehension, my guys were... making love to me.

Water drenched my sensitive skin, feeling like a million raindrop kisses that did nothing to bring me back down to earth. I was trying to hold on to this moment for as long as possible.

"Ah." My back arched, bending as tight as my legs around his head. Legend flicked my clit and I was lost.

Spasms rocked my body, nearly dropping me flat on the porcelain, but my guys held me tight—stroking my heated, sensitive flesh as I spilled sweet juices on Legend's tongue.

"Wow," I breathed. "Why did we wait so long to do that?"

"We won't repeat that mistake again," Roan said. "We do it every day from now on. Three times on weekends."

I didn't even try to tell him we'd probably die from dehydration. Part of me—huge part—wanted to see how long we could keep that sex streak up.

"Hands and knees, gorgeous," Legend ordered.

I moved with eager quickness, getting on my hands and knees between Roan and Legend. Roan stroked himself, dangling his member so tantalizingly close to my lips. My tongue darted out, licking the tip. His sharp hiss of pleasure was as good as sex.

"You want it in your mouth so badly, don't let me stop you. You know I don't play hard to get."

That was all the invitation I needed. Holding his thighs, I swallowed Roan to the hilt. Roan didn't like to play around and neither did I. I set a fast pace—bobbing and sucking till my cheeks caved in.

"Holy fuck." He tangled in my wet strands, brushing them back from my eyes. "You're incredible."

I felt something press against my entrance, heightening my excitement. Believe it or not, this was my first time in the middle. Roan liked to fuck me while Legend did him from behind. When Legend was balls deep in me, it was while Roan watched, jacked off, and told him to pound me harder. And naturally, I loved watching the two of them go at it.

I thought we were out of firsts, but my guys and I always found more.

Legend pushed past my folds, making me moan around Roan. He started pumping, moving my mouth on Roan in sync with his thrusts.

Our grunts, moans, and groans filled the bathroom, echoing in the steamy space.

Roan said I was their perfect third. That they were always a three-some even when it was just the two of them. They were waiting for me to finish the puzzle.

As I crouched between them, receiving more pleasure than a single person could stand, I knew it was true. With them was where I was always meant to be.

I was waiting for the Bedlam Boys too.

Legend smacked my ass.

"Hhmpf," I cried, core spasming. He pushed me higher up the peak, promising that I'd thoroughly wreck myself on the way down.

Roan's shaft slid on my tongue—smooth and pulsating in my mouth. His pumps were getting faster—jerkier. I relaxed my throat, eager to take all he had to give me.

Another swat landed on my ass, popping me off my knees. It was getting embarrassing how much my little backside liked to be punished.

Between Legend's slaps and Roan's pumps, I didn't know which of us was going to come first.

Legend reached under me, rolling his fingers over my happy slut of a clit.

Me. It was definitely going to be me.

My orgasm crested rough and fast, tightening every muscle in my—

"Shit," Roan hissed, thrusting for the final time. He came and I tried to swallow every bit, but he pulled back and finished on my face. That was the final push over the edge.

I came hard, screaming so loud I likely alerted the police to our location. Legend had to hold me up as he spilled inside me. I was limp like an old damp sock, but a thousand times happier than one.

The three of us collapsed in a heap, piled on top of one another. Roan stroked my hair while Legend's fingers ran up and down my thigh.

"Just give me a minute," I gasped, "then we're going again. Roan in the middle this time."

"You saying you want Legend to pound me while I lick your pussy?"

"I want that very much."

Roan looked past me to Legend. "I kept telling you this woman's our soul mate."

"What do you want from me? It took me a while, but I finally came around. Legend and Roan don't make sense without Ivy."

I WOKE UP WITH MY GUYS finally where they be-longed—sandwiched against me. Carefully, I untangled my legs from Legend's and slipped out from under Roan's arm. I left my towel and clothes on the bathroom floor, and padded out naked into the kitchen.

"Oooh." A glance in the fridge revealed someone went out and bought groceries. Necessary since we didn't know how long it'd take to clear the guys' names and end the police search. Jack said he would take care of it. I just had to hope no one would need more expla-nation after the broken and battered man told them Davidson lured him into a trap to take over as sheriff, and smooth the way for the vi-olent pieces of garbage who needed a corrupt cop in their pocket.

"Where is it?"

Jerking, I stuck my head over the door, falling on Cairo in the kitchen entrance.

"Where's what? Breakfast?"

"The deed."

Stiffly, I turned very slowly. "Why would you be asking me about that?"

"You said you wanted to go pick it up from where Dad had it stashed. I'll drive you. Where is it?"

I studied him, wishing not for the first time that there was more to read in Cairo's eyes than... darkness. "You don't need to drive me, Cairo. I can get there myself."

"Sure you can, but why say no?" He cocked his head. "Don't you trust me?"

"I don't know, Cairo." I swallowed the distance, noticing right away as his gaze lingered on my naked body. "Do you trust me?"

"Not even a little." I stopped. "But the way I see it, my blood wronged yours. Amadeo and the Men of Honor he let run free were bastards. But that wasn't who came to my great-grandmother for help all those years ago. Sabrina was alone and desperate, but with all the garbage the Sisters spouted about Bedlam being a safe haven for the damned but determined, they looked at another woman who needed help and saw a target. They looked at two orphaned farm girls and saw a threat."

He stepped forward. "A lot of stuff has gone down between us, but every way I look at it, the betrayal that started this happened decades before we were even born. I'm going to make that right to-day, de Souza."

Hope swelled in my chest. First Legend and now Cairo? Could I be any happier than I was in this moment? I'd gotten all my guys back.

"Then, we'll finally be done."

The smile froze on my face. "Excuse me? Done?"

"That's right." Cairo touched my shoulder, continuing down along my collarbone, tracing the swell of my breasts, gliding over my belly button. His speech so at odds with the gentle exploration. "I'm paying off my family's debt, then you and I will have a clean break. No grudges. No vendettas."

He glanced down at his ying-yang wolf tattoo. "The eternal war is over."

"But..." I searched for words in my dry throat. "I don't want that. Yes, let's end the war, but afterward, I want to start something new. With you, Cairo."

"You can't think that could happen. Your father-in-law would be the man who hid the truth to protect you, but also to protect himself. Your mother-in-law would be a scheming blackmailer who fought to get her hands on your money by any means necessary. Your sister-in-law would be the girl who lived your stolen life in the mansion you deserved, with the family you deserved.

"And your husband, he'd be the fucking blind fool who stole, threatened, beat, and killed to help them all keep you in the dark. We can't come back from that, Ivy."

My heart squeezed. He was finally calling me by my name and not de Souza, and right then it was the saddest word he said.

"I say we can, Cairo."

"I say we can't... and I don't want to."

I rocked back like he struck me, falling out of reach of his stroking fingers.

Cairo tucked his hands in his pockets, turning his green orbs to the sun shining on what was no longer a perfect day. "I'm thinking when all this is over, I'll go away for a while. Bedlam won't need the Bedlam Boys anymore once you take it back. Be kinda nice to find out who I am other than the puppet of my mother and her friends."

"Why would you say we won't n-need you? That I won't need you." My voice cracked. "You're Cairo Sharpe. My wolf. My mate. You protect what's yours."

He turned away. "You're not mine anymore. I said fate would break us. It finally did." Cairo drifted out of the room. "Let me know when you're ready to go."

There on the polished hardwood floors, I crumbled again. That time for good.

THE HOUR-LONG DRIVE to Ashwick, the town north of Hunter's Crest, stretched into an eternity. Cairo and I did not speak the whole way.

Once or twice, I thought about turning on the radio, but my hand didn't move. A dozen to a hundred times, I thought about starting a conversation, but I didn't do that either.

What we learned the day before brought Legend back to me, and drove Cairo out of reach. Over and over again, his speech rang in my head. Cairo was as sick of being everybody's puppet as I was of being everybody's fool. That's where my understanding stopped.

Why did any of that mean we couldn't be together? Yes, his family wronged mine, but that was his family. Cairo was the first person to eat my guilt. To crack me open, find the darkest spots of my soul, and indulge them like a fine wine. He was the first to show me that I didn't have to be strong and ready to fight at all times.

I could surrender. Be taken. Be broken. And someone I loved would put me back together again.

What we have transcended decades' old betrayals. It was me, Cairo, Arsenio, Legend, Jacques, and Roan now, and the day they found out who they were beyond the Bedlam Boys would be amazing... because that'd be the day they found out they were mine.

I wanted to say all of that to Cairo. None of it came out.

The gap between us was widening and I no longer knew how to reach him. According to Cairo, he didn't want me to try.

"I think we turn here," I rasped. "Beaumont Street. Should be the house on the end."

Cairo acknowledged the break in silence by sliding into the next lane. He turned on Beaumont Street, passing by rows of cute little houses and neat lawns. Jack told me the man we were going to see was an old buddy from the police academy. Rhys Martin retired years ago after being injured on the job.

The two hadn't kept in much contact, but Jack assured me he trusted the man completely. He kept my inheritance safe all these years, so I was inclined to trust him too.

"541," I said. "This is it."

Cairo parked on the curb and climbed out. It seemed like he was waiting for me when he paused in the driveway, though the second I stepped to his side, he walked off—taking the laid cobblestone path to the door.

Mr. Martin's place was as charming as the other homes in the cul-de-sac. He planted a little flower garden on the front lawn, and the fountain by his front door was filled with real, croaking frogs.

Cairo shot out, grabbing my hip. "Wait."

"What? What is it?"

"Look," he murmured.

Following his line of sight, I saw what he noticed instantly. The front door was cracked open.

"Why would the door be open?" I whispered.

"Hang back."

"You're not going in there alone. Let's just go slow."

Cairo jerked his head, agreeing. Together we moved to the door, approaching like it might swing out and attack. I flattened my palm on the wood and pushed. My eyes bugged.

"Mr. Martin? Mr. Martin, are you okay!"

I rushed in, ignoring Cairo's shout. A man lay on the living room carpet. Hands and legs bound, he groaned in the pool of blood dripping down his skull.

"Mr. Martin, can you hear me?" I grasped his chin, gently patting his cheek. Martin's lids fluttered, showing me the white of his eyes. "Cairo, what do you think happened? Was he robbed? We should call the police."

"Pretty sure I know exactly what happened."

Something in his voice made me look up, though Cairo wasn't looking back. Dread filling my bones, I shifted toward the hall entrance, and the man stepping out of a bedroom.

Tall. Raven-haired. Silver wings at the temple. Disarmingly handsome.

"Henry Gold."

"Ivy."

"What are you…?" I looked from him to the man groaning at my knees. "What have you done?"

Henry winced. "This is quite awkward. I intended to be long gone before you arrived."

Breath vacated my lungs. Spinning and twisting, my mind strained to comprehend why the well-dressed private investigator was standing in Rhys Martin's home—

I spotted something behind his back. "What is that?" I cried, shooting up. "What are you hiding!"

"Whoa. Relax." Gold raised his arms, and the large brown envelope, beside his head. "I believe this is what you're looking for."

"How do you know what we're looking for?" Cairo gritted. "Did you fucking tie up and beat this guy?"

Gold didn't respond, which was answer enough.

I scrambled for my phone. "I'm calling the police."

"That's not a good—" Gold moved toward me and suddenly Cairo was in our path.

"No, what's not a good idea is getting any closer to her."

"All right," Gold said, sliding back. "No need for that." The guy was still talking like we walked in on him masturbating and were making a big, prudish deal about it. "I'm only trying to warn Miss de Souza that if she makes that phone call, she won't like the consequences. Jack Sharpe revealed a lot of damning information on the bug I planted in his bedroom."

My veins bled cold.

"It'd be difficult for him to clear your names if he's brought up on charges for the many felonies he committed after your grandmother was murdered."

"A bug," I croaked.

Gold shook his head almost sadly. "I'm afraid so."

"Why would you—?"

"Why would you bug my father's place?" Cairo shouted over me.

"I was paid to by my employer."

"I'm your employer," I cried.

"You were until Steven Ellis discovered I was poking around in his affairs, and paid me twenty times my rate to work for him. He hired me to carry out one simple task." Gold opened the envelope, drawing out an old, yellowed parchment. "Find the deed."

I moved first.

Bolting around Cairo, I launched at him.

"Ah ah!" he shouted, whipping out a lighter. "Stay back or it burns."

"Why are you doing this?! That's all it takes for you to flush your self-respect and reputation down the toilet? Throw some money at the coin whore, and he'll beat up an innocent man and steal from a client!"

Rage snapped his calm. "Don't speak about things you don't understand. Self-respect and a good reputation don't pay my wife's medical bills or send my daughters to college. Ellis was contacted weeks ago by a Sheriff Davidson. He told him that Jack Sharpe was in possession of Abigail de Souza's will, and the deed to Bedlam that she willed her granddaughters.

"The man was on vacation, so now was the time to search his home and find where he hid it."

"Double-dealing sack of shit," Cairo growled.

I could not have said it better. I felt twice as uncaring about his death as I did a minute before.

"I searched his place. Cracked his safe. But I found nothing. In the end, I bugged the house in hopes that when he came back, I'd overhear him mention a cabin, a storage facility, a friend—anywhere he might've stashed it. That worked out so much better than I could believe."

I inched to the side, giving Cairo a clear path. "Congratulations, you're a successful thief. But it's over now, Gold. I'm not letting you walk out of here. Whatever leverage you think you have over Jack Sharpe is worthless. That same recording makes it clear he was under duress. A psychopath that's killed before threatened his son. They'll be lenient."

"He'll still lose his job. His credibility will be worthless. Your boyfriends will go right back in a cell."

"My old man is due for retirement, and prison can be character-building," Cairo returned. "Hand it over."

Gold backed away—my deed hovering dangerously close to the flame. His cool was definitely gone. Henry's eyes darted back and forth, looking for an escape.

"Just give it to me and it can all end here." I tried. "There's nothing Steven Ellis can do with that deed. I signed his contract as Rainey de Souza. That's not who I am. It's all void. He should've told you it was over."

"Oh no, Ivy. Nothing is over. Don't you understand?" he hissed. "Steven Ellis has all this property that he now knows doesn't belong to the false government of a fake town called Bedlam, and when this deed is gone... it won't belong to you either."

My spine slackened, rocking me on my heels. "No... But you can't—"

"I can and I will— Don't move, Sharpe! You'd be shocked how quickly old paper like this goes up."

Cairo stopped his advance, snarling.

"Why are you doing this!" Years of pain and frustration exploded from the pit in my throat. "This is my land. My inheritance. You have no right to take it from me!"

"You have no right to claim it! I heard what you said on that bug about making everyone who wronged you pay. You're thinking like a selfish child. You don't understand the weight of the choices that must be made. Bedlam is a home now. People raise their children there. They attend university there. With one piece of paper, you could wipe that all away in the name of greed, revenge, and claiming a fortune that's too big for one mentally deranged young woman to have."

I jerked like he slapped me.

"Let Ellis bring in his bulldozers. Let the mayor fight back. And let those mature enough to decide the future of Bedlam step in and make the right choice for the people, because that person"—Gold set the deed alight—"is not you."

"No!" Cairo and I shouted.

Cairo tackled him, sending them both flying back into the bedroom. The burning deed soared out of his hand, landing on an area rug where the fire greedily consumed it. I dove after it.

A hand shot out and seized my ankle. Gold yanked me back, dropping me face-first on the hardwood. Pain jarred my jaw.

"Get off her!"

"*Oomph*," Gold gasped. The grip on me loosened.

I scrambled to the deed—the last of my family's legacy. The only thing Gran had left in the world to give me. And frantically slapped the flames, uncaring of the heat and flames scorching my palm.

Sobbing, I lifted the charred scraps of parchment... and watched it crumble in my hands.

The deed was gone. It was over.

I SAT ON THE HOOD OF the car, thighs sizzling from the heat, but I barely felt it. Wordlessly, I watched the police drag out Gold, and the paramedics carry out Mr. Martin.

"I have no regrets," Gold shouted at me. "My girls will still get the money. They'll be taken care of."

I hopped off the car.

"In time you'll see that I helped you too," he cried, raising his voice. "A piece of paper doesn't make Bedlam belong to—"

Slam!

I banged the door shut on his ramblings. The police would have questions for me. I'd answer them after that bastard was gone.

Cairo reclined all the way back in the passenger seat, also waiting for the police to leave. I felt his eyes on me, but couldn't meet them. If I did, I'd cry. He and Gold made me do enough of that for one day.

"It's not over. There have to be other ways to prove ownership. A double-dealing, corrupt piece of trash like that can't just burn some paper and take what's rightfully yours."

"But he can," I said flatly. Black crowded in the edge of my vision. Nothing felt real. "Double-dealing corrupt pieces of trash do it all the time. They steal wills and forge new ones. They put traps in con-tracts. They take advantage of the sick, lost, and naïve with a coldness the level of Cavendish.

"I studied law for years, Cairo. No one is tearing down a town and handing me all the treasure hidden in its soil because I ask nicely. That deed was everything. The Sisters knew it. Steven Ellis knew it."

My hands trembled on the wheel. "For over a hundred years—generation after generation—the de Souzas kept that deed safe. I lost what belonged to my family *again* by trusting the wrong person *again*.

"How? How could I be so stupid? How did I let this happen!" I punched the dash, howling. "It was right there. Right in front of me and I lost it!"

Pressure built in my skull. The black bled over everything. I couldn't see the ambulance anymore. I couldn't see Cairo. Or the point of anything. "I shouldn't have waited," I cried, chest heaving. "I should have come straight here... and... and got what was mine... I should've..."

Darkness latched its hooks and dragged me under. The last thing I heard was Cairo's shout.

Chapter Nine

Three Weeks Later

Paris groaned, clapping her hands over her ears. "Fucking nonstop with that racket! All night and day. I don't understand why the construction crews don't have to obey quiet hours. Don't they want to sleep too!" she bellowed over my head and out the window.

I flicked down to the wrecking crew, leveling her former neighbor's mansion. Foundry was stamped on every piece of equipment from the wrecking ball to their hard hats.

They don't have to obey construction laws because the mayor doesn't actually have the power to enforce anything in this paper town. Just like she couldn't enforce the no-development, digging, drilling, or mining laws that she and her buddies skirted as it suited them.

"Ugh." Paris pulled me up from the window seat and tugged me on the bed with her. She hugged me tight, tucking her head under my chin. "What is going on in this town? Foundry is leveling everything in sight. Quinn Cunningham disappeared. Sheriff Davidson is missing. And my brother..."

Paris trailed off, kindly not going deeper into why I spent the last two and a half weeks staying at a motel instead of in our frat house-turned-home on campus. Henry Gold carried out his threat and told the cops everything Jack Sharpe confessed to. Which meant Jack was suspended and under investigation when the guys returned to Bedlam, refusing to spend another day in hiding when Steven Ellis was on the edge of getting everything he wanted.

They came back, and were promptly arrested for escaping police custody, assaulting a police officer, and their connection to Davidson's disappearance. The second charge was bullshit since Peters knew damn well that the guys were in the cell when she was attacked by three masked strangers, but since the guys wouldn't give up who it was, it all fell on their heads.

All five of them were currently in their childhood homes... under house arrest.

Ankle monitors. Beeping if they went out of range. The whole thing. I could only see them on their front lawns or on the other side of their gates, because I wasn't setting foot in those houses with those *women*. I only came to spend a few nights with Paris because her folks took an impromptu vacation to the coast to escape the construction.

"Everything's wrong, Rainey."

I squeezed my eyes shut. It was a dagger through my chest hearing my sister's name. I failed her in every way. First by not getting what she and Gran died for, and then by not getting the monsters who killed her. Jackson Hyde, Thea Wood, Lincoln Roberts, and Everett Cooper were gone.

I returned to Bedlam with my last mission on my heart—avenging my sister. Armed with their names, and pictures thanks to social media, I assumed it'd be an easy hunt.

I was wrong.

All four of them stopped showing up for classes. They weren't in their dorms, apartments, or frats. Their friends said they hadn't seen or heard from them. The fake accounts and numbers I used to message and call them went unanswered. They'd all gone into hiding, but I knew they were still in Bedlam.

Dante's done a show every night since the demolition started.

"It's all so wrong. How did we get here?"

You can blame me.

"Paris," I began. "There's something that I need to tell you. It won't make much sense at first, but I want to be honest with you. You deserve that."

Lifting her head, she frowned. "Wow, very serious. What's going on?"

My lips parted, and I told her everything. Well, almost everything. I told her that after Gran was murdered, I teetered on the edge of sanity. Losing my sister tipped me over for good.

Paris asked a lot of questions about the Rainey period, then even more questions about the person I claimed to be now. I left out the part about Zoey on the bridge with a crossbow, and said it just all came back to me one night. That sparked another round of questions about if the guys knew the truth, and how they handled it.

At the end of my last sentence, I stared at her and she stared at me. I never noticed she shared her brother's ability to hide what she was thinking behind empty, swirling eyes—until that moment.

"Paris, please," I broke. "Don't be angry. I didn't lie to you on purpose. After everything came back, I didn't know how to explain it to you when it barely made sense to me. I lost myself for years. How do you tell your best friend that without her thinking you're"—my lips twisted—"mentally deranged?"

"Hey, don't say that. I don't think anything like that." Paris nudged my shoulder. "I won't lie. This is weird. I'm not sure what I'm supposed to say or do in a situation like this, but... I've also never lost my family in one tragedy after another. First, your parents. Then, your grandmother. Then, your little sister."

I dropped my gaze, shoulders shaking.

"It's understandable that a part of you wanted—needed to hold on to Rainey. Letting her go meant you had no one." Paris rested her hand on mine, surprising me. "I think the truth came back to you, I-Ivy, because now you know you're not alone anymore. You have me,

Amy, Zara, Presley, and Elise. You have my brother and your guys. You're healing, Ivy."

I let out a chuckle that was more a sob. "Doesn't f-feel like healing."

"Getting stronger hurts. Your lungs burn. Muscles ache. You sweat and wheeze and want to give up every day, but then you cross the finish line, and all that pain is amazing. Because it means you accomplished something. It hurts now." Paris's grip tightened on me. "But when you come out on the other side of this, you'll know what it was all for."

Swiping my eyes, I got a hold of myself as her speech penetrated, sinking into the deep hole of despair that refused to believe there was a brighter side to losing your entire family and the inheritance they left you.

"You're really not angry with me? I thought you'd throw me out and yell at the freak to stay away from you."

Paris rolled her eyes, sighing. "Cairo. He handled it like a jerk and that's what made you afraid to tell everyone else the truth, isn't it?"

I inclined my head. "Pretty much."

"Ugh. I love that guy, but you can be sure that whatever his reaction is to something, I will have the opposite and *sane* reaction. We're good, Ivy. You never have to worry about that."

I jumped on her, hugging her so tight, she grunted.

"Gosh, woman, alright. I guess I can throw you one fuck since we're riding on all these fluffy feelings, but just one, and don't go falling in love with me."

I busted up laughing—hugging her even tighter. "I'm going to pass on that, but I'll hold on to the IOU."

"Course you will. I knew you were into me."

"It's because you're way more like Cairo than either of you wants to admit. I don't care that you have different fathers and were born a year apart. You're clones."

"Take that back."

"No."

She scrambled out from under me and seized a pillow. "Take it back, de Souza."

"Oooh," I crowed, reaching for one of my own. "You're gonna have to make me, Keller."

I ducked the first swing and came back fast. Thus began the pillow fight to end all pillow fights.

For one entire night—thirteen hours exactly—I forgot I was still in the lungs-burning, sweat-in-my-eyes, dying-to-lie-down-and-give-up part of the race. I forgot about Gold, Ellis, the Sisters, and even the demolition because for the first time in over two weeks, they didn't work through the night.

Paris and I stayed up watching movies and eating junk. After she fell asleep, I snuck into the bathroom and called my guys. Arsenio told me to send him a video of me masturbating to get him through the night. Jacques listed every legal and illegal method he'd been researching to get my inheritance back. Roan promptly dropped his pants and initiated phone sex. Legend tried to tempt me into coming over, laying it on thick about my promise not to let him sleep alone.

Cairo didn't pick up the phone.

The next morning, I put my things in the back of Paris's car, along with my backpack and homework. I was going straight to the motel when my last class of the day was out. Her parents would be back from their trip that afternoon. The last thing my lifted spirits needed was for the sight of that cold-blooded schemer to harpoon them.

"When are you going to tell Zara, Amy, and the girls?" Paris bounced in her seat, humming along to a decent song on the radio. "Do you want to?"

"I do. It hurts every time they call me Rainey. Plus, the longer I keep silent, the more I feel like I'm lying." I watched the town zip by me, and all the demolition equipment and workers gearing up for another day. "This is a hard story to tell over and over. Even if they take it well, they'll look at me differently. When someone has a complete and total mental breakdown, people hold their breath, wondering when the next one is coming."

"You need to give our friends more credit. Like I'd have anything to do with someone like that. You wouldn't either if they ever gave off that vibe. Admit it," she breezed. "You love us. Have since the first night we hung out. You know we have your back."

I couldn't fault Paris's gift for knowing character. Jacques told me Zara was one of the names on our list of nine. That brief second when a biting chill leaked from her soul, stiffening his spine, reminded him of me, of all people. He said I had the same look the night I jumped from the bridge... and the night I killed Quinn.

Despite what he said, none of it made me wary or question Zara. Like I told him, going through what she did changes a person. Doesn't make her bad, broken, or dangerous. She's different, and she'll always look at the world differently. Finding out all this about Zara just made me think she was someone I could talk to about the things others wouldn't understand.

"I'll think about a good time to tell them. Soon," I promised. "This town is so overrun with secrets and lies. I'm tired of living that way."

"Amen."

Paris drove into the student parking lot beside the poli-sci building. We said bye, going our separate ways to class for Paris, and the student union for me to get a latte and a comfortable spot while I killed an hour.

Drink in hand, I didn't bother looking toward the deck. I didn't want to be out there if I wasn't sitting at the Bedlam Boy table while Arsenio discreetly fondled me. I hated that the judge—not Judge Stone—refused to extend the limits of their ankle monitors to campus. She said they had to watch lectures and hand in their assignments online, and they'd shut up and be grateful Legend's lawyer worked out such a good deal. They deserved to be awaiting trial in prison for attacking cops.

If that judge knew half the horrible things Davidson did, she'd save the outrage for someone who deserved it. I dropped my things on a study table on the second floor and got comfy. *Even though Jack told everyone he lured him into a trap, where he was held and tortured by masked men, the effort the new acting sheriff, Peters, was putting into finding them said volumes.*

They thought Jack was lying to cover for his son. Gold got what he wanted. Jack's credibility was shot.

I was losing my brighter mood fast, so then was as good a time as any. Tugging out my laptop, I pulled up Dante's website and hit play on his latest show. I was hardly going to interrupt my time with Paris to let that man drip his poisonous voice in my ear, but now the reprieve was over. If there was any chance he'd give a clue to where he was hiding or what he planned, I'd be listening for it.

"Evening, Bedlamites, it's day eighteen of the invasion, and yesterday, we watched three homes that have stood for almost one hundred years get reduced to rubble. I'm told they'll take down Westchester Drumlins next week.

"Did your stomach just turn? Did you ask yourself how can they do this, and why doesn't someone stop them? The answer is: they can do this because you're not stopping them. It's up to us to fight *back*,

Bedlamites!" The sudden shout pounded my eardrums. "If you don't fight back against oppression, you're complicit in it.

"Steven Ellis is hosting a town hall meeting this weekend to spout his bullshit that he's doing good for the town, and he'll do even more if the rest of you sell your properties at his suspiciously high offers. Go to that meeting and let him know what we think of—!"

My earbud popped out of my ear. "Listening to anything interesting?"

My breath, my body, my pulse... stopped.

Rigidly, I turned in my seat, gazing up at a tall, fit guy with short dark hair, a square jaw, loam-brown eyes, and a pleasing smile that only made his features more charming.

"Dante."

His smile widened. "Please, we're in public. Call me Lincoln."

Setting down his own drink, he drew out the seat across from me, then sat down and started sipping like we were meeting for a coffee date. After all this time. The searching, the letters, the mental torture, and the actual torture.

"Try something, Roberts. I promise you it won't go down the way you think."

He laughed. "Whoa, easy. I'm not going to try anything. Why do you think I met you in a public place?" Lincoln swept out his hands. "Lots of people around. Plus, two security guards right over there. We can have this discussion civilly."

"I am going to civilly bash your skull in with this laptop, and then tell everyone you told me you had a bomb in your bag and I feared for my life." I closed my laptop, settling the weight on my palms. "Hold still."

Roberts howled, flinging his head back. "Fair enough. If your choice is to sacrifice me, I understand, but you should know you have other choices. We could work together instead. Take back what was stolen from us. From you."

"Excuse me? I could not have heard that correctly. Did you just say we could work together?"

"Yes," he said, laughter draining away. "I mean it, de Souza. Ellis is tearing down Bedlam because he called the mayor's bluff, and she blinked first." Lincoln leaned in, making me snap back. He dropped his voice. "We thought we could stop this without you, but Ellis has ignored every letter we sent. Even when we proved we weren't bluffing."

"What did you do?" I forced through clenched teeth.

"Nothing you wouldn't approve of. Foundry makes their members sign a morality clause. We sent the board, three reporters, and five national news outlets proof of shady deals, bribes, and corrupt business practices. That was a week ago and nothing—"

"Get the fuck out of my face!" My shout broke the normal hum of the union, snapping a dozen pairs of eyes on us. "We are not going to sit here and have some friendly chat. You have five seconds to get away from me, or no number of witnesses will stop me."

Roberts didn't blink. "Okay. Five seconds? Time me, and if you don't want to hear what I have to say when I'm done, I'll tell everyone I said there was a bomb in my bag and I threatened your life. Ready?"

"You—"

"You are the rightful owner of Bedlam and Ellis is digging up your millions."

The laptop slipped through my grip.

"So?" he pushed when the silence spread. "Should I keep going?"

I didn't speak. Wasn't sure I could if I tried. I figured the Black Letter Crew had to know about the deed since Cavendish did. I just wasn't expecting to hear the truth of it from one of the beasts who killed my sister.

"I'm going to take that as a yes," he continued. "We tried to do this for you, but Ellis is too protected. We gambled that he didn't tell the rest of his board what's special about Bedlam. We saw how that gamble paid off when they made Ellis's corruption scandal disappear. The only thing that can stop this now is you claiming your inheritance, and forcing that shit out of our home. You need to do that while there's still a Bedlam left standing."

Nothing came from my side of the table.

"Shit, you really didn't know about any of this, did you?" Cursing, he tossed his head. "That's how the Bedlam Boys wanted it. I knew we should've gotten them away from you sooner. Maybe Davidson did do something right—" Lincoln raised a brow. "I assume he's dead? Quinn too?"

Lincoln nodded like my face told him the answer. "Figured. When they and the sheriff all disappeared on the same night, we knew you got one or both of them to talk. When they didn't come back, we also knew you didn't have use for them anymore.

"But while you were questioning them, did they tell you what the *Bedlam Boys* didn't? Because here's the truth, de Souza. Their mothers are in a group called the Society of Sisters. After the revolt..."

Dante launched into the entire history. From Amadeo de Souza, to the end of the Men of Honor and the rise of the Sisters.

"Then the deed that survived the decades until your grandmother died and the Sisters got hold of it. Cavendish told us they destroyed it and you were no longer any use to us. After you lost it and started calling yourself Rainey, he said to leave you to rot. You'd blow your brains out soon enough."

His words traveled in my ear, stirred no reaction, then faded into vapor.

"But then, around the start of last year, Zoey dug up something and started thinking Scott was lying to us. He said the deed was gone, but one day his girlfriend left her alone in their house to wait for him, and she found research he hid under a floor panel. It was all these private investigator reports on Jack Sharpe and his associates. On top of whether or not the mentally incompetent can leave a will.

"It was obvious he was still scheming to get a deed that supposedly didn't exist. Zoey confronted him and he spilled the whole thing. The Sisters decided to go with mutually assured destruction instead of outright destroying the deed. If we didn't behave ourselves, they'd tell the world the truth about everything. None of us would get a thing."

My eyes narrowed a fraction. *He thinks the Sisters are behind making Cavendish back off? They don't know Jack acted alone?*

"Eventually, he accepted there was no way the Men of Honor could get their hands on Bedlam without the Sisters bringing shit down on all our heads. So he decided if he couldn't have it, no one would."

"What does that mean?" I forced through the needles in my throat.

"It's why he goaded you into killing him. The plan was to trigger the bomb ourselves, except you'd go down hardest of all." His light pools held no trace of deceit. "After you killed him, Zoey would come forward as a witness. They'd find all this evidence in your old barn proving you were obsessed with Cavendish because you thought he killed your grandmother.

"Everything would be there. The real history of Bedlam. Amadeo de Souza. The Men of Honor. A copy of your grandmother's fake will putting Scott in charge of everything. And notes tracking a missing deed that stated you owned everything.

"Once all that hit national news, you'd be in prison, the Sisters would lose control of their stolen town, and the government would slap the town off the land and claim the riches underneath. Cavendish's final sacrifice in the game... was to ensure we all lost."

"But I'm still here," I said cautiously. "No arrest. No prison."

"That's because we protected you, Ivy." Lincoln reached across the table, palm up. "We didn't know who you were when you became one of us. We knew the first Men of Honor owed their existence to one man—their leader and founder. We didn't know that man was your ancestor. Cavendish lied so we'd never guess how important you are, or tell *you* how important you are.

"After he ordered us to kill your sister and you fell apart, the lying bastard finally told us you were *the* de Souza, but with the deed lost to us, you lost to yourself, and what you'd do to us if you ever got your memory back, there was no way you'd take your rightful place as leader of the Men of Honor."

What did he just say?

"He made us your enemies before we ever had a chance, and then he asked us to take it further and destroy you. We let the traitor die and become an unsolved murder instead."

My head spun. This was it? This was the reason Cavendish forced me to kill him? In a nihilistic temper tantrum because he couldn't get his hands on my land or my money, so no one else would have it either?

"But Zoey," I cried. "You didn't want me in prison, but you wanted me to jump off a bridge? What fucking sense does that make!"

That still outstretched hand balled into a fist. "Zoey acted on her own. She took over the Men of Honor after Cavendish, and she wasn't interested in stepping aside for you. According to her, you were still a traitor for choosing Cairo Sharpe over us. We were fighting about it, but I didn't know she was planning to get rid of you for good until it was almost too late. I stopped her on the bridge," he said, thumping his chest. "I protected you. Me. As I'll continue to do until and after you take your rightful place."

"Stop saying that," I snapped, throwing up my hands. "I don't have a rightful place. I'm not, nor will I ever be, your leader. You killed my sister!"

"We were lied to."

"Think I give a shit? Do you think that erases the memory of you guys laughing and making jokes while you ripped her apart?" Burning wetness blurred his impassive handsomeness. Another evil joke. Monsters should look like monsters. "You're going the same way as your buddy, Quinn, and that's a promise. Want to know how she died or should I surprise you?"

Roberts shrugged. "Surprise me. I don't give a shit about Quinn. She was becoming difficult," he said. "Didn't like that every version of this ended with us getting rid of the Bedlam Boys."

My heart thumped an extra beat.

"We didn't tell her to get involved with those guys. Legend decided she was their next girlfriend, and she said yes thinking she could get something on them. Complete waste of time," he said. "They didn't say, do, or leave anything incriminating around the whole time she was in their house.

"The only thing she accomplished was falling for them. She hated that you both stole them and were the reason they had to go." He inclined his head. "Except for Banks of course. Quinn only tolerated him because of Legend. She arranged for him to get stabbed during that brawl. Damn sure wasn't pleased when he walked away with a little cut."

Eyes bugging, that day came into sharp focus. Quinn storming up and loudly shouting Roan's various fetishes until Cairo shut her up. She went straight to attacking Roan even though they all dumped her. No love lost there.

But to think she got one of her buddies to try to kill him? Every day I regret her death even less than I already do.

"Maybe what Quinn hated is that you guys don't make any sense. Why would you have to get rid of them for me? I'm in no danger from them."

The corner of his eyes wrinkled as quickly as his lips twitched. The flash of hatred and contempt was so fast, if I blinked, I would've missed it.

"How can you say that after what I've told you? They've conspired with their mothers to steal what rightfully belongs to you. They took you. *Humiliated* you. You're leader of this town, and they put a leash on you and forced you on your knees. None of that was kink or coincidence," he hissed. "They wanted to break you down and keep you dependent on them, so that if you ever discovered the truth, you wouldn't try to fight against your *masters*.

"It's disgusting," he spat. "A Man of Honor bows to no one. They are beholden to no one. They had to be sacrificed anyway to end the Sisters' legacy once and for all. They all had just the one son. No daughters, and now there will never be any granddaughters. Their treatment of you sealed their fate."

I gaped at him, shaking my head in complete disbelief. "Do you actually buy any of the garbage you're spouting? My protector? Don't make me laugh."

"It's alright if you don't believe me now, because I will subject myself to any form of test you ask of me. We all will," he said, holding out his damn hand again. "You are the true leader of the Men of Honor, and the rightful owner of this town. Others in our group attacked you out of greed and selfishness, but those that remain are loyal to you. We will prove it—simply tell us how." Dante got to his feet. "Once we trust each other again, we can move on to what really matters. Getting Steven Ellis the fuck out of our town.

"When you're ready, send a message through the site," he tossed over his shoulder, walking off. "Use your own name this time."

"Why wait?" I jumped up. "You want to prove something to me, then prove you're not like the rest of these cowardly thieves who steal and lie and hurt innocent people to get what they want. Tell the whole town who you are, *Dante*, and what the new Men of Honor want from Bedlam. Until then, don't expect to survive the next time you ambush me."

Dante didn't slow his stride much less acknowledge that he heard me.

I watched after him long after he disappeared around the corner. His revelations assaulted my mind one after the other. It couldn't be true. This was some kind of hideous trick, and I wasn't looking far enough to see the endgame. Cavendish *and* Zoey *and* Quinn set against me as enemies, but I was supposed to believe the other four in the Black Letter Crew had a huge crush on me? They were *protecting* me?

Roberts was filling my ear with more evil, twisted manipulations. *But why? What does he think he can get from me?*

Gathering my things, I left in the opposite direction—fishing out my phone just outside the double doors. He answered on the third ring.

"Cairo, don't hang up," I rushed out. "You won't believe this. Dante came to see me—in person. He told me the most ridiculous lies, said he'd prove his loyalty to me, then strolled off. What do—?"

"What you do is get over here," he growled. "Now."

He didn't have to tell me twice. There was no chance of my professors seeing me that day after Roberts sat down.

Forty-five minutes later, I was sitting on Cairo's front porch, swaying on the chair swing as he rocked us back and forth with the heel of his foot. I flicked down to his ankle and the monitor. I kept telling myself it could be worse. They could all be in the correctional facility three hours away, but even so, none of this should've happened. They were falsely arrested over a man I killed, and then arrested again for escaping a jail cell they weren't supposed to be in.

None of them gave a hint that they blamed me, though they didn't have to. I was blaming myself plenty for the six of us.

"Stay away from him."

"He came to me, Cairo. Not the other way around."

He shot me a look. "I know you, de Souza. Right now you're thinking of a way you can use this to fulfill your final vendetta. They killed your sister, and now they're here playing nice and spinning bullshit about loyalty and protection. You think you can meet them somewhere alone next time, and take them out.

"Those four didn't get this far by being stupid. They're not walking into any traps, and they're not doing this to help *you* get back what *you* lost. This is all about one legacy—the Men of Honor's."

"I know all the things you're telling me, Cairo. They obviously don't know the deed is gone for good, but all this has to be a plot to do what Cavendish couldn't, and get their hands on it. I just don't know why Roberts believes this is the way to do it. He knows Quinn and Davidson didn't walk away from us. There's no chance I'd have anything to do with the people who killed my sister, but he sat there and spun all that crap about 'putting me in my rightful place.'"

I shuddered. "It was creepy the way he spoke, Cairo. Like I was his possession and he wouldn't have anyone hurt me... other than him."

"You know who you belong to," he said, sweeping over the yard. "And it's not him."

Is it you? Can it be you again?

The questions didn't leave my lips. I had enough rejection from Cairo to break my heart for a lifetime. I couldn't hear no again.

"Anyway, Dante said more important things mixed in with his lies. He said they plan to sacrifice all the Bedlam Boys. Quinn told us they were framing you for murder, but I think he told her that to get her to stop arguing for your lives. He wants you guys dead." Our gazes locked. "I could hear it in his voice. The Sisters' legacy dies with the five of you."

"We know who they are now. We'll take them out long before that. You don't need to worry about us. What you need to do is get your stuff and put it in the guest bedroom. You're staying here until those black letter dogs are put down."

I shook my head. "I'd take you up on your offer if you actually wanted me here. You don't," I stated, blunt as a truck. "This is all about you wrapping up our unfinished business, so you can walk away from me without looking back. Don't ask me to play along, Cairo." His calm pools reflected my glare. "That's the cruelest thing you could ever do."

"My blood wronged yours. If I drop it and walk away just because Gold set a piece of paper on fire, I was never serious about making it right in the first place. I will pay what's owed, but that's not why you're going to stop arguing with me, get your shit, and sleep in that guest room.

"You're doing it because the insane, homicidal bastard who abducted and tortured my father, sat down and had lattes with you today to prove he's not afraid of you, or getting caught. You're not going to be sitting in some crap-ass motel room alone the next time he comes to visit."

"Cairo—"

"Get your stuff, Ivy. Now."

It was my name that did it. Cairo gave me his father's keys and sent me off. I returned with the little I had in the world and brought it into the guest room.

In the Sharpe household, the guest room was a storage space for old case files, Cairo's childhood toys, and a full-size bed beneath a photo of a young Cairo fishing with his dad. I dropped on the sheets and a soft sigh escaped me. The downy comforter was soft, warm, and clean like the mattress underneath. This was already light-years better than the motel.

Knock. Knock.

I jerked awake, squinting blearily at cute little Cairo and his missing teeth. Goodness, I was so comfortable, I passed out fully clothed on top of the bed. That's what happens when sleepovers at Paris's don't include sleep, but do include staying up all night talking and watching movies. As well as early morning phone sex with Roan.

Someone knocked again, dragging me onto my feet. "Cairo?" I called. "Cairo, someone's at the door."

Shuffling out, the sound of running water told me where he was. I left him to his shower and padded across the living room, rising on tiptoe to see who it was. My light, dreamy mood evaporated.

I yanked the door open. "What the fuck do you want?"

Steven Ellis lifted a brow. He was smooth and refined standing there in a pressed, bespoke suit, polished loafers, and the self-assured smile he gave to his sons hanging on his lips. The two personal bodyguards behind him looked a lot more serious.

"Quite a greeting. Come now, young lady. There's no need for bad manners."

"There's every fucking need for bad manners, you thieving, gutless, corrupt, impotent loser. How dare you come here? No one in this house has anything to say to you. Fuck off!"

Ellis shot out, smacking his hand on the wood to stop me slamming the door. "Easy," he said. "I understand your anger, Miss de Souza, but it was you I was looking for."

"Me? How did you know I was here?"

He nodded to the men behind him. "My friends have been keeping a close eye on you ever since you resorted to harassment."

"What? I didn't—"

"I came to return something that belongs to you."

He snapped his fingers, and a guard stepped forward and placed something in his hands. He handed it to me.

"Belongs to me?" I repeated, screwing up my face at the bundle of opened black letters. "I didn't send you these. That has nothing to—"

"Enough games." His voice was slippery and smooth like a black adder slithering over the rocks. "You were upset about the steps I took to secure Bedlam's future, so the resourceful young lady that you are, you hired another private investigator to dig up this fiction on me. A loser indeed. A *sore* loser."

I flicked from the letters to Ellis. "I'm telling you, I have no idea what you're talking about. But if those letters are filled with *fiction*, why would I need a private investigator to make it up for me? Sounds like someone else discovered the real you, saggy-jowled, floppy-dick bastard."

The vein under his brow twitched. "I know you sent these, and now you know that blackmail will not work. My resources trump those of a homeless orphan."

I took the letters, and flung them off the porch. "You don't know anything. I don't sneak around, use PIs to commit crimes, or deliver threats through the mail. Unlike you, I face my enemies head-on. Now get off this porch and go find a pit to fall in. Should be easy? Your crews are tearing up the town."

He swung out, stopping the slammed door again. "No, Miss de Souza. Not the whole town. Only the most favorable places... like your farm."

I froze. "Excuse me?"

His smirk widened, squeezing a band around my chest. "I was willing to be civil and uphold my end of the contract, but then you led my sons into the Bedlam Boys' ambush, and sent lies to reporters and my board. It isn't wise to behave like someone with nothing to lose when your opponent still has a card left to play."

"What did you do!"

"What I was well within my rights to do," he replied. "The sale of de Souza Farm went through days ago. There were hideous, broken-down structures on my property... so I burned them down."

A roaring pressed on my ears, muffling his horrible, serpentine voice—but not enough.

"There were a few items in the barn that looked to be valuable. I considered selling them but, in the end..." Ellis snapped his fingers again and a guard handed him a bag from behind his back. Ellis dumped the contents at my feet.

"No..."

"The real estate agent mentioned these were gifts from your grandmother. She said she had to get them back to you, but I graciously offered to take that chore off her hands."

"No." My face crumpled. Dropping on my knees, trembling fingers picked up the pieces of the carbon arrows.

"The rest didn't survive the fire."

Salty wet drops stained the arrowhead. In the hazy days I was Rainey, I melded her past with mine. Rainey did love archery. It was one thing the social butterfly older sister had in common with her bookworm, sci-fi-loving little sister. But the expert archer was me.

I practiced every morning. I squealed with joy every birthday when Gran brought in another huge, bow-sized present.

I stood behind my baby sister, positioning her tiny hands and teaching her to use her first bow.

This one was hers. I stroked the splintered pieces. *She always favored the carbon.*

"Why-y?" The word choked on a sob. "Why would you do this?"

"Because you and your thug friends don't seem to understand that I'm not a man to be messed with. You've lost. No desperate attempts at blackmail, or laughable threats are going to change that. You—"

"Why!" Screaming, I reared and struck—punching Ellis in the spot that was in closest reach.

"Argh!"

He doubled over, hands flying to his crotch. I pounced on him, bringing him the rest of the way down.

"WHY!!!" Wrapping my hands around his neck, I smashed his head on the wood.

"Hey!" His guards sprang into action—grabbing and pawing at me. I wrenched my arm free and buried my fist in his gut.

One of the hulking beasts tackled me, sending us both toppling over the threshold. I gasped under his crushing weight, but still I fought to get to Ellis.

"That's enough."

The guard stopped abruptly—doing nothing to fight off my pummeling.

"You guys aren't too smart, making trouble in a sheriff's house."

Chest heaving and sobbing, I flipped over, landing immediately on Cairo carrying nothing but a towel slung low on his hips, and a gun. His hand was steady aiming it between my captor's eyes.

"Get off her, then get the fuck off my property. Or I shoot you. Trust me, I won't go down for getting rid of you, Ellis. Not in this town."

I wasn't sure if Ellis heard him. He was still coughing and sputtering on his back.

"Easy, boy," said the guard on top of me. "No one wants—"

"Reach for that and you're dead. All you need to do is stand up, keep your hands where I can see them, and back out the fucking door.

"Now!"

Slowly, they did as he said. Climbing off me, the guys picked up their pale boss and carried him to his idling town car.

"Ivy, what happened?" Cairo helped me up. "What was he doing here?"

Sobbing, I shook him off and ran. I slammed the door on his question, flinging myself onto the bed.

I thought there was nothing more Ellis could take from me. I was wrong.

He could still rip out my soul, and spread it as broken pieces on the welcome mat.

I CURLED UP IN THE middle of the bed where I'd been for hours. Cairo stuck his head in a few times, watched me, and walked back out. The guy wasn't built to give comfort. His idea of giving me a treat was chasing me through the woods and fucking me like an animal wherever we dropped.

Not even that could distract me from the sight of my grandmother's last gifts to me and Rainey in splintered pieces on the ground.

At some point, it was Jack who came in carrying a bowl of chicken noodle soup and crackers. He set it on a tray next to me, where it quietly turned into a congealed bowl of cold, soppy noodles.

Buzz. Buzz.

I glanced at the screen. *Arsenio.*

Cairo didn't know how to talk to me, so it seemed he was calling everyone else to try. Jacques, Roan, and Legend each called twice already. Arsenio was on his third.

Why won't they leave me alone? Why wouldn't everyone leave me the fuck alone!?

Between Steven Ellis, the Black Letter Crew, and the Society, they've taken everything and everyone I care about. How low do they need to bring one twentysomething former farm girl who has never done a fucking thing to them in their life?

Was there another portion of my life that I blocked out, where I committed the horrible acts that earned this karma?

"Help me understand this," I cried, clutching the arrowhead. "Why us, Rainey? Why couldn't we have a happy ending?"

Buzz. Buzz.

"Ugh! Leave me alone!" Snatching up my phone, I swung back to lob it at the wall.

"Ivy? Ivy, are you there?" Paris's voice poured out of the speakers. "Ivy, whatever you're doing, drop it and turn on Dante's show."

I halted.

"You won't believe what he's saying. I mean, it can't be true, right? No one would confess to..."

I dropped the phone, flipping over to get my laptop. Quickly I pulled up his website, hitting play on the live stream.

"—corrupted its history. The Men of Honor were formed to protect this town from the people who would exploit it then, and the man who is exploiting it now. We—Jackson Hyde, Thea Wood, Everett Cooper, and I, Lincoln Roberts—are not your enemies.

"We're not here to run through the town, snatching up virgins, and terrorizing the innocent. We are here to make the hard choices to protect Bedlam."

My eyes widened with every word. I put the phone back to my ear. "Paris," I said, breaking into her chatter. "What has he been saying?"

"He's been admitting to all kinds of crazy things! He said that Jeremy Ellis hired Zoey Mariner to kill the Bedlam Boys in payback, so he killed her and dumped her body off Chaney Bridge."

My jaw went slack.

"After that, he tried to force my brother and his friends into getting rid of the Ellises by having *Davidson* abduct and hold him hostage! But Davidson turned on him and arrested the Bedlam Boys on a false charge. He thought he could force him to kill Jack by making my brother and his friends useless to him, and therefore making Jack a liability.

"Why is he saying these things?" she burst out. "I've known Lincoln for forever. What is wrong with him? Could he really have done this? And if he did, why is he confessing to the entire town!"

My jaw worked trying to find an explanation for Paris, but even though I knew, I didn't have one.

"It's alright if you don't believe me now, because I will subject myself to any form of test you ask of me. We all will."

He's not really doing this. Confessing to crime after crime just because I told him to. This was beyond proving loyalty. All four of them would lose everything to get me to... to what? What did this guy think would happen now?

"—Ellis is corrupt," Dante continued. "The last business he invested in, AgriProspects, wasn't seeing good enough returns. The piece of shit embezzled from the pension fund, then swam clear before the ship went down, doing nothing as hundreds of employees lost everything.

"You're asking yourself if the things we've done are evil, wrong, or unjustified. What you should be asking is what a man like Steven Ellis is doing here? A shady, corrupt, money-hungry robot in a skin-suit isn't tearing our town down for our benefit. You should wonder what he really wants from us, and what we can afford to lose when he inevitably bails out, and leaves us alone in the sinking wreckage of Bedlam."

The broadcast cut off, making me jerk.

"What do you think he means?" Paris whispered. "I mean, yeah, Steven Ellis is another developer determined to take advantage of Bedlam's untouched beauty, but the guy is talking like there's something more sinister about it. He tried to force my brother to *kill him*. Who in their right mind goes that far to stop development?"

"Someone very determined," I replied, gazing down at the arrowhead, "and even more dangerous."

"Is Cairo in danger? Are they all in danger? Dammit, Ivy, they're sitting ducks in those houses."

"No one is messing with the Bedlam Boys." I twirled the piece of carbon, thoughts rushing, swirling, twisting, then aligning themselves in the right order. The right plan. "They keep trying and it never works out for them."

"You're right, of course," she breathed. "The cops are going to find Lincoln and all his psycho friends. Fuck's sake, the guy saves my brother's life, then tortures his dad and tries to turn him into a murderer. What happens to a person that they become that messed up?"

"They lose everything that matters," I rasped, knuckles whitening around the arrow. "So the whole world pays for it."

"Well, he's sick." Paris continued on unaware of what was happening on the other end of the phone.

I clicked on the site's email icon and typed out my message, under my own name.

"Whatever he lost, he doesn't get a free pass to hurt people. He for fuck sure doesn't get to mess with my family."

I hit send, then pushed my laptop away. The chime came as I prepared to close the top.

I opened Dante's message—returned with frightening speed. He knew I'd come to him. He was waiting.

"You're right, Paris. He doesn't get a free pass to hurt people." Steven Ellis floated before my vision. "He doesn't get to mess with my family."

The answer is yes. We will do whatever you desire.

-Dante

"He'll pay for what he's done."

Chapter Ten

I left Jack's bedroom and collided into Cairo's chest. I bounced off without moving him an inch.

"What were you doing in there?"

"We were talking." I sidestepped him and found Cairo in front of me again.

"Talking about what? Why was the door locked?"

"Was it?" I said, tone light. "I didn't notice I locked it. Kind of an automatic thing."

He grasped my chin, lifting my gaze higher than the pecs I was lying to. "What were you talking about?"

"Jack was just giving me tips on what to say at the town meeting today. You know—from his experience as sheriff and a longtime resident. Bedlam has a low crime rate and mom-and-pop shops thrive here. We'll lose all that if we let Ellis turn us into Hunter's Crest."

His eyes narrowed to slits. "And...?"

"Cairo, I don't know what you want me to say. They're giving time for us to voice our concerns, and I wanted to make sure I've got the best speech to sway people. The only thing we have in our favor is that Ellis can't swing his wrecking balls at homes and businesses with people inside. Our last hope is to stop oblivious people from selling to him." I tapped my phone and the speech on it. "That's what I'm going to do."

He didn't move. Cairo's green orbs swept my face, searching for a hint of deceit. I gazed back steadily.

"You come back here straight after."

"Where else would I go?"

Brushing past him, the back of our hands skimmed each other's. I hooked my pinkie around his—just for the barest second—and Cairo... curled around mine.

Letting go, I hurried downstairs and out the door before the urge to stop and think about what I was doing caught up to me. What had to happen next was out of my hands. Their fate was sealed like mine was now.

Fate is what breaks us.

I passed people on the walk to town hall—all of us headed in the same direction. Except for Ruckus Royale, this was going to be the most attended event of the year. Steven Ellis was going to tell everyone how many piles of money he would heap on them for selling up and moving out of this stagnant small town, while the other speakers tried to explain why an overflowing retirement fund was a bad thing.

Yeah, everyone likes watching a lost cause.

They don't know what they're in for. Today will not go down how they think.

The barn-sized, steepled building rose over the horizon, beckoning into its overflowing space. Town hall was actually a cozy little space with seating below and above. They softened the clinical white walls by mixing in a little warm, brown earth tones. In addition to fancy reddish-gold carpet, the town hall was perfect for formal events like prom—which they held there every year.

Not that I've ever been to prom. That life wasn't an option for the de Souza sisters because decades ago, a corrupt judge tossed a few acres of farmland at my great-grandmother and told her to be grateful to eke out a living from the soil, while said judge got rich off her property.

My lips curled at Mayor Creed, Judge Stone, Dean Banks, and Cynthia St. James all standing off to the side, talking about something that wrinkled their manicured brows. As if on cue, Nora left her seat beside her husband and inserted herself in the group.

I forced myself to look away from them and find a seat. Wouldn't do any good to draw attention to myself too soon.

Up front, a long table had been set out, covered with nice linens, and prepared with water and little cookies for Ellis and all of Foundry's board. We'd finally get to see the people behind Ellis, who helped him carve up our town to make themselves rich.

Sliding my bag off my shoulder, I found a spot in the third row and sat down. Paris said she wasn't coming, but a scan of the crowd showed me Zara, Elise, and Amy made it. Actually, a good number of university students were in the crowd. Jeremy Ellis promised them clubs, restaurants, theaters, high-end shopping, and a never-ending party on and off campus. No doubt they were here to listen to Senior repeat more of the same lies.

"Hello." A woman stepped to the podium. She wore a clean-cut gray pantsuit, stylish thin-framed glasses, and her hair in a tight bun. I didn't recognize her, so I guessed she was with the Hunter's Crest crew.

"Evening, everyone. We're due to begin soon, so if you could take your seats. My name is Judith and I'm one of the employees representing Foundry tonight. Allow me to take this chance to remind you that we're hosting a small reception after the meeting. There will be wine, cheese, and finger foods. Thank you all so much for joining us tonight." She beamed. "We're happy to have you."

A snort sounded to my right. "Love how she's speaking to us like we're the guests instead of the other way around."

I bobbed my head. I didn't recognize the short, grizzled man next to me, but I liked him already.

The speaker stepped away from the podium as the side door opened. One by one, Steven Ellis and the Foundry board members filed out. My brows shot up my forehead at the last two people to enter.

Jeremy and Micah Ellis.

They smiled and waved at the crowd, then plopped down on seats on either side of their father and helped themselves to cookies.

It was bold as hell having two of the guys who were out on bail for beating Roan into a hospital bed, strut in here like nothing happened. That was all the proof I needed that this whole meeting was a show. Ellis believed he won. Why not parade his spawn around the town that violently rejected them? They were the kings of Bedlam now.

Eventually, chatter ceased and everyone settled into their seats, looking upon Steven Ellis as he took his place at the podium. It was picturing him howling on the floor, clutching his crotch that cooled my rage enough to keep me in my seat. Everything in me screamed to wipe that smirk permanently off his face.

"Good evening, everyone, and thank you for joining us." Ellis paused for clapping, and got a smattering of it from random people around the room. "Now, we all know why we're here. We've begun the revitalization of Bedlam, and as your partners in this project, Foundry wants to keep the lines of communication open and give you all a chance to share your worries, fears, and hopes as we move forward.

"Before we launch into that portion of the meeting, I'd like to share *our* hopes for Bedlam's future and the projections for the town after the project is complete." The projector screen dropped behind him. "You can see here, bringing new blood into Bedlam will bring in new jobs and..."

I tuned out his speech. Why listen to his fabricated numbers or waste a look at his fictional pie charts? Ellis's plan for Bedlam was to steal every drop of wealth from its soil, then sail off on a five-story yacht with his millions.

"I know change can be unsettling," he was saying, sweeping that charming smile over the crowd. "You hold on to your traditions tight in Bedlam and there's not a thing wrong with that. We should hold on to what makes us great. What makes us unique. But we cannot do so at the expense of progress. I see too much potential in Bedlam to let it remain stagnant.

"A few miles east is one of the top-ranked universities in the country. An achievement that's due to your young people. You are raising the best. They are achieving the most. Then, they are leaving their homes to search for more opportunities. I say enough," Ellis cried, slapping the podium. "Their opportunities are here. Their futures are here. So, let's give it to them."

The audience burst into applause—louder and much more enthusiastic this time. Ellis stepped back, beaming and waving his hands at the crowd. He did an excellent job using all the right trigger phrases and playing on all the right fears. Now anyone who steps up and opposes the "revitalization" is a jerk who hates jobs, money, and wants all the children to grow up and move away.

Nicely played, asshole.

"Wonderful, wonderful," Judith said, retaking her spot at the mic. "At this time, we'll open the floor to questions and concerns—"

"Ahh, no concerns, Judith," one of the board members piped up. "We're all sold after that presentation." He laughed and half the room joined in.

"Right you are, Mr. Conway. What I meant to say is we'll open the floor to questions and praise."

More laughter.

"Please form an orderly line down the row. When it's your turn, step up here and— Oh."

I marched directly up to Judith, smiling pleasantly into her owlish eyes. "May I?" I asked, firmly grasping the mic. "I have a few questions."

"Uh... yes, of course."

Judith moved aside, gesturing me on. I spared a glance at Steven and his sons, and was gifted three hostile scowls. It put a smile on my face.

"Hello, everyone. Many of you probably don't know me. I'm Abigail de Souza's granddaughter." Murmurs and nods rippled through the crowd. I sought his face, sweeping over the audience, and found him posted up in the back.

Our eyes met, and he nodded.

"I don't want to take up too much of your time. My main question is why did you choose Bedlam for this project?"

Conway opened his mouth. "Because Bedlam—"

"Bedlam is a wealth of untapped potential," Ellis sliced in. "With the local university, there will be no shortage of patrons and renters in the new restaurants and student apartments we plan to build."

"I'm so glad you used the word wealth. That brings me to my next question—"

"Only one question per person."

"That wasn't one of the rules," I breezed. "Besides, this one isn't for the board. Mayor Creed, why were the strict no-development policies lifted for Foundry when every other company has been shot down?"

Dozens of heads swung to her, awaiting an answer. Wiping away the initial surprise, Arsenio's mom cleared her throat and stood. "I have gotten that question a lot over the last few weeks. I'm glad I have this chance to address it with all of you. The policies were lifted because I too see a brighter future for Bedlam. One where we're not held back by the past." She smiled at the board. You had to be looking closely to see her mouth was tight around the edges. "I welcome Foundry as our partner in that endeavor."

"Thank you, Madam Mayor. We're honored," said Ellis. "And thank you, Miss de Souza.

"Sir, I believe you're next."

"Before I go, I'd like to give the real answers to those questions."

"Your time is up, Miss de Souza."

"The real reason that Foundry invaded our town has nothing to do with restaurants or rentals—"

"That's enough."

"Matter of fact, I'd be shocked if a single Burger King went up before they all cut and run, leaving us in the dirt pit that used to be Bedlam—"

"I said that's enough!" A chair toppled behind me, hinting that Ellis jumped out of his seat. "Security, escort her out."

"Hey, leave her alone," shouted the same grizzled man I sat next to. "I want to hear what she has to say."

"Forgive us, sir, but we have a lot of people waiting to ask their questions." Ellis tried to regain his charm. "We have to be fair to everyone."

My new best friend turned to the line of people. "Is there anyone here who isn't interested in what she has to say? Or why this guy is so desperate to shut her up?"

Ellis spluttered. "I'm not..."

He trailed off for the same reason disbelief silenced me. One by one, everyone in the question line moved off and took their seats. I was wrong. Looks like they weren't completely swayed by those pie charts and pretty speeches.

"Thank you, everyone," I said. "I'm going to do something that no one has done in this town for over a hundred years: tell the truth."

Mayor Creed stepped forward. "Miss de Souza, I have to agree that this isn't appropriate. There's a proper time and place to air your grievances. This is not it."

"I agree," said Eileen Stone. "And if no one else has a question, I would like to know more about Foundry's plans for community outreach."

"Yes," Conway said quickly. "I'd be happy to answer that for you, madam."

Eileen bore down on me fast. "Miss de Souza, if you would—"

Sometimes a girl has to get to the point.

"The real reason Foundry is invading our town and the mayor can't stop them is because"—I dumped the contents of my bag on the podium—"of these."

Raw, uncut diamonds tumbled onto the wood—knocking and rolling and half spilling onto the floor. Confusion spread through the crowd as people craned their necks to see. The Sisters were having a completely different reaction.

Shock stopped Eileen in her tracks. She looked at me in horror—a look that spread from Marjorie to Cynthia, Nora, and Josephine.

"What are these?" I asked. "These are diamonds. Raw, uncut diamonds mined right here in Bedlam—the town that used to be called Crystal Canyon."

"That's enough," Ellis bellowed. "Security! Get her out of here now. Damn this, where are they? Where's Walsh and Moore?"

Wherever Dante and his friends put them.

"Those can't be diamonds," someone cried.

"Look for yourself."

I lobbed it at the lady in the front. She let out a little scream when it dropped on her. Fumbling, she flung it at her neighbor who recoiled at the half a dozen people who descended on him.

"What is that?"

"A diamond?"

"Can't be true."

"Must be fake."

"They're not fake," I stated. "This is what Dante has been hinting at every day for over two weeks. There's a reason why Foundry is so desperate to buy your land, that they're paying way above market value. It's because they know they'll make it all back and more when they dig up your flowerbeds, and rescue these from underneath."

Holding up a diamond, I raised my voice over Jeremy's, Micah's, and Steven's shouting for their incapacitated security. "I busted these out of one of the locked crates on the demolition site. They cleverly have them labeled 'explosives.'"

"Rainey," Nora screeched. "Stop this. You have no idea what you're doing!"

"I know exactly what I'm doing. I'm helping the good people of Bedlam ask the right questions of Foundry. Like, for example, since the land they've been paying you two hundred grand for is actually worth about two million, will you be getting a check for the difference today, or is it already in the mail?"

"Dammit, bitch. Shut your mouth!"

Hands seized me from behind, wrestling me away from the podium. I'd know Jeremy's gorilla hands and overly sweet cologne anywhere.

"Everything she said is pure nonsense," Ellis rushed, hurrying to the podium. The man shoved the diamonds back in my purse as fast as he could. "These are cheap crystals she found in a shop."

I bucked in Jeremy's grip.

"We know nothing about—"

"Holy shit, it's real." A short man in glasses and suspenders had gotten hold of the diamond I threw at the crowd. "She isn't lying. This is real!"

"How can that be?"

"How much is it worth?"

"Liars!" My grizzled friend leveled a shaking finger on the board. "Thieves!"

Steven looked from him, to the board, to the bag of diamonds in his hands...

...and ran.

"Boys," he shouted at his sons. "Go!"

"Stop them!"

Jeremy dropped me. The three of them beat it for the door. I shot to the side, rolling out of the way of the ten, thirty, fifty stampeding townspeople giving chase.

"They're in the crates," I screamed. "Take back what's yours. Bedlam now!

"Bedlam forever!"

I thought I knew chaos the night Cavendish lit on fire, and the entire party ran screaming in every direction. I had no idea.

Bodies collided in the entrance—all of them pushing, straining, fighting to get the fleeing Ellises.

I crawled under the table, beating it to the other side door. I escaped into the hall and stumbled outside to the most beautiful sight.

Foundry, in their wisdom, decided to live stream the meeting for everyone who couldn't attend in person. Just in case, I had Dante tap into the feed and broadcast it as tonight's show. Almost everyone in town heard the truth... and the streets were filling fast.

"Diamonds?"

"My land is worth millions?"

"Where are they hiding them?"

"That girl said they're at the construction sites!"

"Con men!"

"Liars!"

"Cheats!"

Those last shouted insults were for the board members who followed me, thinking they were wise to go in the opposite direction of Ellis.

Bang!

A gunshot rang out, ripping screams from everyone—including me. "They're shooting at us," I shrieked. "Foundry's shooting at us!"

"What? No!"

"Beasts! Monsters!"

Missiles flew through the air. Hairbrushes, glasses cases, shoes, bottles—pelting the panicking bunch of suits.

I ran before it got ugly. There was no need to see which Man of Honor—Lincoln, Thea, Jackson, or Everett—fired the gun. I just applauded their perfect timing.

Running around the building, I skidded to a stop before the parking lot. Steven, Jeremy, and Micah made it to the car, but that was as far as they got thanks to four popped tires and no spark plugs.

"Thieves!" A dozen people rocked and pummeled the car, rattling the shouting occupants inside. "Give us back what you stole!"

"The diamonds are at the construction sites!" I called. "They're taking what's yours! Get it back!"

Part of the mob broke off, racing across the street. Foundry really had moved in on every inch of our town. There were two sites just in my eyeline, and another one a block behind me.

Bang! Bang!

More gunfire. More screams of fear... and outrage.

Townspeople were flooding in from everywhere—shouting, screaming, running, demanding. The sun was setting on Bedlam, nurturing the kind of savagery that could only come out at night.

But not enough.

I crossed the street, ducking into *The Last Call*. No one was in the bar, not even the bartender. Bold as ever, I hopped the bar top and started taking down bottles.

"Where are the—? Ah," I said, grabbing the bin of washcloths. "There you are."

With steady and clear focus, I popped the tops and put the rags in their new proper place.

The doorbell chimed, snapping my head up. A young brown-haired woman in jeans and a band shirt stared at me. I smiled.

"Hello, Thea. I believe these are for you." I handed her my Molotov cocktails. "Don't hit any Bedlamites."

"Wouldn't dream of it."

She walked out, already clicking the flames of her lighter.

Sighing, I shut my eyes—taking in the moment. They took everything from me, thinking that the little orphan farm girl was too weak and stupid to fight back. They should've known—

"The blood of revolutionaries runs in my veins."

I found a booth, kicking back to relax while the shouting, car horns, and crashes got louder outside. My phone buzzed five minutes in.

Paris.

"Ivy? Ivy, where are you? Are you okay?"

I dropped my voice. "No! Bedlam has gone mad, Paris. I just wanted people to know the truth. I didn't realize they'd lose their minds!"

"This isn't your fault. It was Ellis running off like the con man criminal that he is that did it! Talk about an admission of guilt. I can't believe this." Paris was talking so fast, I could barely keep up. "We're sitting on diamonds? How did Foundry know? How did you know?"

"Jack told me. That's why my grandmother was k-killed," I cried. "The whole time, the truth was worse than I could have imagined."

I wanted to be honest with Paris. I truly did. Maybe after all this was over, I would, but right then, I couldn't make her complicit in what would happen that night.

"Are you inside?" I asked. "Are you safe?"

"Yeah. I'm at Marshall's place, but the dumbass isn't. We were supposed to hook up after watching the meeting, but he took off two seconds after hearing diamonds. His parents also sold to Foundry," she said. "I want to go after him but—"

"Don't. It's dangerous out here, P. I heard gunfire when I was running out of the square, and someone's throwing Molotov cocktails."

"Fucking hell!"

"Just stay where you are," I said, casually rising and stretching my back. "This will all be over soon. Stay safe."

"*You* stay safe. Where are you?"

"I found a bar to hide in. No one else is in here. I'll be okay."

Paris fussed some more but I finally eased her off the phone.

Smiling, I stepped out to my new favorite sight. Fires burned in different places on the square. Cars were overturned. Mobs ran through the street.

I followed one group, guessing where they were going.

The demolition crew was still working under high-powered lights and lamps. A fact they had to be cursing their bosses for.

"Are you people insane!" Hard-hatted, orange-vested men formed a line, pushing back against the growing mob. "Those are explosives!"

"Yeah, right. Sure they are."

"Open the crates."

"Show us what's inside if they're only explosives!"

I really had to stop grinning. It was highly obscene at a time like this, but I was loving how easy all this was. Saying the diamonds were in the explosive crates would naturally force the construction workers to defend them and force people away. As a result, Bedlam would fight harder—convinced that's exactly where their riches were.

"Back off!" A worker lashed out, shoving a woman off her feet.

"Keep your hands off my wife."

He was socked across the jaw, snapping his head nearly all the way around. A vicious fight broke out quick and brutal.

I continued on, leaving them to it. My work was done.

From that point on, no one connected to Foundry would have a second's peace in this town. No one else would sell to them, and their sites would constantly be raided for the treasures they tried to hoard.

Something a smart man like Ellis realized when he found himself before a bunch of angry townspeople holding a bag of diamonds. In his hands was the only payout he was destined to get from this project, so he tried to run with it.

I'm just glad Jack was willing to part with his stash.

Jack told me his family had been stealing from mine since his grandmother's generation. I asked him on the off chance he had any diamonds stashed away that his wife didn't get in the divorce. He said yes, he kept those in the floor safe that no one—not even Cairo—knew about. He kept those back to give to his son after he died. I convinced him that it was a better idea for him to give them to their rightful owner instead.

The Sisters were no doubt emptying their stashes right about now too. In twenty-four hours, Bedlam would be trending on national news. Everyone would know about the diamonds. People would come in to stop the fighting. Even more people would come in to see if it was true. A spotlight would be thrown over everything they tried to hide.

I left the square behind, dodging the hooting, hollering rioters running in the opposite direction. My work was done here. Might as well go back to Cairo's and see what's for dinner.

The porch light was off when I arrived. I knocked a few times and rang the bell twice.

"Cairo? Cairo, it's me. I know you're in there because you can't be anywhere else. Let me—"

The door flew open. A hand grabbed my wrist and tugged me inside.

"What the fuck did you do?"

I looked up into furious, fiery greens. All of a sudden, madness not unlike the fervor gripping everyone outside overtook me. I rose up and captured his lips—kissing Cairo wildly, passionately, dangerously.

Tangling in my hair, he ripped me off, growl leaking through his teeth.

I had woken the wolf, and my rising pulse knew it. But I didn't care.

It was the wolf who loved me.

"I came back like you told me to, baby."

"You did more than that." Cairo forced me back and against the wall. I gasped as he tipped my head back, baring my neck. "You started a fucking riot. How? Why?"

"I did what I had to do," I rasped. "Bedlam is mine. If I can't have it, no one else can either."

"Who helped you?"

"Why do you think someone—?"

A warm, calloused hand closed over my throat. "Who helped you?"

My swallow bobbed against his palm. "Dante and the Men of Honor helped me. They proved their loyalty."

His lips peeled back from his teeth, leaking a sound even worse than his growl. "You lied to me."

"I had to! I was ending this once and for all, Cairo, and you couldn't be a part of it." I shoved his shoulders. "I wasn't going to let you think this was the one. This was your last act of penance, and then your family's debt is paid. Now you get to *leave me*. It will never be paid, Cairo! I will never let you go!"

"Ivy!"

"You promised that I would decide when fate broke us. Well, it's not done with us yet."

"I promised you too many things if you believe that's how this works."

"You—"

Bang!

The front door flew in and busted a hinge crashing into the opposite wall. Cairo and I flew apart.

"Oh my..."

A broken, bleeding wreck of a man staggered over the threshold.

Gone was his expensive gray coat and one of his shoes. The clothes that were left were torn and covered in blood—hanging off him like rags. His mouth bled heavily. Patches of his hair were torn from his scalp. A nasty wound on his leg turned his pants scarlet. But none of that raised the hairs on the back of my neck.

It was the gun Steven Ellis trained on my face that did.

"Where are they?"

"What? Who?"

"Where are they!" he roared.

Cairo shoved me behind him. "Where is who?"

"My sons. My boys." Ellis dragged his bad leg over the mat. "Your savage friends busted the windows. Pulled them out of the car. I tried—tried to get to them—" The gun shook. "They took them. You know where they are."

"I don't—"

"Don't lie to me!" He fired at the ceiling, rocketing my heart into my throat. "You planned this. You wanted this to happen! Where did you tell them to take my boys?" He swung the gun back on us. "Stand aside, Sharpe."

Cairo's fingers dug painfully into my hip, keeping me behind him. "I'm not going to do that."

"Stand aside!"

"She doesn't know where they are! Fucking look outside. Does it seem like anyone has control over what's going on out there?"

Mania twisted Ellis's face—even more terrifying for the streaks of blood running down his forehead. "I won't tell you again."

"She doesn't know where they are," he shouted. "But my father's the sheriff. He's not here right now, but I'll call him." Cairo moved us both toward the phone. "He'll get the whole station out looking for Jeremy and Micah—"

Ellis pulled the trigger.

"Ahh!" My scream echoed through the house.

Cairo dropped like a stone, collapsing at my feet.

"Cairo, no. No, no, no," I cried, dropping next to him.

"Get up."

"He needs help! I have to call Doc Nash." I lurched for the phone and found myself staring down his barrel.

"I said get up!"

I screamed as he yanked me up by the hair, throwing me against the wall. Ellis fell on top of me. I froze when he pressed the gun muzzle over my left eye.

"This bullet goes right into your brain, you little hick bitch, unless you tell me where Micah and Jeremy are right now."

"I don't—"

"Tell me!"

Spittle showered my cheeks, mixing with salty, stinging tears that weren't for me.

Cairo. My Cairo.

All he wanted was his own life, free of people's lies and manipulations, but I couldn't give him that. I had to own him like the Sisters. Like his obligations as a Bedlam Boy. Like his duty to his broken and drunk father. And in the end, I let him pay the price for my war.

Heavy, shuddering sobs ravaged my chest. "Cairo..."

"Give me back my boys." His finger twitched on the trigger. "Right now."

"I s-swear, I don't know. I don't know!" I exploded. "I didn't tell anyone to kidnap your twisted monster spawn. What the hell would I want with them? It's you who destroyed the only thing I had left of Gran and Rainey."

"So you're getting your revenge by destroying what's important to me."

"No!" My teeth gritted as he pressed the gun harder. "I had nothing to do with the mob snatching your sons. You can shout and threaten all you want, but my answer is not going to change."

"No?" His voice went flat, dropping the temperature twenty degrees. "Then, what good are you?" Ellis drew back on the trigger.

"Nooo!"

"Uh." Ellis jerked—his hands suddenly going slack and dropping by his sides. The gun clattered to the ground as he tipped over, falling face-first on the hardwood.

I gaped at Cairo, and the hard glass bowl he bashed over his head. "Oh, baby." I threw myself in his arms, ripping out a shout. "Are you okay?"

"I've been better," he gritted. Cairo doubled over, clutching his arm under the fading surge of adrenaline. "Fuck it, woman. That's the second shoulder I've messed up for you."

"Cairo, I'm sorry. I'm so sorry." I kissed his mouth, nose, cheeks, eyelids, everywhere. "You've fulfilled your penance. If you want to go, I understand. I won't stop you. I love you," I cried. "I just want you to live. Even if you don't live that life with me."

Beads of sweat coated his forehead. "Thanks for the permission, but if you could stop kissing me for a minute and get me a doctor." His legs gave out, dropping him on his knees. "That would be great."

On the longest night of my life, I drove Cairo to Doc Nash—his ankle monitor beeping at us the whole way. That night I held his hand while the fires and fighting raged outside.

I haven't lost everything, I thought, tracing his sleeping face. *Fate brought me five guys who ate my pain and soothed my soul.*

"And one day it'll bring us all back together, Cairo. I know it will."

"IVY. IVY, WAKE UP."

I cracked a lid open. *Where was I? What—?*

It all came back to me. The town hall meeting. The riot. Ellis's attack.

"Cairo!" I shot up, nearly falling off Doc Nash's worn, squashy couch.

Doc Nash's practice was pretty much the first floor of a residential home. He converted the living room into a place to see patients, and the den was where he kept overnighters that weren't going anywhere unless it was into an ambulance to take them to the hospital. A gunshot wound was an automatic ride to Hunter's Crest Hospital, but Doc Nash was worried no ambulance drivers would risk themselves in the riot.

"What is it?" I croaked. A glance out the window told me the sun was just beginning to rise. "Is the ambulance here?"

"No."

"Do you need something?" I went to his bed and lifted his blankets, checking him over myself. "Are you in pain?"

"Did you mean what you said?" Cairo broke in. "I'm released from my penance. The debt between our families is paid."

My chest squeezed. "Yes, Cairo," I forced myself to say. "It's paid. I hope that you do find out who you are away from Bedlam. Its secrets have hung over your life since before you were born. It ripped your family apart, and forced you on a different path. You deserve to find your own way, and you can't do that with a constant reminder by your side."

I was proud of myself. I got all of that out with dry eyes.

"Just be happy, my wolf. Heal your wounds."

"Hmm." Cairo gave me a long, measured look. "Bullshit."

I blinked. "What?"

"Everything you just said is bullshit. You don't want me going anywhere. You want me chasing you through the woods for as long as I can pounce and mount you like the tasty little prey that you are."

"No, I—"

"So, fine. I will."

My heart. My breath. My mind. All of it stopped.

"What?"

He heaved a sigh. "I've decided I'm not giving you up. All the shitheads you named have screwed up and knocked my life off track. You're the first thing I've had that's mine. That I chose for myself. I won't lose my mate so soon after finding her."

This couldn't be real. He wasn't saying what I thought he was saying.

"Besides, I've taken an arrow and a bullet for you. By my calculations, it's you who owes me penance. Start with making up for lost time." He smacked his thigh with his good arm. "Climb on."

A smile teased my lips. "Okay, but one thing first."

I leaned over, and socked him in the jaw.

"Agh! What the hell?"

"That's for cheating on me." Temper coated my good mood fast. "If you ever mess around on me again, I'll kill you." I stuck my face in his. "Look in my eyes and tell me if I'm lying."

Cracking his jaw, Cairo chuckled. "Oh, I believe you. Lucky for me I didn't cheat on you the first time, so there definitely won't be an *again*."

"What do you mean? That girl—"

"My lab partner," he finished. "I kept blowing her off that week because I was focused on getting my dad back. I finally told her I had time to work on it that night. It got late and she doesn't live on campus, so I let her crash."

He shrugged one shoulder. "She was going to sleep on the couch, but then I heard you in the hall, and decided to piss you off instead."

"Why would you do that to me?"

"Because you weren't Rain, and I couldn't stop punishing you for it."

I was quiet, letting that sink in. "And now?"

"Last night I almost lost you too, and it woke me the hell up. I chased Rain through the woods, but I pounced on you. You're the one who fights me. Who bows before my domination but never surrenders. You're the one I love, and none of those things changed after you did."

Tears prickled behind my eyes.

"You're everything I wanted in a mate and more." He caught a droplet on my cheek and gently brushed it away. "Past time I stopped bitching about losing the side of you that was never real."

"Goodness, Cairo." My throat choked up. "I'm definitely going to ride your cock in this doctor's office now."

"Don't wait for an invitation. Drop your pants."

Giggling, I hastily shed my clothes in a pile and hopped on the rising mound beneath his sheet.

Cairo was my mate. The one who claimed me and brought me into my new pack and family.

Arsenio—whose dark side danced with mine.

Roan—who pushed me past every comfort zone and made me laugh the whole way.

Legend—who closed himself off completely, except at night when he held me in his arms and told me things he never told anyone.

Jacques—who challenged my thinking as much as I challenged and pushed his.

We were only ever meant to be with each other.

I bounced on Cairo's cock, making him wince with each buck, but damned if that wasn't making him harder. His fingers were mercilessly twisting my stiffened nipple. I was trying my best not to make noise, and failing spectacularly.

I didn't know what was next for the six of us, but I trusted there was a better life for us away from Bedlam and the hold it had on everyone who set foot on its soil.

It was time we found out who we truly were outside of a Bedlam Boy, an orphaned farm girl, or a secret heiress.

I threw my head back, spine arching as my orgasm gripped and wrestled me under. Pleasure shuddered my body—turning my muscles to jelly as hot ropes of Cairo's cum burst inside me.

I collapsed on his chest, totally spent. "I swear we're going to start our new life together soon," I huffed, "but there's one more thing I've got to do first."

I RECLINED ON THE OLD rickety steps, munching on an apple. They came out of the shadows like vapor, lining up before me.

"Hyde. Wood. Everett. Lincoln," I said, nodding to each Man of Honor in turn. "Thanks for coming."

"Where else would we be? We struck Foundry a fatal blow. Literally fatal in the case of a few board members and Steven Ellis," said Lincoln. "Found out this morning that he bled out from his injuries."

"Shame," I said, voice flat. "At least he didn't take this place before he went." I looked around Westchester Drumlins—where my journey with the Bedlam Boys, and the journey back to myself—truly started.

"Any word on what happened to Jeremy and Micah?"

"They were found tied naked to a tree in the woods," Thea said. "They got the hint. Those two won't set foot in Bedlam again. Why? Should we kill them?"

"There's no need." I crunched another bite. "Foundry is dead in this town. The diamonds are all over the news. From here on, no one can dig up a rock in Bedlam without the real and only half as corrupt government knowing."

"All the officials, agents, assessors, and investigators they sent in, have to leave sometime," Roberts said. "When that happens, it'll be time for the Men of Honor to step up and protect Bedlam as it once did. We'll get rid of the Sisters and the Bedlam Boys for good, then there's no one left to interfere."

"This town will be a better place under us," said Jackson. "We'll punish those who take advantage of the weak. What the Bedlam Boys were supposed to do if they weren't too busy making their mommies rich."

"No poverty. No crime. No mercy for those who disobey us," said Everett—a tall, square-jawed guy who had strands of premature gray in his dark hair. "Thanks to the riot, the world has already seen what we're willing to do."

"Thanks to Ivy," Lincoln corrected. "I told you she was the one meant to lead us." He turned to me. "Just tell us what to do first."

"Ah, yes." I sat up, wiping off my hands. "First thing and most important"—my face changed—"this is for my sister."

Four figures emerged from the living room and grabbed each Man of Honor from behind. They sliced their necks in one smooth arch before the shouts left their lips.

Their bodies flopped on the floor. I stepped over them, kissing Arsenio, Jacques, Legend, and Roan.

"Thank you, loves. Did everything go okay the other night?"

Jacques looked down at his silent ankle monitor. "Stupid fools thought a man with a genius-level IQ couldn't hack into their little toy. Yeah, everything went down like they knew the entire plan," he said, looking down at the bodies. "I disabled the monitors and we followed the Men of Honor through the riot, getting video of them throwing Molotov cocktails, flipping cars, and firing gunshots in the air.

"The cops will be looking at them, not you for inciting a riot. Of course, they'll never find their suspects and everyone will believe they're on the run."

"Love it." I wrapped my arm around Legend and reached for Roan's hand. The red-haired imp bypassed my hand and grabbed my ass instead. "That's a happy ending if I ever heard one."

"Not quite. We haven't dealt with our mothers yet," said Legend.

"After we do, what do you think about transferring out of Bedlam U?"

"Huh. I wouldn't hate that."

"It'd be nice to fuck you all over a different campus," Roan mused.

"Be just as nice to get out of Bedlam," I said. "Find out who we really are."

"I can save you a pointless trip of self-discovery," Arsenio replied. "Who you are... is ours."

Epilogue

C*airo*

I watched her in the lounge chair—the picture of contentment as the sun soaked her skin.

"Stop staring at her like a lovesick puppy."

Rolling my eyes, I glanced at my sister. She was in the middle of loading up her tray with prawn balls and spiced tortilla chips.

"Paris, you should pack your stuff. This is your stop."

"We're in the middle of the ocean."

"Did I stutter?"

She laughed, ignoring me completely. Paris carried her tray out to my dad, where they picked up their conversation.

It was hard to believe four years ago, we were at Bedlam University—the kings of a small school, but the pawns of a small town. Now...

I passed a smirk over our five-story yacht, *Rainey Seas*. We liked to sail most of the year. Why spend your time in one place when there was so much world to see? Thanks to Jacques, we could afford it.

The guy told Ivy he was working on a way to get her inheritance back—legally or illegally. Turned out he was tracking down each of our mothers' secret bank accounts... and draining them dry.

Between the five of them, their mothers, and their grandmothers, they saved up about sixty million dollars combined. Jacques took it all and gave it to Ivy.

Don't worry, we didn't leave them destitute. They did give us life after all.

Jacques left them the equivalent of their actual salaries in their savings. More than enough to make their pretend lives as simple judges, deans, mayors, and charity organizers—their real ones.

None of them have spoken to us since.

"What about Italy?" Arsenio leaned over and dropped a kiss on Ivy's lips. "Haven't been there in months."

"There's a reason for that," Jacques said. He found himself at Ivy's feet. Lifting them onto his lap, he rubbed her arches, eliciting a soft purr. "It's too soon."

"Korea?" Roan offered from the hot tub. He and Legend bubbled in the steamy water. Both of their hands had been under for a suspiciously long time. "We'll hit Jeju-do this time. I could do with a little island living, and it'll be good for our girl."

"Guys, I'm fine," she protested. Ivy lovingly rubbed the swollen mound her two-piece bathing suit did nothing to cover. "We're fine."

Our daughter was in there. No matter how many times I told myself that, it didn't seem real.

Ivy used to joke that a baby would soften us. The joke was fucking on us because we ripened like mangoes in the sun two seconds after we saw the pregnancy test. Roan once said you don't ride an injured horse. Turns out we can't punish a pregnant Ivy either.

Roan put away his crops. Legend locked up his paddles. Jacques only used his belt to hold his pants up now. Arsenio was still a prick who dominated her in bed, but afterward, he spent the night cooing at her belly, so he was having a hard time maintaining his rep as the most dangerous of us. And our rough consensual rape sex was very light on the rough lately.

Sometimes Ivy complained about it, and tried pushing our buttons to get us to break. But she loved us pampering her too much to really fight it.

"Why don't we go Stateside?" Paris spoke up. "When's the last time you and I bought out every shop in New York, Ivy? I gotta start showering my niece with gifts now."

"Oooh, that does sound fun."

"What do you think, Dad?" Paris asked Jack, brightening his face as it always did.

She still called her own father Dad of course, but Nora didn't take it well when Paris refused to take her side, or pressure Ivy into giving her the money back. She kicked Paris out of the house, and my sister took it as the chance she'd been waiting for—to finally get out of Bedlam. Ivy invited her to spend a week on the boat with us, and that was it.

She and Jack got close again. Closer than Dad and I ever did. I suspected it was her influence that helped him hit four years sober.

"I think New York sounds great. Don't know if I told you I've got cousins there," Jack said. "We can make a whole vacation of it. You ladies relax and have some fun while I catch up."

"Three votes for New York," said Legend. His and Roan's shoulders were jerking in their sockets. That confirmed I'd be staying out of the hot tub for the next few weeks. "Arsenio?"

My phone went off, pulling me away from the conversation.

"What?"

"Ah, that lovely greeting and dulcet tone could only be Cairo Sharpe."

I frowned. "Who is this? How did you get this number?"

"I was given this number, so I could collect when the day came."

Something about the voice tickled my memory.

"Come on. Don't you remember me? I busted you out of jail four years ago."

Adriel Burton.

"Again, what do you want?"

"What do you think?" he snapped. "I'm cashing in that favor. I got into some trouble down here in Miami. My boys can't make the charges disappear, and I'm not going down for this. I broke you out of jail, now you're going to do the same for me."

"A Miami prison isn't on the same level as a small-town sheriff station guarded by two and a half inept cops. Neither is the trumped-up charge we were brought in on the same as whatever your boys can't get you out of. Am I right?"

"Doesn't matter," he gritted. "That favor was a blank check. Legend and I agreed. And don't pretend you can't do it. Your reputation is international, Bedlam Boy— Oh wait, you call your gang the Fates now.

"Cairo—the enforcer. Arsenio—the hit man. Roan—the interrogator. Jacques—the brain and lawyer. Legend—the trap. Pretty Boy St. James charms your targets into being in the wrong place at the right time. I need some of that for the bastard who *framed* me!

"Make it happen, Sharpe. It's not a good idea to break a deal with me."

"Hmm. Looks like in the last four years, you've dropped the innocent act too."

"There's a lot of that going around. So, what's it going to be?"

I shrugged. "Why are you asking me? All requests go through the boss."

"What? Who—?"

Crossing the deck, I handed over the phone. Ivy cycled through a few expressions as she listened. Confusion, surprise, mild disgust, annoyance, then—

"An open favor? I see. I'll be in touch." Ivy hung up. By the cut-off shout, it was in the middle of the conversation.

She smiled at us—the radiant goddess, more brutal and deadly than we could ever be. "Sorry, guys. We'll have to put New York on hold. It looks like we're heading to Miami."

"Hmm, I'll like you in Miami." I threaded my fingers through hers, lining up our wedding rings. She had two more on this hand and two on the other. "Beaches, Cuban sandwiches, palm trees, ocean sex."

"Mmm," she purred. "It's a date. Oh, but first, we have to kill a guy."

"Then, it's our kind of date. Even better."

"I love you guys," she said, "and I love our life together."

"We love you too," Legend replied, "but let's be honest, we didn't give you the choice to do anything else."

Keep In Touch

Join Ruby's mailing list for news, teasers, and more:
https://www.subscribepage.com/rubyvincentpage
Join Ruby's Facebook Reader Group:
https://bit.ly/3bNuCOq

ABOUT THE AUTHOR

Ruby Vincent is a lover of all things romance and every kind of bad boy you can twist around your finger. She loves saucy heroines, bold alpha males, and weaving a tale where both get their happily ever after.